LACHLAN SMITH

LION PLAYS ROUGH

headline

Published by arrangement with The Mysterious Press,
an imprint of Grove/Atlantic, Inc.

First published in Great Britain in 2014 by
HEADLINE PUBLISHING GROUP

First published in paperback in 2014 by
HEADLINE PUBLISHING GROUP

1

Cataloguing in Publication Data is available from the British Library

ISBN 978 1 4722 0139 3

Typeset in Palatino by Avon DataSet Ltd,
Bidford-on-Avon, Warwickshire

Printed and bound in Great Britain by Clays Ltd, St Ives plc

Headline's policy is to use papers that are natural, renewable and
recyclable products and made from wood grown in sustainable
forests. The logging and manufacturing processes are expected to
conform to the environmental regulations of the country of origin.

HEADLINE PUBLISHING GROUP
A division of Hachette Livre UK Ltd
338 Euston Road
London NW1 3BH

www.headline.co.uk
www.hachette.co.uk

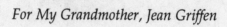
For My Grandmother, Jean Griffen

Chapter One

It was Saturday. I'd just biked to the top of the Bolinas-Fairfax Road and was turning onto Ridgecrest when I heard a car round the bend behind me – too fast and too close. The car was there before I could react. The bumper clipped my heel and sent me off onto the shoulder. As I went over the handlebars I saw a blue Pontiac convertible flash past.

I'd been pedaling uphill, so I hadn't been going fast; I rolled once and ended up sitting on my rear end in soft pine needles and dirt. As for the bike, the back wheel was bent and wouldn't turn. I was twenty miles from where I'd left my car, less than halfway through my ride.

It was eighty degrees in the shade, and the air was absolutely still. If the bumper had been a few inches to the right, I told myself . . . While my hands were still

1

shaking but my breath was starting to slow, the convertible came back.

The driver stretched her long legs as she got out of the car. Her hair was straightened, spider web-fine, and she wore a cream-colored blouse, khaki shorts, and sandals. A spray of freckles ran across her upper chest.

I knew I should be angry with her, but I was glad to be alive. 'You're goddamn lucky you didn't kill me,' I said.

She looked me over. 'Not a scratch on you. Thank goodness.' She clicked her tongue at the bike. 'You're not going anywhere on this.'

She opened the trunk and I put the bike in.

'Leo Maxwell,' I said. 'Thanks, it's the least you can do. My car's down in Mill Valley on Highway One.'

She took my hand coolly. 'Lavinia Martin. You know you swerved right in front of me.'

'That's not the way I remember it.'

She drove with both hands on the wheel, her eyes focused ahead. Alone with a beautiful woman in a convertible. It was a rare opportunity. These days I hardly ever talked with anyone who wasn't from work.

I tried again. 'Is it my lucky day or do you have a habit of running down strange men on lonely roads?'

2

In response she reached back for her purse and opened it on the console between us. I looked down and saw a snub-nosed automatic, nickel-plated. 'My husband bought that for me.'

'So you're married,' I said. After a moment she closed the purse and returned it to the back. It wasn't that I'd never seen a gun. I'd had guns pointed at me on occasion, even fired in my presence. It hadn't all been desk work. But still, I let a few miles go by before I spoke again.

'I prefer a forty-five,' I finally said. 'Revolver. But I'm also the kind of guy who owns a typewriter. It's just style, I guess, personal preference. A forty-five was the gun my brother always kept. I'm pretty confident that when I squeeze the trigger a bullet's gonna come.'

Lavinia had her arm out of the car, her fingers spread in the wind. 'Your brother a cop?'

'Criminal defense attorney. He was, anyway. His name is Teddy Maxwell. Maybe you heard of him.'

She looked like she was about to say yes, then shook her head, distaste showing in the set of her lips. So she was one of those who see criminal defense lawyers as little better than criminal accessories after the fact. Too bad.

3

'He was one of the best defense attorneys around. Then about two years ago one of his clients shot him in the head while we were eating lunch right across from Civic Center in San Francisco.'

She worked the gears, accelerating more aggressively into the curve, but otherwise showed no reaction.

'I was just out of law school, working for him.' She didn't reply, which had the effect of making me fill the silence.

And so I ended up telling her more than I intended, about the months in the hospital, then the half year in the rehab clinic where Teddy'd had to relearn how to swallow his food, dress himself, speak coherently.

'What does he do now?'

'Comes to the office every day. Does this and that. A little research, sits in on client meetings. He had to give up his bar card. He can't practice. For now we've got a place together, but I'm hoping that someday he'll be ready to live alone. That's what he wants, I know.'

We came out of the woods and into the sun. To our right, a green hillside sloped down toward the trees. As Ridgecrest Road climbs Mount Tamalpais, it offers some of the most glorious coastal views anywhere in California, sixteen hundred feet above the foaming sea. She didn't once turn her head.

4

At Panoramic she headed toward Mill Valley. I didn't try to talk to her again. You don't chat about the weather after you've told someone about your brother catching a bullet and relearning to feed himself. I would have liked to have gone on and told her how even now, two and a half years later, I still kept waiting for some flash of the old Teddy's formidable intelligence, how I suffered from the creeping illusion that he was faking it. Snap out of it, I kept wanting to tell him. Be yourself. Talk right.

I directed her to the parking area off Highway 1 at Stinson Beach where I'd left my car, Teddy's old Rabbit, not dead yet. 'Look,' I said as I got out. 'I'm a nice guy. I'm not going to sue you, but a new wheel is going to set me back about two hundred bucks, and that story about me swerving in front of you is bullshit.'

I did what nice guys do: I gave her my card and told her that she could send me a check.

Chapter Two

By eleven thirty I'd been home, showered, changed, and walked over to our offices at 580 Grand. On weekdays I was usually at my desk before seven. Jeanie, who commuted from Walnut Creek, would arrive around eight, our assistant, Lynn, at nine, and Teddy by nine thirty or ten.

Weekends I usually had the place to myself, unless we had a meeting with a client or a witness. I was the eager beaver, looking to make a name for myself, so that I'd be ready to strike out on my own when Jeanie finally said the hell with private practice and went back to the PD's office. Along with being my boss she was my brother's ex-wife. My real legal education had begun with Teddy that summer before the shooting, and in the past three years she'd finished it. I had two dozen jury trials under my belt, half of them felonies

– and I'd won most of them. I was on a roll, brimming with self-confidence.

From my desk I heard Teddy when he showed up around one. He'd been to his brain-injury rehab group and had taken the bus up Telegraph to Berkeley and back by himself. Unmindful of social niceties even before the shooting, he didn't look in to say hi, but I heard him puttering around in the conference room.

At one forty-five Jeanie bustled in, keys jangling, phone chirping its low-battery warning. As usual, her presence raised the office energy level twofold. She was my height, with fine brown hair and a broad face; her beauty was in the way she carried herself, in her intelligence, in how she looked at people.

'Are we ready to go?' she asked as she passed my door without glancing in. 'Coffee brewing? Got your game face on?' I heard her keys hit the desk in her office. 'This guy's gonna be thinking about folding,' she went on. We couldn't see each other but we often held conversations from our desks, talking in raised voices through the doorways. 'He's gonna be scared shitless. He's gonna ask you to call the DA and find out if that shitty deal's still on the table. What are you going to say?'

'Jeanie, relax.'

'You going to tell him what happens to child molesters in prison? Or are you going to do a number, convince him Leo Maxwell's the second coming of Clarence Darrow?'

'Am I supposed to notice your good mood?'

'Yeah, you are.' She now appeared. Teddy had come out into the hallway and stood looking at her from the doorway of his little office, not seeming to register my presence, though I was directly in his line of sight over Jeanie's shoulder. Ever since the shooting he had eyes only for her, eyes haunted by waste. 'You know why?' she taunted.

'Why?'

'Because it's your fucking case, and I'm collecting the fee. That's why.' She turned. 'And you,' she said to Teddy. 'You'd better work on pulling a rabbit out of that Swiss cheese brain, because your little brother's going to trial in nine days and he hasn't got shit.'

'That's not true,' I protested. But I was following her script. 'There's the girl's family life. Two years ago when all this started her parents were talking divorce. Then she comes forward with these allegations and voilà, they're back together. So that's motive. Then there's the cops, the suggestive interviews . . .'

'So it's liar, liar pants on fire.'

9

'Someone molested Erica Lawler. We're not denying that. She just went and transferred the guilt outside the immediate family. Someone safer for her to accuse than her own uncle. By now she probably believes the story she's been telling.' I nodded to the binder containing the report of the expert we'd hired to testify on the subject of kids making false allegations of sexual abuse.

'Sounds like reasonable doubt to me. But that's not what wins child sex-abuse cases. Reasonable doubt is for running stop signs, for shoplifting.'

'It's a theory of innocence.'

'And it's going to crumble to dust when they put that little girl on the stand so she can describe how her best friend's father raped her during a sleepover.'

'Okay. Then what do you propose?'

'Soft-pedal the divorce stuff. You can't push it too hard. Otherwise, she seems calculating, which is the one thing she surely is not. You can hit the interviews pretty hard. The DA wants the jurors to be afraid of a sex offender running loose, so you scare them with these so-called experts planting false accusations in the minds of sweet kids. Neutralize fear with fear. What if it was your kid they'd gotten hold of, your name they were asking her about? So that's your lizard brain appeal. You get the uncle on the stand, rip his guts out. Then reason with them. Appeal to the mammal brain; make them see how the brother fits. It's a hit job, pure and simple. Okay? Ready?'

In fact, she'd given me my trial plan back verbatim, only with an overlay of the lizard/mammal brain dichotomy she'd slapped on to every case ever since she'd picked it up in some CEB seminar. But there was no point calling her out. Scare the jurors then reason with them was Jeanie's basic trial strategy in all hot button cases. The DA's case invariably tapped in to undercurrents of primitive anger, primitive fear. We couldn't win such cases by appealing to reason and evidence until we'd neutralized the DA's fear-mongering by scaring the jurors with our own primal nightmares.

The phone rang. 'Leo? It's Marty Scarsdale. I'm downstairs.'

I went out to the hall to meet him. He was tall, in his late thirties, with thick, dark hair and a gray, pinched face. His palm was damp when we shook hands.

'How you holding up?' I asked. 'How's the living situation?'

He was on bail, but his wife had thrown him out. The last I'd heard, he was staying with a college friend.

'I had to move out of the place I was in,' he said. 'I ended up checking in to this hotel out near the airport. Weekly rates.'

His stressful living situation meant the trial would be even more draining. He would probably come across as that much more guilt-ridden to the jurors as they studied his demeanor, looking for any sign he'd done what the DA said.

I led him into our offices and back to the conference room. Car was supposed to join us later. For years he'd been Teddy's go-to investigator; now he was Jeanie's. Car and I didn't get along, but his work was first-rate.

'So this is the first of many times we'll be sitting down together in the next few weeks,' I said once the three of us had our coffee. 'You go to trial on June nineteenth. That's a week from Monday. But it won't necessarily start that morning. We'll be trailing, which means that each morning we'll know by ten AM whether there's going to be a courtroom available. If there is, we go. If not, we wait another day. But criminal trials have priority, so we won't be waiting long.'

I recapped the case up to the present, listing the motions we'd filed to exclude various crucial pieces of evidence, reminding him of the preliminary hearing last winter in which he'd been held to answer based on the testimony of the investigating detective. I summarized the evidence the DA had turned over in discovery, including the videotaped interviews with the thirteen-year-old victim, Erica Lawler, in which she told of being sexually assaulted by Scarsdale while spending the night with his daughter, Angela, her best friend.

When I was finished Scarsdale looked up. 'I've been thinking maybe you could talk to the DA again and there wouldn't be a trial.'

'I could talk to her,' I said. 'But all along she's been saying they weren't going to let you plead to anything less than five years, with a lifetime sex offender registration requirement. That's five years in the state prison as a convicted child molester. It's not going to be easy time.'

'You don't think the DA might back down now that we're so close to trial?'

'I can talk to her and feel her out. But no, I don't think there's any chance she'll back down.'

'I didn't do this. I wish I understood why this was happening.'

'If I didn't think we could win, I would tell you, Marty. I think we've got a real shot. We've got a fantastic expert, a psychologist who has testified dozens of times about the phenomenon of an innocent person being accused when the child can't bring herself to name the true perpetrator. I've spent hours with her, and she's going to be a very convincing witness.'

I went on to reiterate the basic theory of our defense: that Scarsdale was innocent, and that Erica had in fact been having sex with her uncle, who was living with the family at the time of the alleged rape but moved out shortly after she'd come forward with the story about Scarsdale assaulting her during the sleepover.

Scarsdale listened intently, giving little nods as I went on. 'We'll hit the police hard for not exploring alternate theories. At least in the initial phases, no one once asked her about the uncle. She named you, so they ran with it. We'll be able to show that from the beginning the cops were focused on making their case against you rather than learning what actually happened.'

The door opened and Car slipped in. He had his BlackBerry in one hand and a coffee cup in the other. Thickets of tattooed foliage ran up his arms. His head was shaved, his face unlined. He looked half his true age of forty-five.

14

'So you can show that they ran a cruddy invest-igation,' Scarsdale said. 'But what about Erica's story? She's sticking to it, right?'

'We have to show that she might have a reason to lie, without making her look calculating. The jury's going to believe she was sexually assaulted. The question is who did it. Car's done the legwork. He can tell you what he's found out about the family situation.'

Car finished whatever he was doing on his BlackBerry and tucked it away. He succinctly summarized the parents' deteriorating marriage. The uncle, the wife's younger brother, had been living with the family after losing his job as a teacher; he'd been the girl's nanny, basically, picking her up from school, taking her to friends' houses or home, watching TV with her. While he lived with them, Erica spent more time with him than with her parents. Then she'd become pregnant and the uncle had taken her to have an abortion. She hadn't told her parents until after the procedure. Then she accused Scarsdale.

The uncle had refused to talk to Car, which suggested he had something to hide even if he didn't. In the meantime, we'd kept the pressure up. Car had showed up at the guy's new job and apartment, until he hired a lawyer who told us to stay away. I had the uncle under subpoena. When we finally met in the court-room, he was sure to be hostile and scared. In the meantime, Car was looking into his background, turning over stones.

'So you're going to concede that she was molested,' Scarsdale said when Car and I had finished.

I shot a glance at Jeanie. 'Probably.'

'There's no chance in your mind that she's just making it all up, trying to get attention.' His breath was short now, his cheeks flushed, and I saw that over the past few months he'd grown capable of hating this little girl. Even if he were innocent, even if we managed to clear his name, some vestige of this hatred would remain, like the scar from a burn, the lasting damage that always results from prolonged involvement with the criminal justice system.

If the emotion I was seeing now surfaced at trial, we were in trouble. On an impulse I took a DVD from the file. 'This disc has the interviews the police videotaped with the girl.' I held it out. 'It's the story she'll tell in court.'

He shook his head. 'I don't want to look at it. That's your department.'

'You have to. And you need to do *more* than just look

16

at it. You have to live with it. Take it back with you to that hotel and watch the whole thing. Watch it again and again. Every day until trial starts, whether you can stand it or not. I want you to keep watching until you can hear her talk about you doing these things without getting mad, without flinching, without so much as raising your blood pressure.' I shot Jeanie a glance and saw her pensive frown. This wasn't the plan, but we had to do something to neutralize the reaction we'd just witnessed.

'It's a good idea, actually,' she said. 'You might see something we haven't seen. You know Erica better than we do. She's your daughter's best friend. What we're looking for is something that doesn't sound like her own words, some turn of phrase that gives us an opening on cross-examination.'

Jeanie gave me a look of apology, but we'd already agreed that she would be doing the cross.

'I don't know if I can do this,' Scarsdale told us.

I sighed. 'Then you might as well plead guilty. Because if the jury sees the look on your face that I saw a few minutes ago, you're done. Look, you can't show anger. You have to pity her. Find a way. That's your task over the next eight days.'

Car was on his BlackBerry again. He shook

Scarsdale's hand, then ducked out of the conference room. Scarsdale rubbed his bloodshot eyes, and I realized we'd probably done all the work we were going to be able to do today. I suggested we wrap it up and meet again on Wednesday.

When I returned from walking Scarsdale out, Teddy and Jeanie were at the conference table, Jeanie on her laptop, Teddy gazing out the window toward Lake Merritt. I sat back down at my place.

'So do you think he did it?' my brother asked after a minute.

There was a pause. The old Teddy would never have asked that. Not only would the question never have occurred to him, but also the answer wouldn't have mattered. The scar in his brow was little more than a dent, half-covered by a lock of hair that had come back gray. Its fissures, though, ran deep.

'Probably,' I said. 'Either way, his money's the same shade.'

Jeanie squeezed Teddy's shoulder and went out of the conference room. A moment later I heard her leave. When she'd gone, Teddy retreated to his office. His limp was barely noticeable these days until he got tired. I watched him as he went, and then I looked down with impatience. The old Teddy would have known how to win Jeanie back, but the old Teddy had used up all his chances.

He'd raised me after our mother's death and our father's incarceration. Now it often seemed that the wheel had come full circle, Teddy dependent on me and me the one in practice with Jeanie, who'd once been Teddy's law partner as well as his wife. I'd had to beg her for this chance, and ever since she'd hired me I'd focused all my attention on showing her she'd made the right decision.

If by some miracle I managed to win the Scarsdale case, doors would open for me. I could start thinking about getting out from under Jeanie's wing, opening my own practice, choosing my clients. I was ready – or I thought I was. All I had to do was prove it.

Chapter Three

The phone rang as I was polishing my black shoes. It was 8:00 PM and I was still at the office. I almost didn't pick up.

The operator asked if I would accept a collect call. I told her I would. Jail calls were always collect. 'Leo Maxwell?'

'That's right.' I held the phone against my shoulder as I rubbed the cloth over the toe of the left shoe.

'The criminal defense attorney Leo Maxwell? Teddy Maxwell's brother?' The voice could have belonged to a black man or a white man. It could have been a white man trying to sound black, but that didn't occur to me until later.

'He's not practicing anymore. Are you an old client of his?'

'Nah, but I need a lawyer. Guy in here told me about you.'

I steadied the phone between my shoulder and ear. 'Yeah? Who?'

'Just a guy here in Santa Rita.'

I didn't have any clients currently in Santa Rita Jail. I wiped my hands. 'I've got a pretty full caseload right now. Why don't you give me your name and jail number and tell me what you're charged with. Just the charge.'

'Robinson, Jamil.'

'Jail number?'

He gave it to me.

I prodded him again for the charge. 'Nah, you got to hear the whole story. And it says here on the wall that these calls are recorded. No way can I tell you what I need over the phone. This is some sensitive shit.'

'Fine. I probably don't have any time to take on a new client right now in any case. Good luck with finding yourself a lawyer, Mr Robinson.'

I was about to hang up when he said, 'My sister's on her way to see you. She'll tell you what you need to know. She's the one who gave me your card, dawg. You met her this morning.'

'I'm still going to need to know what the charge is.'

'My sister will tell you all about it. You at 580 Grand?'

'That's what it says on the card. You going to tell me the charge?'

'You make up your mind. There's plenty of lawyers in the book.'

Less than ten minutes later the phone rang again. 'Mr Maxwell? This is Lavinia Martin. We met this morning. I'm here on behalf of my brother, Jamil Robinson. Are you going to keep me standing on the sidewalk at this hour, or shall I come upstairs?'

'I'll buzz you in.'

She'd changed clothes since I saw her. Now she wore a navy-blue suit over a blouse with a plunging neckline.

'You don't waste time,' I said. 'You got your checkbook along?'

Her hand lay on mine. 'I'm sorry about what happened this morning, and I'm sorry if I seemed preoccupied, Mr Maxwell. It's just that my brother—'

She broke off, seemingly overcome. I cleared the mess off the extra chair in my office and she sat. 'I pride myself on not being an overly emotional person. Jamil—'

23

I got the box of tissues from the drawer, but she ignored it, closing her eyes and pinching the bridge of her nose.

'Take your time.'

Finally she opened her eyes and let her hand drop from her face. Her eyes were perfectly clear, a striking auburn brown, a shade lighter than her freckled skin. It was as if she'd wadded up the emotional part of herself and thrown it away.

'I suppose I should begin by telling you that my brother has a lengthy criminal record.' She spoke slowly. 'Most recently he did two years for robbery.'

'Two years isn't so long.'

'Daddy's a man of the cloth. He had work lined up for Jamil when he was released. Nothing glamorous. Janitor work. It wasn't good enough for Jamil. He'd met some men in prison, and some friends of theirs gave him a job when he got out. Security work, supposedly.'

'Daddy,' I repeated.

She went on. 'Jamil was pulled over on San Pablo last night. The police searched the car and found a gun.'

'The DA's office will violate him in about half a minute if he's on parole. If he'd been an ordinary citizen, and wasn't drunk or high or doing anything

24

else obviously illegal, we might have a chance, but the cops can search a parolee anytime, anywhere. They don't even need a reason.'

'My brother and I both realize that a return to prison probably can't be avoided. The question is how long and whether he'll be getting out. You see, according to Jamil, the gun they found in the car was used two weeks ago for a murder. Sooner or later the police are bound to discover this weapon's provenance and charge my brother with that crime.'

'Provenance.' I gave her a hard look, feeling a pulse of excitement at the thought of a murder case. There was no way to keep her from telling the police everything Jamil had told her. 'You'd better start at the beginning.'

She leaned forward. 'The murdered man was a local businessman. Some say in reality the head of a syndicate of drug dealers and shakedown artists. Maybe you heard about it.'

'I only know what everyone in this city knows,' I said. 'That the real issue is the white establishment's inability to stomach black economic independence. That we can't hear about a black man dying violently without thinking he must have done something to deserve it.'

I'd heard about the murder she'd mentioned, of course. It bore all the marks of an internal struggle for control over Oakland's drug trade, which is how the killing had been reported in the papers for about a day and a half, before they moved on to the next one.

'I suppose you think that because you've represented black men in court you can talk about our community like you're some kind of insider, someone who knows how it is.'

I wasn't going to rise to the bait. 'This afternoon you were driving a convertible in Marin County, but I actually live in this town.'

'And I don't?'

'In the hills, maybe. But the hills aren't Oakland. You've got a gun in your purse and you're still afraid to stand alone on Grand Avenue after dark – yet you come in here on your high horse.'

She paused, then sighed. 'It's true that I've left my roots behind. I was right to get out when I had the chance. My husband doesn't know anything about what I'm trying to do for Jamil. And I'd prefer to keep it that way.'

'Don't look so excited when you mention your husband,' I said.

'Mr Maxwell, I'm not here to discuss my personal life.'

'Let's knock it off, then. Either you finish telling me what your brother told you, or there's the door. Before I decide whether to take your brother's case, I have to know everything. Because if he was dumb enough to confess to his sister, I don't want anything to do with him.'

'This is confidential?'

'Anything that incriminates your brother would be confidential between you and me, yes. But I'd be free to divulge anything else you tell me, even if it hurts or embarrasses you. If you told me that the gun in the car was yours, for example – I'd hang you with it. You see, if your brother becomes my client, I'll smear anyone I can if I think it might put him in the clear. That includes you, your preacher father, your little dog.'

'I see.'

'How does Jamil know it was the gun used in the execution?'

'He knows.'

'How?'

'He does,' Lavinia said. 'And I believe him.'

'He knows because he's the one who pulled the trigger, and he was stupid enough to hold on to the gun.' I put down my pen. 'I'm sorry if I sound

27

callous, but wanting Jamil to be innocent won't make it so. That gun isn't motive or opportunity. It's not eyewitness testimony. It's only evidence. It's only the murder weapon. It's only enough to convict your brother and send him to prison for twenty years.'

Her tone now was icy. 'You haven't given me a chance to explain.'

I waited, and so did she, both of us hanging, as if she wanted me to beg to hear what she had to say. And I did want to hear it. But I was willing to wait. Finally she broke the tension by running a hand through her hair. Her lips parted, and I noticed the space between her top front teeth. She hadn't worn perfume this morning, but she was wearing it now, a blend of cinnamon and eucalyptus and roses.

She took a breath and let it out. 'Jamil was pulled over at ten thirty. The officers put him in the back of the squad car. After twenty minutes an unmarked car pulled up, and this detective got out. Detective Campbell. He searched the vehicle while the officers stood off. Campbell found the gun.'

'You're saying he planted it?'

Instead of answering she opened her purse and took out an unsealed envelope filled with cash, placing it on the desk. 'Your retainer.'

28

If the bills were all hundreds like the bill on top, there were several thousand dollars. I pushed it away. 'This isn't the way we do things around here.'

She made no move to take it back. 'We need someone with courage to break this case open. More courage than most of the lawyers I spoke to over the phone this afternoon.'

I looked down at the envelope. Maybe I could find a way to make this good with Jeanie. 'That much money will buy you some courage. The question is how much. It'll cost a lot more than that to take a case like this to trial.'

'Oh, there isn't going to be a trial. My brother's a good soldier. He's confused, and he's scared, and he hates the police, but if someone tells him to confess, he'll do it. Men like my brother, they either live by the rules of the street or they die by them. And right now he's scared.'

She stopped, staring hard at me. '*Please.* My brother needs a lawyer.'

Caught by the intensity of her gaze, I told her I'd look into the case.

When she left, I realized I'd forgotten about the bicycle tire.

Chapter Four

After counting the money – an even ten thousand – I taped the envelope closed and sat with my hands folded across it, lost in thought. Then, locking it in the safe, I turned out the lights and left.

Our building was across from the lake. The other offices were occupied by criminal and divorce lawyers, an insurance agent, a drug-testing agency, a finger-printing business, and a bodyguard company that marketed its services to gospel singers and celebrity preachers. On the ground floor were a boutique clothing store and a casket outlet.

The string of lights around Lake Merritt wavered in the rippling water. Just up Grand the theater marquee told me what to think of the president. I trudged up Elwood onto Santa Clara, turned right onto Vernon, then left onto Moss. Our condo building stood about halfway down the quiet street.

When I got upstairs, Teddy was on the couch in the front room watching *Shawshank*. He'd remembered to heat up a TV dinner, and he'd eaten half of it; once a glutton, now he rarely finished a serving. He'd dropped eight inches from his waistline. The headshot diet, we called it, but he was still huskier than I was. I popped popcorn and joined him.

'Home from the salt mines,' he said. 'You crack the case?' It was what he always said when I came in. Since the shooting he'd become almost affectless, no longer subject to the mood swings that once had put such distance between us. His passivity grated on me more than his moods used to.

'I may have gotten us a new client. Guy got pulled over last night with the murder gun from a major drug hit in his car.'

'The cops had a—?'

'Warrant? No. Someone tipped them off. I haven't talked to the client yet. Potential client. His sister came to see me. What he told her is that he got pulled over by a couple of officers in a patrol car. They had him wait until this homicide cop showed up. Campbell. He searched the car and found the gun.'

'Huh.' Teddy was watching the screen. 'You going to see the guy?'

'Yeah, but I'm not sure when. The sister told me he'd be calling me from jail in the morning.'

'And he's claiming the detective planted the gun.' The crease in Teddy's brow deepened. It was a story so outlandish that it might as well be a lie, a story that all but disqualified Jamil from taking the stand in his own defense, the kind of story that would force any defense attorney to consider putting on a false case even if he knew his client was telling the truth.

I should have considered all this before, but it wouldn't have mattered.

Teddy was still frowning. He unlocked his eyes from the TV and jammed his fist into the popcorn bag. 'The sister told you this gun-planting story?'

'That's right.'

'So maybe she got it mixed up. Maybe he never told her anything about a gun being planted. Maybe he was just holding it for someone.'

Teddy pushed popcorn into his mouth, his eyes going back to the screen.

I'd lost him, but not before I saw where his thoughts were leading. His words called to mind a key ethical principle for the criminal defense lawyer, a principle that dictates that as long as a lawyer is not absolutely sure a client is lying, the lawyer is obliged to let the client testify and help him tell whatever story he wishes.

To put it bluntly: if I want to preserve my client's ability to lie, I must take care not to know the truth.

It followed, therefore, that I must not allow Jamil to tell me the story he'd told his sister, not until I'd had a chance to show him how unworkable it was, and to make him see that no jury would believe that a detective had planted that gun.

I'd seen *Shawshank* dozens of times, but I stayed up to watch Andy and Red's reunion. Later I lay awake, but I wasn't thinking about Scarsdale. Instead I was rehearsing how I would convince Jeanie to let me take Jamil's case.

Chapter Five

The phone rang in my office at seven thirty Sunday morning, just as Lavinia had told me it would. I'd gotten up early and come to the office just to take the call. Again I accepted the charges. 'You talked to my sister?' the voice asked.

'I talked to her.' It was already getting warm in the office. 'She's a persuasive woman.'

'Tell me about it.' A laugh. 'But she's fine, ain't she? Rich, too, thanks to that husband. He's the man we both have to thank.'

'What's he do?' I asked, thinking of the gun in her purse.

'He's flush. He ain't never wanted anything to do with any of Lavinia's people. He told her she had to make a break, and she did, except she couldn't turn her back on me.'

'I think I learned enough from your sister to get started. In fact, for now I think it's better if we don't talk about what happened the other night. I want to come over to the jail and meet with you this afternoon for half an hour or so. Have you been arraigned?'

'Yesterday morning. Just the felon in possession, though.'

'Okay. If there are other charges we'll take them as they come.'

'I don't want you coming over here this afternoon. There's other things going on then you need to be worrying about.'

'Like what?'

'She don't need to know nothing about this. You know that guy she told you about – but we don't need no names over the phone. Call him Mr Soup.'

It took me a moment to get it. Like Campbell's soup, for the detective who'd found – or planted – the gun.

'Most Sunday afternoons Mr Soup has a meeting with a friend of his. Old friend, from back in the day when they was kids. Call him Spoon. Spoon's also a friend of mine. That's how I happen to know about these meetings. You follow?'

'I think so.' He could only be referring to the survivor

of the drug trade power struggle, the man supposedly behind the murder he was accused of.

Jamil went on. 'Soup don't want to be seen with Spoon, and Spoon don't want to be seen with Soup, but they got important business. Still with me?'

'I think I am.'

'Now given the recent developments, and me being where I am, Soup and Spoon going to have to meet for sure. Soup got to say, Hey Spoon, I know you surprised at how hot I been getting, but don't worry, I ain't gonna let that mouth of yours get burned. And Spoon got to say right back, Soup, I'm gonna keep on slurping you up.'

'So there's going to be a meeting. Where?'

'Know Pinehurst Gate, off Pinehurst Road? A little parking lot up there. Another parking lot down in Canyon Meadow. Around three o'clock Soup parks at Canyon Meadow, laces up his running shoes. Spoon parks up at Pinehurst, walks in. I guess they meet in the middle, hike down a little side trail to a spot you can't see from above. Mr Spoon always had me wait in the car, so I don't know what kind of things they talked about. But you can bet it wasn't what to get their mamas for Valentine's.'

'What do you expect me to do about it?'

'I think this is one of those situations where like they say, a picture is worth a thousand words.'

After all the buildup I'd been expecting something more substantial. 'You give me a call tomorrow morning and I'll let you know if anything comes of it.'

He must have heard my disappointment. 'Look, I ain't playing. There's damn good reasons why Soup and Spoon have their meetings so far out of the way.'

'It's pretty last minute to be hiring an investigator.'

'If you can't get this done, I'll just call Lavinia and tell her to come get her money back. You got eyes. You must know how to use a camera. You got a finger for pushing the button. You a little green, from the sound of it, but you keep your head on straight you'll be all right. They ain't going to shoot no white boy if they can help it.'

I wasn't comforted.

I called Car. I thought he was going to laugh at me for swallowing Jamil's story, but after hearing me out he was merely firm. 'This is precisely the kind of job that could get me killed. And not in the name of virtue. It's a dirty job. Doesn't require any skill. I won't do it, and you ought to turn and walk real fast in the other direction.'

It was bad practice not to use an investigator. Anything an investigation turns up is liable to become evidence, and a lawyer must always avoid having to call himself as a witness. Without an investigator, there is no one to say that the photograph is what the lawyer claims.

There's good practice, and then there's the reality that sometimes there's no one else. 'Maybe I could borrow some equipment,' I heard myself say.

A pause. 'You said borrow, but there's no borrow, not from me, especially not to you. Rent, buy, or steal is the universe of possibility you and I are working with. I'm not a rental agent, and you don't have the balls to rip me off.'

It sounded like he was by the water. I heard gulls, maybe the bark of a sea lion, but I couldn't be sure. I always regretted calling Car. But he always came through, even if it cost me more in pride and money than I'd bargained. 'I don't have much of a budget.'

'You said you needed equipment? We talking a backhoe, posthole digger? Or something a bit more intimate?'

'A camera with a telephoto lens.'

'I can set you up with two-year-old equipment, my old stuff. All digital, works fine, good condition. Since we're friends I'll cut you a deal. What do you say a thousand for the setup?'

'The best I can do is five hundred.' I knew he was cheating me.

'A thousand. If the price is too steep maybe the case isn't worth taking. Spying on people's shitty work. It only takes getting burned one time to spoil the fun. I'm speaking from experience. A thousand bucks shouldn't sound like a big investment. If it does, better to back out and go jerk off to all the money you saved than regret it later when someone is shoving a thousand dollars of camera equipment up your ass.'

I closed my eyes, took a deep breath, then opened them. 'How soon can you meet me?'

'Forty minutes. Pick me up at the MacArthur BART. Oh, and Leo, I get paid in cash, I don't write receipts, and I don't take returns. I'll show you how to use the stuff, and after that you're on your own. I don't want any panicky phone calls.'

'You won't get any.'

'Right. Be seeing you.'

Chapter Six

From the BART station I drove up into the hills. The grass on the slopes was such a brilliant white gold it hurt my eyes. These hills had burned in the firestorm of 1991, killing twenty-five people. I remember my father driving me to the top of Potrero Hill to watch the fires at night. Even so far away I did not feel safe. I hadn't been. A few years later my mother was dead, my father imprisoned for murdering her, a crime he insisted he didn't commit. How, as lawyers, we came to be on the side of perpetrators rather than victims is something outsiders seldom understand.

My father was an unsuccessful lawyer; Caroline, my mother, sold makeup and jewelry at Macy's. She was unfaithful, and he was jealous. As far back as I can remember, our house was filled with raised voices or a silence I never mistook for peace.

My father could never be innocent where my mother was concerned, but after all these years I'd come around to believing that he didn't commit the ultimate crime. It was Teddy who put the pieces together. Then, as a reward for solving the decades-old mystery of who really killed her, he got a bullet in the brain.

I exited at Redwood Road and parked at the Canyon Meadow Staging Area. Some kids were running on the playground, oblivious to the heat; it must have been over ninety-five.

I knew these hills well. Teddy and Jeanie used to live just on the other side of the county line, and Pinehurst and Redwood Roads were one of my favorite road biking routes in Oakland. The spot Jamil had described was a bench on a little spur beneath the ridge trail, a steep hike up through toyon and oak.

I started my climb, and soon left the noise of the playground behind. I heard no traffic, no sirens, no sounds other than the titter of birds from the thickets and the buzz of insects from the shade beneath the spreading oaks. It was peaceful, all right. You could drag a body off into the woods and probably no one but the deer would ever find it.

I climbed one more thigh-burning rise and came to a hilltop clearing. Below was the little spur trail, almost like a game trail, which led to a secluded bench where I guessed the two would meet.

Green brush stood out against sun-bleached grass on line after line of hills. The pyramid-shape mass of Mount Diablo rose above the trees. Living all your life down in Oakland, you would never know how much space there was up here.

I found a place where I could see the bench without anyone using it being able to see me. I hoped. The hot wind was relentless. My tongue felt shriveled and dry.

I left my hiding place twice, worried I'd guessed wrong about the meeting place. I was coming back the second time when I passed a fit black guy in a Police Association T-shirt jogging the other direction. Detective Campbell. A surprisingly small man with a build like a dancer's.

He was in his late thirties, early forties. A handsome face – it would have looked fine in marble – with a shaved head, hollow cheekbones, brooding eyes.

When I reached the top of the other hill I looked back. He stood with a leg propped on the bench, stretching his hamstring. I went on over the hill, then worked my way through the brush, creeping on hands and knees the last twenty feet.

I peered through the camera and saw Campbell turn

to meet a guy who'd just come down the trail from the other direction, dressed in slacks made of some loose, light fabric and a silk shirt. I snapped picture after picture, swiping the sweat away from my eyes with the back of my hand.

I saw Campbell try to shake hands. Spoon, slapping away the hand, drew a gun. I was too nervous, having trouble keeping the camera in focus. I wondered what I would do if Spoon shot him.

Campbell's hands soothed the air. After a minute Spoon began to nod, then tucked the gun away. They bumped chests in a one-armed macho hug, then went to the bench.

The years seemed to fall away from Campbell's face; he was no longer the hard-faced detective I'd seen on the trail. Before my eyes, the boys they must once have been together seemed briefly to eclipse the men.

After half an hour Campbell looked at his watch. They slapped hands and went their ways, Spoon down the trail toward Pinehurst, Soup back toward me, running with the same athletic bounce in his step as before, despite the heat.

The wind whisked through the bushes and made the oaks creak. When I was sure it was safe I crawled out of the brush and went back down the trail.

Chapter Seven

Back in my office I loaded the pictures from the camera onto my computer, then began pulling up newspaper articles about the murder. None of the pictures showed the mystery man. I wasn't done. Knowing the murdered man had a legitimate front as a local businessman, I searched for his name. In one of the articles that came up I found a picture of the man from the hills. His name was Damon Watson. He owned a private security business operating out of East Oakland.

I called Jeanie. 'I want to bounce something off you.'

'Do you know what my one overwhelming consideration was in hiring you? The knowledge that if someone had to work on Sunday night, it wouldn't be me.'

'I had a call yesterday from a potential client, and

I've done some investigating on my own. I thought it was time to bring you into the loop.'

'How could I possibly be out of the loop, being your boss?'

'Two nights ago the police stopped a parolee and found a gun in his car. Jamil Robinson. He'd heard my name, and he called from jail, and his sister came to the office last night and told me some things he didn't want to talk about over the phone. Evidently the gun the police found is the murder weapon from the killing of a big player in the drug trade a few weeks ago.'

'How does she know?'

'I have only the client's word for it. Prospective client.' I told her what Lavinia had told me, the story of the client being pulled over, made to wait in the car, then Campbell arriving and discovering the gun. 'I don't like it any more than you do. I still don't like it, but it just might be true. The new guy in charge, he and Campbell go back I guess, and it looks like Campbell may have been protecting his boyhood pal. What he gets in return I don't know.'

'We don't have time to take on a new client right now,' she said. 'We need to focus all our energy on Scarsdale.'

'When I talked to Jamil on the phone this morning he told me about these Sunday afternoon meetings between Damon and Campbell up in the hills. So I thought I might as well head out there with a camera and see what I could see. And what do you know, I've got a series of pictures of Damon pulling a gun on Campbell and Campbell talking him down.'

'Leo, Jamil's just going to plead out. They always do, these guys, these low-level gangsters. We don't want to get mixed up with these people.'

'I've got a feeling about this one. I really think our guy might be innocent. Wouldn't you like to be on the right side for once instead of defending scumbags like Scarsdale?'

'No. I want to make enough money to retire in fifteen years. That's what's left of my idealism. I hate to break it to you, kiddo.'

'I already took the money. She gave me a ten-thousand-dollar retainer.'

'You did what?' Her voice was icy. 'You're at the office? I'm coming in.'

'We can talk about it in the morning,' I said. 'You don't have to drive all the way over here.'

'No, *tonight*. Because I'm not going to sleep otherwise, and if I'm not going to sleep, you shouldn't, either.

Just when I was starting to think it was going to work out, you go and pull something like this.'

'Something like what?'

'Just wait there. I'll see you in half an hour.'

An hour later Jeanie and I were in the conference room. She kept pacing from one side to the other. The envelope of cash Lavinia had given me was lying on the table, but we hadn't gotten there yet. I'd shown her the pictures. Neither of us had said a word.

'Is he your client or isn't he?'

'I can't take on clients without your approval.'

She was as angry as I'd ever seen her, and she wasn't a woman to disguise her emotions. 'The point isn't what you or I think. The point is what he thinks.' She picked up the envelope and tossed it at my chest.

I caught it. 'He's my client.'

'What happens now?'

'Turn the pictures over to the DA. Jamil walks; Leo's the big hero.'

'These pictures don't prove shit. They don't show shit. And you don't even have enough money there to get you through the prelim.'

'Maybe it won't come to that.'

'I'll tell you what happens now. You give me one

reason not to put you out on your ass. You and your ten-thousand-dollar retainer.'

Up until now I'd just been trying to weather the storm, thinking that she would rage for a while, and then we'd get down to business. 'You're thinking of firing me.'

She looked at me steadily. 'I warned you when I hired you that I had doubts about your professionalism and your judgment, and that I was going to keep you on a short leash until those doubts were gone. I wonder if I made the wrong decision.'

'Look at the pictures. Damon's holding a gun on him, they're hugging, and then they're talking like long-lost brothers. I found myself wishing this afternoon that I'd gotten it all on tape, but it's actually better this way. The pictures tell as complete a story as you could ever want to tell.'

'If you'd taped them you'd really be in trouble. You'd have broken the law.'

'Jesus, I know that. I did a damn good job.'

'Looks to me like you had it gift wrapped for you. How'd you say this person got your name?'

'He said he got it from someone in Santa Rita. He didn't tell me who.'

'No, I don't like it. If you'd come to me when you

should have, I'd have said pass. It doesn't sit well, cash in hand and this unbelievable story and then these pictures. We're lawyers, not private detectives.'

'So what do you want me to do?'

'Turn the pictures over to the DA's office. Return the money to the sister. Tell Jamil you're sorry, but you can't take the case.'

I swore and threw back my chair, standing and turning to face the darkened window. I wanted to walk out on her, walk out on the practice, take Jamil and Scarsdale with me, and for a moment it seemed that I would. But she'd taken a chance on me, and I owed her too much.

'Fine,' I said through my teeth.

'Other lawyers, not just the DA's office but other defense lawyers – everyone respects a lawyer who plays to win. But when you cross the line, start breaking rules—' She paused. 'I'm not saying that's what you've done, but it seems to me that's where this is leading. If you're going to work for me, we need to be crystal clear. We play by the rules.'

'And yet you worked with Teddy all those years and you had no idea that the entire city of San Francisco believed he was buying testimony wherever he could get it?'

She didn't answer.

'Fine,' I said. 'I'll take the photos to the DA tomorrow and after that I'll tell Jamil he needs to find another lawyer.'

'Focus on Scarsdale. It's a good case. You can win it if you keep your eye on the ball. Something like this Jamil thing, when it seems too good to be true – the real ones are never this easy.'

She left. I locked the money in the safe and went out for a drink.

Chapter Eight

At 9:00 AM I called the Oakland DA's office and asked for the prosecutor on Jamil's case. The receptionist put me through to the voice mail of Christopher Fowler. I left a message identifying myself as Jamil's lawyer. A series of photographs documenting a conspiracy between a man named Damon Watson and Detective Eric Campbell had come into my possession, I said. 'I'm hoping to give you the courtesy of reviewing this evidence in the privacy of your office rather than having to see it on the evening news,' I said. 'Please call me back.'

The phone on my desk rang twenty minutes later. 'Mr Maxwell, this is Kip Fowler.'

'Thanks for returning my call.'

'I'd like to have a look at whatever you've got. How's ten AM?'

I checked my watch. 'That's fine. One thing. I'd like my client to be present.'

There was a pause. I was sure Fowler would object. But he said, 'Fine. Better make it eleven, then. Give them time to fish him out.'

At ten forty-five I drove around the lake to the courthouse. I passed my briefcase through the screening device, walked through the metal detector, and took the elevator up to 9. After I told the receptionist who I was, she lifted the phone and spoke into it. A moment later a tall, pencil-thin man with glasses and a silver crew cut appeared and shook my hand. 'Mr Maxwell. Your client hasn't arrived, but he should be here shortly. Why don't we go on back.'

He led me down a hallway past several rows of cubicles into a conference room with a table much too large for the space and a view of the lake. Sesame seeds were scattered across the tabletop, and a trio of dried-out-looking bagels sat on a plastic tray beside a half-excavated carton of cream cheese.

'Do you have an A/V system, or shall we just use the display on my laptop?'

'No money for high-tech conference rooms, I'm afraid. We spend too much prosecuting criminals.'

'That's something we can agree on.'

'If we stopped doing our jobs, where would that leave you? The public defenders are always lecturing me on the folly of the drug war, overly zealous prosecution of petty offenses, that sort of thing, and with some credibility. They're in the same boat we're in. None of us is getting paid by the hour. It's the private defense attorneys who take the system to the bank.'

'That's how I came to be wearing these diamond cufflinks.'

He glanced sharply at my wrists, then a slow smile spread across his face. 'Well, you're young yet. But you'll catch on.'

I was opening my laptop at the head of the conference table when the door opened and a woman came in. She was tall, with long, dark hair and pale skin – Japanese Irish, I knew. Her name was Cassidy Akida, and we'd been in law school together.

Fowler introduced her. 'We've met,' I said.

'Ms Akida will be prosecuting you.'

'I thought you were handling this.'

'I'm handling the case against your client. Ms Akida will be prosecuting you. You've passed the bar, Mr Maxwell, so you must be aware of Penal Code Section 632.'

Cassidy had a thick bound copy of the California

Penal Code under her arm. Opening it, she read aloud, '"Every person who, intentionally and without the consent of all parties to a confidential communication, by means of any electronic amplifying or recording device, eavesdrops upon or records the confidential communication, shall be punished by a fine and imprisonment in the county jail not exceeding one year. Except as proof in an action or prosecution for violation of this section, no evidence obtained as a result of eavesdropping upon or recording a confidential communication in violation of this section shall be admissible in any judicial, administrative, legislative, or other proceeding."'

I listened with the admiration I reserve for audacious acts. She did it well. I'd have preferred she were reading something else, like maybe Cleopatra's final soliloquy. I'd have preferred that she were almost anything but a prosecutor.

'Excellent,' I said. 'Maybe a slightly heavier stress on *imprisonment*. The word "and" is important. Also of significance is "amplifying or recording device". Ditto "eavesdrops". None of that applies to cameras.'

'Ms Akida?' Fowler prompted.

She had a case printed out, passages highlighted. Again she read, '*People v. Gibbons*, 215 Cal. App. 3d

56

1204, First District, 1989. "In other contexts, communication has been recognized to include not only oral or written communication but communication by conduct as well. We acknowledge that certain terms used in the privacy act, such as 'eavesdropping', 'amplifying device', and 'telephone', might suggest a narrow definition of communication, synonymous with conversation. However, Penal Code Section 630 expressly states the intent of the Legislature to protect the right of privacy of the people of this state. Consistent with the express declaration of intent and in the absence of any express statutory limitations, we find that 'communication' as used in the privacy act is not limited to conversations or oral communications but rather encompasses any communication, regardless of its form, where any party to the communication desires it to be confined to the parties thereto.'"

'You still wish to proceed, Mr Maxwell?' Fowler asked.

'Sure. That's the case about the guy who secretly filmed the girls having sex with him, right? You want to prosecute me for taking pictures on public land, in the open air, of a cop and a murder suspect? Go ahead. Let's have a jury trial.'

Fowler smiled indulgently. 'Now that we've called

your attention to the statute, you must realize that no illegally obtained evidence can be used in court on your client's behalf.'

'California's wiretapping statutes predate Proposition Eight, which we both know makes any evidence not excluded by the federal constitution or California's hearsay rules admissible. You guys are the ones who usually catch the benefit of that, but this time it works in my favor. The pictures come in.'

His face tightened. 'We'll see. In any case, they'll come in against you, too.' He nodded to Cassidy.

'Prosecuting criminal defense attorneys for blowing the whistle on the Oakland Police Department should make for great press. I'll have those cufflinks before you know it.'

It was Cassidy who spoke. 'If you still have a law license, that is.'

If I'd broken the law, I would subject myself to discipline by the bar and the possible loss or suspension of my license. But I was certain that in this case the law *and* the ethical regulations were on my side.

I began packing up. 'You've played this one wrong, Kip. You can catch the pictures showing the meeting between Detective Campbell and Damon Watson on the news. You can see along with the rest of the world what a conspiracy to frame an innocent man for murder looks like.'

I slammed shut my laptop. Fowler made soothing motions. Cassidy was smirking.

A knock on the door. Fowler answered it. Three deputies stood in the hallway with a man in orange between them. A big, slouching guy with fuzzy cornrows and a potbelly. His hands and feet were chained to his waist.

'Finally,' I said. 'I'd like a moment alone with my client.'

Fowler glanced questioningly at the lead deputy, a husky man with a moustache. 'No can do,' the deputy said. 'Not here. This is an unsecured area. You want to go down to the holding cell and meet him in an interview room we can arrange that. Up here, the escort will remain with the prisoner.'

The man, Jamil, was frowning at me. 'What do you mean, your client?'

Jamil's voice over the phone had been brash, but now it was high and whining, with a faint lisp.

I turned to Fowler with a sickening plunge. 'Take this man back downstairs and bring up Jamil Robinson.'

One of the deputies reached down and checked the

prisoner's jail bracelet. 'Jamil Robinson.' He read off the number and looked up at me.

Jamil looked from one deputy to the other. 'You told me I was going to meet my lawyer,' he protested querulously. 'This guy ain't her. I ain't talking to some lawyer you picked out.'

'You hired me,' I said. 'We spoke on the phone. Remember? Your sister visited my office.'

'My sister?' he said, his voice rising with indignation. 'My sister? Man, my sister dead.'

There was no blood left in my face. My mind was occupied with visualizing the path I'd taken to get here, the long walk I would have to retrace before I was out of this place and alone with my shame.

'Who's your lawyer?' Fowler asked.

'Nikki, man. Nikki Matson.'

Not the name I'd wanted to hear. Amid the Bay Area criminal defense community, there was no lawyer more feared for savagery and vindictiveness.

Fowler turned to me. 'You see this man is represented.' To the deputies he said, 'Take him back to Santa Rita.' To Cassidy, 'Get Ms Matson on the phone.' To me, 'You can bet Nikki will have your bar card.'

'Come on, Kip,' I said when the deputies and Jamil

Robinson – the real Jamil Robinson – had gone out of the room. 'I was set up. Someone claiming to be Jamil Robinson called my office, and a woman claiming to be his sister paid me a visit. Obviously neither of these people was who they claimed.'

Fowler seemed unable to decide whether to believe me. Cassidy looked skeptical. 'You took the case without ever meeting the client,' Fowler said.

'I was set up,' I repeated. 'Plain and simple.'

They were unlikely to see it that way, and neither was Nikki. I could only hope that she'd be interested enough by what was in the pictures to overlook my apparent attempt to poach her client.

Cassidy stepped out into the hall with her phone. Fowler and I didn't say anything. We were in the soup, and it was my fault. A moment later Cassidy reappeared and said, 'Nikki Matson is on her way. She's pissed.'

Fowler's face puckered. 'You're not going anywhere,' he told me, though I hadn't moved. 'I'm sure as hell not going to answer for dragging Nikki's client out of jail and over here without his lawyer present. Jesus,' he said, and he grabbed a chair and threw himself down in it, probably realizing that his case was devolving into a fiasco.

I went to the head of the conference table and set up my laptop again. Whoever had hired me had lied outrageously, but the pictures were real. Jamil had been framed, and my employers wanted the world to know about it.

What I was about to do was worth ten grand to someone. Later, the question would be to whom and why. Now, all I cared about was salvaging what was left of my career.

Fowler was paged and went out. I heard Nikki as soon as she was through the secured entrance. 'Where is he?' she stormed in her deep smoker's voice. Her anger preceded her, rattling the plaster. 'What did you do, set him up with a dummy lawyer and put a wire on him? Where have you hidden him? Probably in a cell with a snitch, now that your plan has failed. Why even bother with a snitch? Take it from me, Kip. It's much simpler just to write out a statement and forge his signature. It's more direct and there are fewer witnesses to bite you in the ass.'

They came through the door. Fowler's face was flushed and his lips were thin with anger. 'Ha!' Nikki pointed a long purple fingernail at me. 'You're dead. Boy, you are *so* dead. Nobody fucks with my clients. Did you think you could snatch him away from me? Is that what you were planning? Is that how this latest crop of attorneys does business? Well, it's the last business you'll find in this town. My clients are loyal. They don't jump ship.'

She was a huge woman, just under six feet and well over three hundred pounds, wearing a steel-gray suit and coming to a halt like a battleship docking. Instantly she focused on me, glaring malevolently.

'I was set up,' I told her. She made a noise of disgust.

'Get out of here. Go on home,' she said. She had her briefcase open and was taking papers out. It appeared, amazingly, that she already had a motion drawn up, though it had not been twenty minutes since Cassidy called her. She slid a copy toward Fowler. 'This is being filed as we speak. Consider yourself served. That's a motion for sanctions and for a protective order. I'm going to ask that the judge admonish you, fine you, and hold you in contempt for willfully violating Mr Robinson's Sixth Amendment rights by initiating contact out of my presence.'

Fowler had a sheen of sweat on his forehead. He fingered the motion, then pushed it aside. 'Mr Maxwell represented himself to me as Mr Robinson's attorney. He requested this meeting and demanded that Mr Robinson be present. He claimed to have evidence of a conspiracy between Detective Eric Campbell and Damon Watson to frame your client for murder. And now you know everything I know about this mess.'

'If that's the case, then these pictures are potentially exculpatory evidence. I demand that you turn them over to me at once.' Nikki pounded the table, looking at Fowler with her jaw set and amusement in her eyes.

'I would be happy to, but they aren't yet in my possession. Mr Maxwell has been trying to decide whether to show the pictures to us and expose himself to prosecution under Section 632, or crawl back under whatever rock he crawled out from.'

'Oh, nonsense. You think the pictures will disappear if you prosecute someone for making them? Only if it's not as bad as you think. Otherwise it's a murder case, not an eavesdropping case. And you *must* think it's bad, or we wouldn't be here.'

'Murder and conspiracy,' I said.

She ignored me. They all did.

'Let's see them,' Fowler said, turning to me. 'Time to put the cards on the table.'

I shrugged. It was what I'd come here for, but Nikki had already done the unpleasant work of relieving me of responsibility for Jamil's case. The problem was I still had Lavinia's voice in my ears. And I still wanted to bring Campbell down. Then I remembered what Jeanie had said about my reputation.

I displayed the pictures without comment, one after the other in rapid succession, like a stop-frame movie showing the sequence of the two men meeting, the gun coming out, then going back into Damon's waistband, finally the two sitting together and talking on the bench.

Afterward no one said anything for nearly a minute. Cassidy glanced at Fowler, her eyes narrowed. Nikki stared down at her knuckles, her brow furrowed, her face intense but unreadable.

At last Nikki let out a long sigh, pushed back her chair and stood up. She gave a rueful laugh. 'The way I see it, Kip, you have three choices, all of them equally bad. You can drop the charges and open an investigation of Campbell. You can pursue these charges against my client and watch it blow up in your face. Or you can go in the bathroom and put a bullet in your head.'

'You forgot one,' Fowler said. 'Run our own investigation independent of the police department and bring down the whole pack of them.'

'Hm,' Nikki said with a tight-lipped smile. 'I'll hear

from you,' she told Fowler. Then apparently to me, though she didn't look in my direction, 'You come with me. I'm not finished with you yet.'

I just wanted out of there. 'You let me know if you want me to surrender,' I said to Cassidy as I gathered my stuff.

She didn't respond. From my suit pocket I took the CD I'd burned of the photos and slid it down the table toward Fowler. 'There are other copies of that in existence. Fair warning.'

'Fair warning indeed,' Nikki said.

We went out through the secured entrance of the DA's suite of offices, then took the elevator together to the ground floor of the courthouse, Nikki's wheeled briefcase rumbling along behind her. As we were leaving the courthouse, Detective Campbell was just walking in. I froze for a second, no more. He ignored Nikki's saccharine greeting, but he looked straight at me, turning his head to follow as I passed.

'He's going to have a shock,' Nikki said, as if remarking on the weather. 'If he doesn't already know it was you, he will soon. He doesn't have much to worry about, unless there's more of an evidence trail than I suppose. The union will take good care of him.' She glanced at her watch. 'Lunchtime. As a rule I eat alone but today I'll make an exception. The DA may swallow that shit about a setup, but you'll have to come clean with me if you want to stay prosperous. Here's my car.'

It was an eighties-era Cadillac, white with red leather seats, parked in a handicapped spot out in front of the courthouse on Lakeside Drive. She wheeled her bag up to the rear passenger door and made a signal toward me. Obediently I opened the door and lifted the boxlike briefcase onto the floor of the back seat. It must have weighed fifty pounds.

The car rocked underneath her as she sat behind the wheel.

I got in on the other side. 'Was that supposed to be a threat?'

She started the engine. 'What do you think?'

'It's hard to tell, coming from someone who'd joke about Fowler blowing out his brains.'

'That was no joke. The man is high-strung, and you just handed him the crap sandwich of the week. No matter what he does, he loses, and his boss will be the one with egg on his face. If Fowler can't get this conviction, and I don't think he can, he'll never go higher in that office. That's too bad. I've always had him wrapped around my middle finger.'

'Little finger. Wrapped around my little finger.'

'I say what I mean to say.'

She drove us to a Lao restaurant just west of Lake Merritt. I went with her because I wanted to know who'd set me up and figured she must have a better idea than I did. What I was going to do with that information once I had it was another matter.

It was a little place with linoleum floors, folding tables of the kind you might find in church basements, and vinyl tablecloths. In the back corner a TV played Laotian music videos, a karaoke ball bouncing along the bottom of the screen. We were shown to a small table near the back. Nikki ordered for us both: rice-ball salad for two, green curry for her, red curry for me. She said something in what I assumed was his language, and the waiter grinned.

'You must be a regular here.'

'Oh, I'm a sponge for culture. Enough about me. Let's talk about you. Who hired you to take those pictures?'

While I was pondering my response, the waiter came with tall glasses of iced green tea sweetened with condensed milk. He was still grinning.

'My employer's identity has to remain confidential. Why do you want to know?'

'Because it concerns me. I need to know who's fucking me so that I can fuck them back. If you don't want it to be your ass, you better tell me who hired you.'

'Go ahead. File a bar complaint. You'll have to get in line, though. Right behind Fowler.'

She gave a sharp laugh. 'Is that what you think this is about? Ethics?'

'Since you brought up the subject of ethics, who hired you is the question. Who pays your fee for defending Jamil? I'm guessing this guy Damon, judging by your reaction to the tape.' She had a reputation for defending gang members – taking money from the men at the top and copping pleas for foot soldiers – just the sort of thing that appeared to be happening to Jamil. She might even be in on the frame-up, if there were one.

'It's none of your business who my clients are. Jesus, that I have to sit here and take this shit from a kid still in diapers.'

The rice-ball salad came. With her fork she picked off individual grains of fried rice and speared rings of green onion. After every bite she patted her lips with her napkin.

'You know why you got burned on this one?' she

said after she'd taken the edge off. 'It's because you haven't had proper mentoring.' She took another bite. 'You've got discretion, even though you've been made a fool. I'd love nothing more than to help you settle your score with whoever did it, but you don't want my help. Fine. You want to be a courthouse joke, I won't stand in your way.' She studied me over her fork, then pointed it at me and said, 'Your brother and Jeanie must have warned you about me. They must have advised you never to have anything to do with me. That must be it.'

I began to smile, knowing her reputation for unscrupulous, unethical practices. Then I remembered that I was the one who'd blundered into her case, interfered with her client, and the smile fled, and I didn't feel like eating anything more. 'I'm afraid Teddy never mentioned you. I could ask him. You never know who and what he'll remember. But I try to avoid reminding him about the past.'

'Yes, I suppose that's all over now. Poor bastard. I bet he wishes that gunman's aim had been just a little better.'

I pushed back my chair. 'You watch your mouth.'

'Come on. Sit down. It's just my way of talking. Everyone knows I say what's on my mind. Don't let it bother you.' Her gaze grew inward, thoughtful. 'I've been looking for a new associate. Maybe you were made a fool, but you went out and got those pictures. You got them. That tells me something about you, that you're not quite the helpless child you appear to be.'

'You can't seriously be offering me a job.'

'I could use someone who's not afraid of getting his hands dirty – someone who cares about results, and the truth above all else.' In her mouth the word sounded like a euphemism. 'What are you making with Jeanie, fifty, fifty-five? I'll pay you ninety.'

I sat looking at her, the numbers ringing in my ears. 'You and Campbell, you're two gears in the same machine, aren't you? His role was to make sure Jamil was arrested with that gun. Your job is to make sure Jamil doesn't turn on his boss. I'm the wrench in the works, and you figure you can buy me off, take me in hand until you find out what you want to know, use me to put some distance between yourself and the dirty work.' I stood. 'Ninety isn't nearly enough.'

'It's not just the salary. I'm offering you guidance, protection. Take a few days and think about it.'

'I've thought plenty.'

'Fair warning, then. Watch your step. Oh, and I'll take my copy of the CD you made for Fowler.'

I dropped the extra CD I'd made on the table and walked out of the restaurant just as the waiter came with our curries. The food smelled good.

Chapter Nine

I managed to avoid Jeanie and Teddy when I got back to the office. I closed my door behind me and looked longingly at my bike. I lifted the rear wheel and spun the pedals, checking the motion of the chain. I wondered how long it would be before I took another afternoon off to ride it.

The thing to do now was check on Scarsdale; make sure we were still on for our meeting. I called his hotel room, letting the phone ring and ring, but there was no answer. I tried the cell. No luck. He wasn't exactly staying in the kind of neighborhood that made you want to go for a stroll. I called the front desk of the hotel. 'I'm trying to reach the guest in 205.'

'If your party isn't answering, you're welcome to leave a message,' the woman said.

'I'm a bit worried about him. He's been depressed.

73

His wife kicked him out and he lost his job. Is there any way you could check on him?'

I heard her hitting keys on her computer. 'The room hasn't been cleaned in two days. I can see on the hallway security camera that the DO NOT DISTURB sign is hanging on the door. Is this an emergency?'

I hesitated, then told her no.

I was already out the door.

'Marty!' I called, banging on the door. 'It's Leo. If you're in there, open up.'

The woman from the front desk hovered beside me. I wished she would go away. From the room I heard no sound of movement, but there were voices, a child's with an adult's voice interjecting. The volume was low, but I recognized the soundtrack of the police interviews with Erica, the child Scarsdale was accused of molesting.

I pounded the door again. 'Marty, if you don't open now, I'm going to have them call 911. And then the paramedics will come here and break the door down. If you don't want that to happen, you'd better open up right now!'

I heard what sounded like a groan, the creak of the mattress, and then the door was unlatched. I stepped into a dank human smell, as if all the excretions of all the lonely people who had slept here hung like a vapor in the room.

The curtains were drawn. By the light of the little girl's scared face on the screen I saw Marty sink to the floor and take a drink from the glass he found there. I turned on the light, and he flinched, lifting an arm to his eyes. The AC was going full blast. He pulled the grimy bedspread down over his shoulders. He was wearing the shirt and slacks he'd been wearing Saturday at the office.

His voice was scratchy, as if he'd been crying. 'I want to plead guilty. Everything she said, I did it, and more. I just want it all to stop.'

My anger surged. Now that he'd confessed to me I wouldn't be able to put him on the stand. 'Get up off the floor and pull yourself together.' I stabbed the TV's power button and threw open the curtains. 'You want to go to prison, Marty? You know what'll happen to you there?'

He sat blinking. 'I want help. It's the only way I'm ever going to stop.'

'No one's going to help you. They're going to throw you in prison and leave you there for years. And eventually someone in there is going to kill you for what you did. I think if you wanted to die we'd have found you dead in here.'

The front desk clerk was still standing in the door. 'He's fine,' I explained. 'There isn't going to be any trouble.'

When I looked again the door was closed and she was gone. I took the glass from Scarsdale's hand. He was shivering under the blanket, squinting against the sun from the window. His eyes were bloodshot, red rimmed, his face pale and unshaven, with dried spittle around his mouth. I felt an urge to kick him, and saw no reason to resist.

He didn't respond except to grunt and stop shivering. I kicked him again, harder, squarely in the ribs. It felt good. I was bracing to give it to him again when he stood. 'In the bathroom,' I told him. 'Shower, toothbrush, shave.'

He lurched past me. Humiliation was all right. We could work with humiliation. I surveyed the wreck of the room, wondering when he'd last eaten. There was a box with three-quarters of a pizza.

In the mirrored wall I caught sight of my reflection: a smaller man than I thought of myself, too wiry, shoulders stooped with a bully's malice, eyes half-lidded as if I were the one with a guilty conscience, a flush of contempt on my freckled face.

While the shower ran I found him some clean clothes and put them on the bathroom counter. When he came out he was abashed, not sober by any means but with the fight gone out of him. He wasn't going to be pleading guilty. I would bring the topic up again when he was in better shape, but I saw at once that from now on he'd do what I said.

'You got somewhere else you can stay?'

He shrugged, sitting on the edge of the bed. 'Another hotel.'

'I don't think you should stay here, do you? You look like you've had a rough couple of nights.'

'You told me to keep watching the video.'

'Yeah, well, maybe you've watched enough. Let's pack. What you need is a change of scene.'

I helped him check out and took him to the Ramada across the street. New room, clean sheets, band of paper around the toilet seat, everything fresh. It wasn't the second start he needed; it wasn't a new life. But for the present it was the closest we could get.

I went to In-N-Out and brought back burgers. As I walked back to his room from my car I heard the sound of kids splashing and yelling. Before I left again I told him to stay away from the pool.

Chapter Ten

Teddy and I were sitting on the couch waiting for the news to start. We didn't usually watch it, but tonight I figured I'd better. I reminded him of the potential client I'd mentioned the other night, filled him in on what I'd done up in the hills, and explained what had happened to me at the DA's office this morning.

'Bottom line is my client's not my client. Someone set me up. Jamil's real attorney is Nikki Matson. She threatened me, trying to get me to tell her who hired me. I pretended I knew, but I don't have the foggiest.'

'You told Jeanie what happened?'

'I've been managing to avoid her.'

'Nikki,' Teddy said. 'I remember Nikki. She's one of the people I wouldn't have minded forgetting.'

'When she got done threatening me she tried to give me a job.'

'You're not gonna quit Jeanie.'

I shook my head. 'Lavinia could have planned it, I suppose. Hitting me with the car. She could have been following me. She saw an opportunity and she took it. But an opportunity for what?'

'To expose this detective.'

'There were two of them in on it. Lavinia and the guy who called me pretending to be Jamil. If they knew so much about what Campbell was up to, why couldn't they blow the whistle themselves?'

'How much do you remember about the car?'

'I didn't get the license number. A blue Pontiac, fairly new. She seemed to have money. She said she was from Oakland but seemed freaked out to be standing on the street outside our office. You're not from Oakland if Grand Avenue makes you nervous.'

'Unless you're afraid someone's going to recognize you,' Teddy said.

I hadn't thought of that. For the umpteenth time I caught a fleeting glimpse of my brother's old intelligence, gone again even as it flashed into the light.

The pictures I'd taken yesterday appeared on the screen in sequence, telling their silent drama.

'Nikki fucking Matson,' I said.

'What was she supposed to do with them?'

'You're right. No real downside for her in giving the photos to the news, letting the DA sweat it out.'

'Maybe she was the one who set you up. You dig up the dirt, she and what's-his-name get the benefit.'

I shook my head. 'Nikki has a little conflict of interest. The other guy on the tape, Damon, I'm pretty sure he's her client, too. In fact, she may have been in on the frame-up. As Jamil's lawyer she was in a position to make sure he pleaded guilty like a good soldier. That's one of the reasons I'd hoped we'd have a few more days to figure out what's going on, not to mention how I can get out of this mess.'

But I wasn't getting out. Seeing my name flash across the bottom of the screen, I turned up the volume and heard, 'Oakland attorney Nikki Matson, Jamil Robinson's previous lawyer, said she had nothing to do with the pictures, and that Mr Robinson had fired her. Robinson's new attorney, Oakland criminal defense lawyer Leo Maxwell, issued a written statement today refusing to comment. Quote, "These photographs speak for themselves".'

'Jesus fucking Christ,' I said aloud. 'I'm not his lawyer. I didn't say that.'

'Sources in the Alameda County district attorney's office pointed out that the person who made the photographs would be subject to prosecution under certain interpretations of California's wiretapping statute and could face up to a year in jail. When asked if Maxwell would be charged, a spokesperson refused to comment, stating that office policy forbids discussing ongoing investigations.'

The story ended, and I killed the volume. 'Nikki fucking Matson,' I said. I didn't know what made me angrier, that someone had issued a statement in my name or that the DA's office thought they could intimidate me with threats of prosecution.

We were silent for a moment. Then Teddy said, 'Did you issue that statement?' But he knew the answer.

I let out a long sigh. My cell phone rang and I pulled it from my pocket. Jeanie. Crap. I got up from the couch and went into the kitchen.

'Jeanie, I *didn't* make that statement.' Hearing the tinny sound of my own voice, I knew that she wouldn't believe me, and that even if she did take my word, she wouldn't trust me after this. She'd known me too long, and too well, and she would be all too ready to conclude that I hadn't changed a bit.

'You screwed me, kid. So I'm going to have to cut you loose.'

'Jeanie, I—'

'Don't. You knew last night what you were going to do, and the least you could have done was level with me. I'm perfectly aware that sooner or later you're going to want to get out on your own. I guess that time is now.'

'Jeanie, I know it's hard for you to believe, but honest to god, I'm telling the truth. I was just about to call the TV station and demand a retraction.' Now I wished that I hadn't avoided her all day, that I'd gone immediately and explained. It was all too much to lay on her now.

'What you said last night about this thing seeming too good to be true, you were absolutely right. I saw Jamil at the DA's office. He claims he didn't hire me and we never talked on the phone. He doesn't *have* a sister. He clearly wasn't the guy who called me. The voices are different. Jamil never fired Nikki. She fired *him*. I'm pretty sure she was the one who gave those photographs to the TV station. She must also have sent them a false press release in my name.'

'How does that work?' Jeanie demanded, angry and incredulous.

'She doesn't want to be his lawyer anymore, because she represents his boss, Damon. That's the guy in the pictures with Campbell. If the pictures came out on their own, it would be obvious she's got a conflict of interest. Either she was in on framing Jamil to take the fall for Damon, or she stood by while Jamil stabbed Damon in the back. By giving the photos to the press with that phony statement, she makes it look like Jamil hired me without her knowledge, like he fired her instead of her firing him.'

I looked up and saw Teddy standing in the kitchen doorway.

'So?' Jeanie asked, still not buying a word of it.

'So now Nikki's off the hook. She's not responsible to Damon for Jamil and whatever he might tell the police, and she's not touched by the frame-up. She manages to cover her ass both ways.'

'Leo, the Scarsdale trial starts in six days. These excuses are beside the point.'

'Excuses?' I needed to make her understand. 'The thing is, however ridiculous the situation may be, I'm the one who got myself into it.'

'What's that supposed to mean?'

'This morning I was ready to turn over the pictures and walk away from this. I can't do that now.'

'What's it about, a point of honor?'

'Something like that.' I'd messed up, and I needed to do what I could to make it right.

Jeanie picked her words carefully. 'In that case, the

question in my mind is whether you stay on for Scarsdale or whether I cut you loose immediately. I'm not speaking out of anger. This is the reality of running a practice. I need an associate capable of making good business decisions. You want to be Don Quixote, go work for the public defender.'

'It's not of much benefit to Jamil to dodge a murder rap if he comes out smelling like a snitch. But he's basically got no choice now, after those news reports. Meaning, turn snitch for real. That is, if the police could protect him, which I doubt, given that evidently he was framed by a cop. It's probably a stroke of luck that Nikki dumped him, but I don't think he's going to see it that way. The least I owe him is to talk to him. Even though it may cost me this job.'

'You talk to him if you feel you have to. If he tells you to go to hell, which I certainly would, given the mess you've already made of things, you and I will sit down tomorrow or the next day and have a discussion about whether we're going to have to ask for a continuance on Scarsdale. I can't justify entrusting one of my clients to someone with no future in this office.'

I remembered the kick I'd given Scarsdale this afternoon, the man's sniveling confession, and felt a flash of shame.

'In the meantime, you'd better make sure your files are up to date.'

I was on a high wire with Jamil Robinson, but if I could just manage to stay there, it could be my big case. 'Fine,' I told her. 'I'll write you a letter of resignation. You can keep it on file. If you decide to tear it up, okay. If not, I understand. You're running a business. You've got to make decisions based on that.'

At last the bitterness broke out of her, her voice thickening. 'You'll do fine on your own. Better than fine. In this business it doesn't pay to have too sharp a conscience.'

I swallowed the sting. 'I owe you a lot, Jeanie.'

She'd already hung up. Teddy was still standing behind me.

'You should call the TV station and demand a retraction,' he said.

I turned away from him, opened the fridge, and stared into it. 'Right now I'm going to drink a beer and go to bed. And first thing in the morning I'm going to drive out to Santa Rita.'

Teddy didn't reply, his face neutral, or nearly so. After a moment he held out his hand. Forcing myself to see what was before my eyes, I passed him a beer.

Chapter Eleven

By nine thirty the next morning I was through jail security and waiting in an attorney meeting room. Santa Rita Jail is a huge place. With benches and trees and a wide lawn like a college quad, the exterior tries to camouflage what lies beyond the gates. Inside, it's the same as any other jail, with the stink of unwashed bodies and low-nutrition food, anger and fear, sickness and desperation.

Where I found myself waiting was like all such rooms: small, with concrete block walls, a flimsy table and two plastic chairs. The deputy had locked me in. I heard him returning along the echoing hall, and then the door opened and admitted Jamil, wearing an orange jumpsuit identical to the one he'd worn yesterday at the DA's office. The deputy closed the door behind him.

I stood and shook his hand. This time he wasn't shackled. 'I wanted to apologize,' I said.

He stared with an intent urgency into my face, his eyes bright. He seemed smaller today than he had yesterday. 'No point apologizing,' he said in his high voice. 'What's done is done.'

'I came to see if there was anything I could do to help. You must have heard by now what was on the news.'

'I heard. Nikki dumped me.' He wore his vulnerability all on the surface; in a place like this such naked weakness could only lead to subjection. A man like Jamil would be on the lookout for a protector, a leader, a father or brother figure. He could easily have committed the murder he was charged with. Inside or out, whatever his daddy of the moment said to do, he would obey in a snap.

'A woman came to my office a few days ago pretending to be your sister and hired me to be your lawyer. Then someone pretending to be you called me on the phone and gave me the information about the meeting with Damon and Campbell.'

'Like I told you yesterday, I don't got no sister.'

'You talked to Nikki recently?'

'I thought I would get with her yesterday, but they

just drove me to the courthouse, brought me up to see you, then took me back. And then last night I hear about this shit.'

'You probably heard that a statement went out in my name, claiming to be your attorney. I didn't make that statement. For me to be your attorney I'd need a piece of paper with your signature on it saying you wanted me to represent you. You haven't given me anything like that. We never talked before yesterday. So I can't very well be your lawyer, can I? You need to understand that.'

He wouldn't meet my eyes, and he slumped so low that he seemed to melt into the table. 'Doesn't matter what you did or didn't do. The whole world gonna think I was behind those pictures, that I hired you to stick your nose in something that ain't my business, that sure as hell ain't yours. The whole world, man. Me and you, we like one dead man talking to another. There ain't no point.'

'Someone's been messing with both of us. I didn't issue that statement. What are you talking about? Who's going to want us dead?'

He didn't answer the question. Maybe he thought it was obvious. I guess it was. Instead he said, 'How come they said that statement was from you, if it wasn't? How come they *said* you was my lawyer?'

I measured out a precise square on the table with my hands. 'You might want to ask Nikki about that.'

He sat up. 'Nikki!'

I looked at him. 'Think about it. She represents Damon, doesn't she? And Damon's your boss? And he's the one your lawyer has to point the finger at now that everyone has seen those pictures?'

'So what if she represents Damon? She represents everyone who works for him. How else you think she came to be my lawyer? You think I got money to pay her?'

'The way things stand, it's him or you. And which one do you think she's gonna choose?'

'You're telling me Nikki set me up. Fine. And I'm telling you I'm a dead man.' Again he seemed to melt.

'I can't prove it. But that press release makes you look like someone who tried to save his own skin by hiring your own lawyer and getting him to spy on your boss. Life would be a whole lot easier for Nikki if I'd been your lawyer all along. Then Damon doesn't have to wonder where she's at.'

'Nikki dumped me. And she ain't even going to come tell me to my face.'

'You were supposed to plead guilty anyway. Isn't that what she's been telling you? So what do you even need a lawyer for, if all you had to do was roll over?'

'I been in prison before. Like I said, in here, out there, don't matter. I'm through.' He looked up with a sudden idea. 'How can Nikki make people believe you been my lawyer, when you've just been telling me you never was?'

'The thing is, I *could* be. These people who hired me in the first place, whoever they were, they paid me a lot of money. I guess they wanted to get your boss and Campbell pretty bad. The way I see it, that money rightfully ought to go toward paying for your defense. You can hire me, but you don't have to. You want to go with another lawyer, that's fine. Whoever he is, I'll pay him.'

I hadn't planned to make such an offer, but that money was dirty. Jamil deserved to choose his own lawyer – even if it was inevitable that he'd take me. The last thing I wanted was to make another link in the chain of pressures that had been applied to him.

'Guess I'll go with you,' he said after a pause. 'Not that it matters. I'm finished. And so are you.'

I hoped, for both our sakes, that he was wrong.

Taking a retainer form from my briefcase, I filled in the blanks, acknowledging receipt of the ten thousand dollars. We each signed it. Now it was official: now I was working for him. Which meant Jeanie and I were done.

'All right, man, now that we've got that cleared away, let me tell you what happened,' he said.

I rose. The pictures were evidence that the relationship between Campbell and Damon was more complex than it ought to be, but I wasn't ready to hear the story of the planted gun from Jamil's mouth. 'I'll need to know what happened, but not yet. When the time comes, I'll ask. For now, just try to remember as much as you can.'

'Shit, man,' he said. 'Nikki didn't want to hear it either.'

'Don't worry. When I've finished my investigation, we'll talk.' I rapped on the door. 'There's no chance of getting you out on bail, unfortunately, since you were on parole when you were arrested. So you'll just have to sit tight.'

'Yeah, man,' Jamil said.

The rest of that day his despairing tone kept ringing in my ears.

* * *

Back in my office, I wrote out my letter of resignation, signed it, and left it on Jeanie's desk. I called the district attorney's office and asked for Fowler. He wasn't there. I called again and asked for Cassidy. When she came on the line I explained that Nikki no longer represented Jamil Robinson. I was taking over.

'Okay,' she said skeptically.

'How about me?' I asked.

'Officially, I can't say.'

'And unofficially?'

'The only advice I can give you is to consult an attorney.'

I laughed. I almost wanted them to go ahead and charge me. Almost.

Later that afternoon I heard that the Oakland PD had temporarily assigned Detective Campbell to patrol duty while the department investigated his ties to Damon.

That evening Jamil's body was found hanging from a bed sheet in his cell.

Chapter Twelve

Reading the story in the *Tribune* in the morning, I felt a helpless rage. I had Jeanie tear up my resignation letter, but neither of us really believed it was over, that I was finished with it. There were too many loose ends. For now, though, I sought to lose myself in the Scarsdale case.

I spent Wednesday working on a motion to exclude the videotaped interviews of the child victim at the trial. Defending an innocent man is like walking a tightrope; you fear the tiniest slip. When you know the client is guilty, on the other hand, you're an acrobat a foot above the ground.

It was an interesting, complex motion, and putting it together absorbed me entirely, in the way that only legal writing does. Wednesday night I was at the office until 1:00 AM. Thursday morning's breakfast was cold pizza from the night before.

I shouldn't have spent so much time on it, but I needed to keep from thinking about Jamil hanging there in his cell, needed to keep from wondering what his last moments had been like. Whether the videos came into evidence or not, the girl herself still had to testify, and it was her live testimony that I was afraid of. I couldn't very well keep her from taking the stand.

I could, however, keep my client from testifying, and I was faced with the task of finding a viable defense without him telling the jury he didn't do it. Though we hadn't definitely decided that Marty would testify, we'd proceeded under that assumption. Jeanie hated putting clients on the stand; she believed that it was at best a roll of the dice, and that most of them would, in the end, lack the composure to do anything but hurt themselves. Trust yourself, trust your evidence, trust the Constitution: that was her mantra.

And yet there's no substitute for the horse's mouth. No matter how relentlessly we attacked the police interviews, no matter how many motives we could give Erica for making up the story of Scarsdale molesting her, it was a child sex-abuse case. The law says it's the prosecutor's burden to prove the defendant guilty beyond a reasonable doubt; still, none but the greenest attorney believes the jury in a child sex-abuse case will follow that instruction. Given the revulsion such cases arouse, a defendant is effectively charged with proving himself innocent.

On the bright side, I wouldn't have to babysit Scarsdale all week, wouldn't have to spend those hours I'd dreaded rehearsing his testimony, wouldn't have to hold his hand, coach him, warn him, reassure him. Now we wouldn't have to go through the whole sticky pageant of rehearsal and cooperation. I was free to forget him, there in his hotel room, until the day of trial, free to set aside the human element and distill the case to a series of rhetorical formulations.

The trouble was the human element never stays down for long. Yet it wasn't Scarsdale; it was me. I couldn't stop thinking about Jamil – and about Lavinia.

'I know who she is,' I said to Teddy when I got home after filing my motion Wednesday night. 'Or who she must be, at least.'

Teddy was parked in front of the TV watching *SportsCenter* with a beer, eating a bowl of cereal.

'She had inside information, which makes her connected either to Damon or to Campbell. She knew about their relationship and about their meetings. She didn't seem like a gangster girlfriend, so I figure she's got to be a cop.'

Of course the people who'd hired me, who'd set me up, were cops. I figured that the two of them must have wanted to expose Campbell but didn't want to take on the career-ending alienation and contempt that comes with the code of silence, the thin blue line. Whatever was going on here, it was identical to the code of the streets.

That gun in Lavinia's purse hadn't been a cop gun, though. I just couldn't imagine an off-duty officer carrying it. Nor was a Pontiac convertible a cop car. So maybe she'd been a cop but now was paid better. In any case, she had the inside scoop and wanted to do the right thing, wanted to see a crooked detective exposed.

In the morning I called two friends from law school who worked for the Alameda County public defender's office. Neither of them could recall an officer who matched the description I gave. The hesitant quality of their voices told me it wasn't much of a description. The only part of her I could picture clearly was her legs.

There was no official, public directory of Oakland police officers, certainly none with photos, but I knew that group portraits of every graduating academy class for the last fifty years hung in the public hallway of the headquarters building on Frank Ogawa Plaza.

It's strange for someone like me, an attorney, to enter police headquarters without official business. I told myself that I was on public property, that as a citizen I had the right, but I still felt as if I were walking into enemy territory when I arrived just after eleven.

Lavinia was probably young enough to have become a cop during the last ten years. Two academy classes per year, about two dozen portraits to check, each showing between thirty and fifty new cops all dressed in identical uniforms. My job was made easier by the fact that there weren't many women, and few of them were as tall as Lavinia.

I was contemplating the portrait of the second academy class of 1994 when a voice close to my ear whispered, 'Lost?'

I turned, bumping into someone, stepped back, and met Campbell's stare. He was dressed in a patrol uniform with his uniform hat under his arm. It looked wrong on him, clownish, making me wonder how long it had been since he'd worn anything but a suit. He seemed perfectly calm until I noticed the vein at his throat pulsing. Then his gaze shifted from my face to the picture I'd been studying. The caption beneath the photo listed her name as Lavinia Perry. She'd told me her real first name.

Campbell studied it for several moments, then with a kindly smile turned his gaze on me. But the smile didn't reach his eyes. They were like pieces of glass underwater. 'You know me,' he said, not a question but a statement of fact. 'I know you, too,' he continued. 'The dude with the camera. Leo.' His eyes moved to the class portrait. 'Nineteen ninety-four. Seems like yesterday, doesn't it?'

He began to whistle as he walked off, his hat still under his arm.

Back at the office, I was aware something was coming to a boil inside me. There was no question in Campbell's mind that Lavinia Perry had been the one to hire me, and he knew where to find her, too.

She owed me an explanation, and perhaps she deserved a warning. Maybe while Campbell remained under the microscope of a departmental investigation he'd try to keep her out of it. She obviously knew more than she'd told me. No doubt her career would be hurt if it came out that she'd blown the whistle on her fellow officer. But if she were forced to tell everything she knew, Campbell would be the one hurt more.

A second call to the public defender's office produced better results. When I mentioned the name, my friend Henry put the phone down and came back ten minutes later with a full report gathered from his colleagues, several of whom knew her as one of the most prolific earners of overtime for the Oakland Vice Squad. Another thing: she was an officer with a reputation for stretching the truth.

At 10:00 PM that evening I was sitting in my car down on International Boulevard, keeping an eye on Lavinia Perry. I'd followed her as she left the station garage in an undercover vehicle. She was dressed in high heels, fishnets, a short skirt, and a flimsy top, undoubtedly wearing a wire as she set off to work the corners of East Oakland. Her partners in the unmarked car were never far away. I'd watched them snag three johns in the last hour. At the moment of agreement, the lights and siren would swoop down.

According to Henry, during the last twelve months, Lavinia Perry had earned something close to seventy grand in overtime with her hooker act. One of the misdemeanor attorneys in the office had gotten the number out of her when he was grilling her on the stand, trying to make her look like someone who'd say anything for money. She was a good actress. I knew that. And she looked the part. In the streetlight, her halter top sliding down, her hair pulled back, she was the very ideal of what a lonely guy might be dreaming of, too good to pass up even if somewhere deep down a voice he didn't want to listen to were telling him a real whore on these streets would never look so fine.

There were girls every block or so, most of them alone. Occasionally there'd be two or three standing together on a corner, punctuating the landscape of bodegas and auto parts stores. I'd been trailing them – Lavinia and her backup – from corner to corner, watching from a careful distance as they worked their routine. When after the three arrests they took up a new position at International and Thirty-Eighth, I got out. I didn't know what I was going to say. Mostly I just wanted her to see my face.

I weaved and stumbled, stopping to kick an imaginary bit of debris out of my way. I didn't look up until I was close, about ten paces.

She spoke first. 'Hey baby, want a date?'

I stopped. I looked at her. I took two more steps, then stopped again. 'Vinnie. Lavinia Martin. Wow, I haven't seen you since school.'

'For fifty dollars I'll be whoever you want, but I don't know any Lavinia Martin.'

I moved into the glow of the streetlight. I tried to sound uncertain. 'You're right. You couldn't be Vinnie – not dressed like that, not in this neighborhood. No, Vinnie's dad was a preacher . . .'

Her mouth parted in a silent oh, but she hid her surprise behind a screen of impatience. A car slowed, veering toward the curb, then cut back out into the lane, engine revving. Lavinia – Sgt Perry – swiveled her head, tapping her foot and thrusting out her elbow, for all the world like a hooker trying to reel in lost business.

'But wait a minute. Maybe I'm right after all. Come on. We used to sit in the cafeteria and share a bowl of soup. Campbell's soup.'

I was aware that every word I spoke was being overheard by her partners in the squad car. No doubt she was thinking of them, too. 'If you don't want a date, then beat it. I don't know you, man.'

'I heard what happened to your brother. That they got him in his cell, strung him up, made it look like suicide. Not a nice story.'

'Get out of here!' she hissed. 'We don't know each other.'

'Are you going to make me pay fifty bucks just to have a conversation with an old friend?'

'Look, I'm a cop. You want to sleep in Santa Rita tonight, be my guest.'

I broke character. 'You're going to have to turn off that wire first. You've got nothing on me. But I've had a talk with our mutual friend. Mr Soup.'

From my left I heard a low warning whoop from a siren, then blue and red lights began flashing. The unmarked car pulled to the curb and two cops got out. One shone a flashlight in my face. Blinded, I felt a tick of fear.

'Officers, this woman solicited me for prostitution,' I explained.

The stockier of the two patted me down. Ignoring me, he asked, 'What was going on here?'

'I thought I recognized her. That's all. But I didn't know she was a cop.'

'You knew enough to call her by her first name,' the other noted.

The one with the flashlight told me to turn and put my hands on the brick wall. I felt my wallet being fished out of my back pocket.

I glanced over my shoulder at Lavinia. The second cop now had his handcuffs out and was gripping my wrist behind my back. The stocky cop was going through my wallet, studying the ID in the beam of his

Maglite. Finally Lavinia said, 'Screw it, Danny. Let this one go, won't you?'

The one holding me gave me a shove. 'Lucky break. Beat it.'

My wallet landed on the pavement at my feet. I grabbed it.

Later I realized it was lighter by forty bucks.

Chapter Thirteen

The next morning, Friday, I looked out the window and saw a Bronco idling on the curb. From my balcony I could see a figure sitting in it, but not who. Since Jamil's death I didn't leave the house anymore without first scanning the street. I'd also started varying my route. At night the slightest of sounds awakened me.

Nonetheless, I had to prepare for trial in the Scarsdale case. And I also had to shop for Teddy and me. More than anything, though, I needed to escape the near-ceaseless blare of the television and my brother's hulking stupor before it. He was slipping downhill, no doubt about it. He'd been out of rehab three months, and each day was putting in more and more TV time.

When I finally sucked up my nerve to walk downstairs, the Bronco pulled from the curb and shadowed me. Sgt Perry, rolling down her window, ordered, 'Get in. We need to talk.'

'You want to talk, you park and we'll go have coffee like civilized people.'

'We can't be seen together.'

'You probably want your ten thousand bucks. Where'd it come from – the evidence locker?'

We both knew I was only putting on an act. I'd sought her out.

'I can't leave my dog in the car,' she said. 'If you don't want to ride with me, you can follow me to the Berkeley Pier.'

Her back windows were tinted. Until then I hadn't noticed the animal in the rear cargo area, an enormous beast that seemed to have to crouch to fit back there. 'Okay,' I said. 'I'll go get my car.'

She waited until I pulled onto the street in the Rabbit, but it was all the allowance she made. At the top of our street she turned hard right toward MacArthur and the freeway. Changing lanes down the hill, she sped through the yellow light.

I waited, took the interstate to Berkeley and exited at University Avenue. She was already out on the pier with the dog when I parked.

It was a chilly morning. The heat wave had passed,

and the weather had returned to its summer pattern of morning fog. Lavinia wore a black Raiders sweatshirt and no makeup, her hair pulled back in a ponytail. It didn't matter. She was as attractive as ever. The dog walked beside her on its leash. It was like a husky but huge, with a massive head and ears like the scoops in the bulk-food bins, one eye blue and the other milky white. Its head rose higher than my waist and it ignored me utterly. One leg was sheathed in a purple cast, forcing it to walk on three legs.

'It comes off in a week and a half,' Lavinia said, noticing my attention.

'He seems to be coping pretty well.'

'He'll cope with anything if I tell him to.'

'I guess he heard what they do to horses.'

'You wouldn't believe his bills. No workman's comp for Trigger.'

The fog was starting to lift. The tops of the East Bay hills had come into focus, but across the water the buildings of San Francisco remained draped in clouds. Not for the first time, I found myself wishing that Teddy and I had never left the city for Oakland.

'You spoke to Campbell,' she said.

'I was at police headquarters, looking at pictures of graduating academy classes. He came up behind me when I was looking at the picture of your class. He must have had an idea who set him up.'

'Damn, damn, damn.' She stopped. A trio of kite surfers carved and bounced across the waves, their colorful parachutes sawing the air. Finally she turned to me. 'Look, you've got to keep quiet about this. If you use my name I won't back you up. I'll deny everything.'

'I almost lost my job.'

'I'll lose my job for sure if they find out I gave you the dirt on Campbell. Then what? I spend the rest of my life nabbing shoplifters?'

'Why should I protect you? You set me up.'

'Meeting you like that, knowing who your brother was, it was too good a chance. You've got to understand. I was desperate. You learn to let a lot of things slide, working in this city. But for me, there comes a point where you have to say *enough*. Only I didn't have proof that Campbell was protecting Damon.'

'You still don't have it. The pictures don't prove anything.'

'That's why it had to be you rather than me.' Her lips tightened. 'A defense attorney doesn't need proof to make accusations of police corruption.'

'Without proof, a month from now Campbell's right back where he started.'

'Unless . . .' she said, the word hanging in the air.

'Unless what?'

'Unless something more turns up.'

'Meaning what? Jamil became my client after you scammed me. Nikki Matson cut him off like a moldy piece of cheese, and now he's dead. And that means there's nothing to keep me on the case. I'm a defense attorney. I work for living clients. They're the ones who pay.'

'What was it you said to me last night? It stuck in my mind. You said they got him in his cell, strung him up, made it look like suicide? Who did you mean, they?'

Those were my words, all right. Yet I knew, as she did, that it's no easy task to have a man murdered in jail. I thought of how despondent Jamil had sounded when I talked to him, of how little help I'd been. Could he – could anyone – have reacted that way? Preferring suicide to execution? I realized I wasn't sure. 'You think he was murdered?'

'I'm just repeating what you said. Jamil apparently hires you to take some pictures, and *they*, whoever they are, they see all of a sudden he's not going to plead guilty the way he was supposed to. So *they* arrange for a little accident.'

'They meaning Damon Watson.'

111

'I didn't want this to happen. Neither of us did. But it happened, and now the question is what are we going to do about it?'

She had me. Whether Jamil had been killed or had committed suicide, his death was the direct result of our meeting, of Lavinia's meddling and my ensnarement in her trap. I sighed and leaned my elbows on the railing. 'If you expect me to trust you, you're going to have to give me some answers. You could start with how you knew about that meeting in the hills.'

'I thought you had it all figured out. Call it intuition.'

'Campbell knows you. That's pretty clear.'

'He ought to. I'm married to him.'

I felt a shock, as if the pier had without warning tilted beneath me.

'I thought you were an idealist. I thought you wanted to expose a dirty cop because it was the right thing to do. This sounds like a vendetta.'

'Believe me. I wouldn't go out of my way to hurt him if it weren't the right thing. That's what makes it so hard. That's why it can't come out that I was the one who hired you. How could I ever explain to my baby that I was the one who brought his daddy down?' She patted Trigger's head and he glanced up at her appreciatively. Her baby.

'You haven't answered the question. How did you know about the meetings?'

Her voice came fast and low. 'I thought he had a regular girl he was cheating with Sunday afternoons. He always gave this bullshit story about going to meet an informant. Anyway, I had a tracking device installed on his car.' Her face was intent, her eyes taking on an obsessive gleam. I stiffened, but she didn't notice. The dog licked at her ankle. 'He was cheating, but not on Sundays.' She looked away. 'We're separated now.'

'Is there any way he can argue Damon was a legitimate informant?'

'That's what he'll say, I'm sure. I'm sure that's what he told himself. They grew up together. I'm sure he thought better the devil you know. But he didn't have control. Any time you start framing people to protect even a legitimate informant, well, it's clear you've crossed the line.'

'You make it sound like a given that Jamil was framed, a given that Campbell planted the gun. But so far I haven't seen any proof. Maybe Damon put the gun in the car and told Campbell. Maybe Jamil was the lone killer and he was dumb enough to hang on to it, like I said the first time we talked. And Damon tipped Campbell off. Either way, Campbell's in the clear if he can explain those photographs. Unless you're holding something back.'

'Even if Jamil pulled the trigger, he didn't act on his own. Someone ordered him to do it. The logical person is Damon, and Campbell has clearly been protecting him. It could be he thinks he's playing a deeper game. But I doubt it.'

I doubted it, too. I'd seen the look on Campbell's face when Damon pulled the gun. I remembered Damon's twitching anger, my sense that the finger and not his brain would decide whether to shoot. No one in his right mind would play games with such a man.

'We're going to work it up front this time,' I said. 'No lies, no games.'

'No games,' she promised. 'It's only a matter of time before they expose themselves. Campbell's in too deep. Damon owns him. I've got a transponder on Campbell's car. When he trips up, when he says he's one place and he's really somewhere else, I'll know it, and I'll call you.'

'And I can do what – take more pictures?'

'I'm just a source of information, Leo. What you do with that information is up to you.'

'Bullshit. You want something or we wouldn't be

here. What makes you think I'll take the information you give me and run the way you want me to?'

'Because you're a good man, I can tell that about you. The point isn't to bring Campbell down. The point is to stop Damon Watson, to see him prosecuted for Jamil and all the others, the ones we don't know about yet.'

I thought of Scarsdale's trial starting Monday, his hotel-room confession. I wanted to believe what she'd said about my moral courage, but I knew it was a scam. I wondered how much she knew about her husband's friendship with Damon Watson. 'Who or what is Jamil Robinson to you?' I asked.

Trigger lay down with a sigh, and Lavinia leaned against the railing, watching the sea gulls swirl and cry. She seemed like she might answer, but she just shook her head as if I couldn't possibly understand.

I was back on the freeway before I realized I hadn't asked her who her partner was, the man who'd impersonated Jamil on the telephone.

Chapter Fourteen

On Monday morning Scarsdale's case was the first called in master calendar, and we were sent to Judge Conroy's courtroom for trial forthwith.

I'd tried several previous cases with Conroy. He struck me as fair in the sense that he seemed to relish peeling the skin from an erring lawyer on either side of the bar, but old-fashioned in his seeming belief that perjury simply could not occur in his courtroom, except perhaps from a criminal defendant. The idea that an officer of the law would take the oath and lie was so repugnant to him that he refused to consider it.

Conroy was quick to speak when he disliked a line of questioning, and his impatience was so caustic that inexperienced lawyers usually moved on. Those who'd been around longer knew that his bark was worse than his bite, and that he would rarely go so far as to forbid a legally relevant, admissible line of questions. The crucial calculation had to do with whether it was worth proceeding under a hail of abuse.

The case was being prosecuted by a career DA named Chris Mooney, with none other than Cassidy Akida in the second chair. For about half a second I considered objecting, then decided to ignore her presence.

Mooney and I spent all of Monday and half of Tuesday questioning prospective jurors, finally whittling the field to the standard twelve with two alternates. All through jury selection Scarsdale sat quietly beside me, shaved and presentable but wholly immobile and remote, showing only fleeting interest in the people who would decide his fate.

On Tuesday afternoon the judge sent the jury home, heard argument, and granted my motion to exclude the videotapes. My victory was hollow, like a cheap run against the Yankees in the top of the first. After other preliminary matters he told us to be ready with opening statements the next morning at 9:30 AM.

Jeanie congratulated me as we headed back to the office. She'd sat at the defense table all morning, helping me with jury selection but letting me run the show. 'Want to go over your opening before I take off?'

'I have all the pieces, but I need to figure out how I'm going to stitch them together.' I hadn't told her about Scarsdale's confession. I'd been trying not to think about it, because whenever I did, a cloud of anger and depression fell on me, blotting out all the landmarks on the path I'd charted to acquittal.

'You going to hit the uncle hard or soft?'

'I think hard,' I said reluctantly. 'Both barrels. The more I think about it, the more I realize that we can't tiptoe around. If we're going to smear him, we've got to smear him good.'

She drove in silence. 'You may be right,' she finally said. 'The risk being that they don't trust you yet, that you don't have the authority to make that kind of an accusation. But innuendo isn't exactly going to get the job done.'

I kicked the underside of the dash, and she shot me a surprised glance. 'But we know the uncle didn't do it, and what I say may ruin his life, especially if the papers pick it up. Yet I'm not supposed to let that bother me. Because it's my job, right? I survey the available strategies, look at what's permitted by law, and choose the best. "Best" meaning most likely to result in acquittal.'

'Sounds like you're starting to wish we hadn't taken the case.'

'Too late for that.' I thought bitterly how she'd handed this one off to me. An opportunity, she'd called it. A test. Well, I was learning my lesson now. I was learning what happened to eager young criminal lawyers who bite hard without tasting first.

'We weren't thinking about the uncle when we agreed to represent him,' Jeanie said. 'Maybe it happened just the way you said. The uncle did it and psychologically she couldn't handle the truth. So in her subconscious mind, in her memory, she changed the identity of the molester. It's reasonable doubt. Hell, it's more than reasonable.'

'It's a disaster. Why don't we just go all the way and frame him?'

'This is the work, Leo. The system hurts people. Is that supposed to be a news flash? Of course it does. It's designed to hurt anyone who gets caught up in it, because everyone's story has to be tested. Witnesses, victims. Into the fire. And if we don't bring the fire, no one will.'

I didn't say anything. I knew she was right. The

revulsion I was feeling was something I'd experienced time and again, and in the heat of battle it would pass. It was just that I'd never been in quite this position before – the position of accusing an innocent man to defend a client I knew was guilty as hell.

Jeanie wasn't my mother, wasn't my sister, wasn't my lover – though I'd spent a number of years wishing her into these roles. She was my boss, and no matter how many clichés she invoked, the fact remained that Scarsdale was my responsibility and my problem.

I ought to have told her about his confession. But, as usual, when professionalism and dispassionate judgment should have guided me in my relationship with her, old resentments resurfaced. I stared out the window and kept my mouth shut.

'If you don't want to practice what you've got so far for the opening, I won't come in.' She pulled to the curb by our building and turned to gaze at me in that way she had of seeming to strain for a glimpse through a crevice in my facade – a look that used to split me open but now just made me want to chink up the cracks.

'I'll be here in the morning by six thirty,' I said. 'Let's do a run-through then.'

'Fine.'

I slammed the door and she drove off.

I worked until 1:00 AM, hashing out a rough, unsatisfactory outline of my opening, then walked home for a few hours' sleep. The kitchen light was on, the apartment reasonably neat; from Teddy's bedroom came deep snores. I opened a can of beer and drank it standing at the sink, feeling that what had happened to Teddy had happened primarily to me.

I couldn't help thinking that if Jeanie hadn't divorced him before the shooting, she would have been the one stuck with him. What about her vows, I wanted to ask. In sickness and in health.

With another beer these thoughts crumbled and fell away, and I was left alone with the fact of myself, standing in the kitchen in the middle of the night, feeling haggard and unprepared. In the past, my trial strategy had always crystallized during the final week before trial; this time, the opposite had happened. Everything had shattered. Easy, I told myself. Time to sleep. Exhausted as I was, I knew from experience that the only thing to do was close my eyes and trust that things would seem easier in the morning.

I must have slept for at least an hour, but when the phone rang it seemed that I'd just closed my eyes. It was Lavinia Perry, but she didn't give her name. 'It's me,' she said.

'Do you know what time it is?'

'Campbell's not where he claims to be. He tells the dispatcher he's down at the Coliseum but the GPS puts him almost in San Leandro, near Oak Knoll.'

'What do you want me to do about it? I can't take pictures in the dark.'

'I don't *want* you to do anything. I told you I'd call and I called. This might be your big chance, or maybe he's just getting a blow job. Take it or leave it. Go back to sleep for all I care.'

I hesitated, but I suddenly felt wide awake. 'Give me the coordinates.'

I plugged what she told me into Google. It spit back a spot on the map in the hills above San Leandro.

What the hell do you think you're doing? I asked myself. You've got to give an opening statement in four hours; you've got to find a way to win this shitty case. Already, though, I was out of bed, pulling on my pants and a sweatshirt, thinking of Sgt Perry when I'd first seen her driving that convertible, of Jamil in his cell. I was accustomed to sleep deprivation. I told myself that a mere three or four hours would only dull the edges.

Teddy's voice stopped me at the front door. 'Leo, you going out?'

'Yeah.' My hand on the knob. 'I got a tip. It's about that case.'

'Wait a second. I'm coming with you. I can't seem to sleep tonight.'

He often suffered from insomnia. I should have told him to stay, but I didn't. He was out in a minute, having dressed faster than usual, dark jeans and a sweatshirt. It felt good to have him with me, not thinking about his debilities, just the two of us. As we drove I remembered in a vivid flash being six and Teddy taking me on the bus to school. Back then I'd still believed he could hold back all the harms of the world. Now I was supposed to keep him from harm.

We drove south on the broadly curving 580 Freeway beneath the brow of the hills, the lights of the flatlands beneath us, the more distant ones of the cities across the bay rising occasionally into view. We crossed into San Leandro and I exited. Soon the headlights picked out a sign that read NAVAL MEDICAL CENTER OAKLAND but there were no lights anywhere beyond the locked gate. According to the directions I'd printed out, the coordinates I'd been given were behind it. I continued past the entrance, then turned left on a road paralleling a fence topped with razor wire. The moon was full, showing strips of eucalyptus bark caught in the chain link. The shedding trees' medicinal tang came through the window.

We passed a parked Crown Vic, unmarked but with a bank of lights in the back. I froze, gripping the wheel, but it was empty. Following the directions, I turned left, keeping to the fence line of the abandoned hospital. It had been closed after the 1989 earthquake; last I heard they'd been planning to turn it into a housing development. There was a driveway, then an open gate. I parked on the side of the road fifty feet farther along on an upscale residential street.

I didn't know what I thought we were going to do. I hadn't even brought the camera. But I was here.

'So I guess we'll just go take a look around,' I said as we got out of the car.

'If I had a jury case in the morning I would be at the office.'

'That where you think I should be?'

'I don't give a fuck, Leo. I'm so indifference, I might just cease to exist.'

Indifference, indifferent. It wasn't worth correcting. Hearing him actually put in words the attitude I'd been observing for months scared me, as if we'd reached a new and more dangerous stage.

125

'I care,' I said. 'That's why I can't figure out what the fuck I'm doing here, except that Campbell must have a good reason for being here, and I'm hoping we'll get lucky and learn something that'll help us figure out where he stands.'

'Thanks for bringing me, anyway. Makes me feel almost alive.'

We went down the drive and through the gate, where the padlock and chain hung from the hasp, and down into a parking lot with weeds growing up through the cracks. Nearby was a once-grand stucco building with a bell tower, built in the mission style. Mats of vegetation grew from its tiled roof, and mold streaked the walls. Spindly trees grew from the foundation. There was a courtyard with a large oak visible inside it. Above the entrance a sign – half-obscured by a bay laurel – read CLUB KNOLL.

We walked beneath it into the overgrown courtyard, where rainwater that had collected in a stone-and-mortar fountain reflected the moon.

I smelled marijuana smoke a moment before I heard the voices. They were above me, I realized, then went still. I grabbed Teddy's arm, heard a metallic sound, then the fountain seemed to explode beside me, spraying my face with sharp bits of stone.

126

Teddy hit me hard, and we ducked behind the fountain. I lay listening to my heart beat, the shots ringing. Teddy was breathing hard. 'Up on the balcony,' he said, and I heard the sound of running feet on stairs, then a final slam. A powerful light blinded me. Two men stood above us. 'Let's get those hands where we can see them,' one of them said.

I rolled onto my back, showing my hands, blinking against the halogen beam. 'Now get up real slow,' he said. I rose, telling myself that if they'd meant to kill us we would be dead.

The one with the shotgun was middle-aged and bulky, in a black hoodie and baggy jeans. The other was younger, wiry, wearing a dark shirt, cargo pants, and work boots. He carried a handgun in addition to the light. 'Pull your wallets out of your pockets and toss them on the ground,' the older one said, and the younger one came forward with the light to scoop them up. Then he patted us down and took our cell phones and keys.

Our captors conferred. The older one got out a radio and walked off into the darkness. I made out Teddy's name and mine, then caught the phrase, 'those fucking pictures.'

'Going for a little ride,' he said, coming back.

127

'I'm an attorney. I'll be missed if I'm not in court in the morning.'

'Don't worry. It ain't far. Better than being blown away. Maybe we ought to have blown you away, you and that pervert you represent. Mr Leo Maxwell. Esquire.'

'Alleged pervert,' I told him as I rose to my feet.

He touched the shotgun barrel very gently to the side of my head, and in the grip of terror I couldn't shut up. 'So you boys must be Damon's muscle. Where are you bringing us? To meet the man?'

'Boys? Who you calling boys?' the younger one said, and slashed me behind the ear. I doubled over, feeling a hot flood in my scalp, seeing the flashlight beam again. But my hand came away dry when I touched the spot.

They led us past the fountain and inside the building.

'Have to bring you back afterward, drink us some fine Cabernet up there on the balcony,' the man with the shotgun said.

'Why you always have to be joking?' his companion asked. 'You know these two ain't coming back.'

From there we proceeded down the back stairs to where a Lincoln Navigator waited with two more men sitting in the front. Once we'd been shoved into the middle seat, the original pair got in on either side of us. I pressed against the warmth of Teddy beside me, inhaling the funk of his body and middle-of-the-night breath.

'Don't worry,' Teddy said. 'Nothing's going to happen.'

'Where we going?' I felt a shrug on one side of me. I thought of Teddy lying in a coma after being shot all those months ago, how I'd believed then that if he'd had any choice he'd want to die rather than live. I still didn't know whether I'd been right or wrong to think that. I hadn't ever gotten around to asking him. Now it seemed that maybe I never would.

We drove a short distance through the old hospital grounds, then came to another gate. Before the car came to a full stop, the man in front was already out and unlocking another chain. With the car stopped again I felt the muscles in my legs tightening to spring, but there was nowhere to run as they walked us through knee-high grass. I kept telling myself, I will stop, I will make them do it here if they are going to do it. At last I fell to my knees. 'I'm not going any farther.'

'Boss doesn't want the car down there, so we got to walk the rest of it,' the older man said, in the even, apologetic tone of a someone who intended no harm, handling me as easily and gently as he handled that shotgun.

'Where are we going?'

'Boss wants you in the pool room. I told him he could kill you up in the club as easy as anywhere, and if he's not going to kill you, why, it's a shorter walk back to the car. But he don't care what I think. "Bring them down here," he tells me. So I'm bringing you.'

Beside me Teddy stood with his arms folded. 'What about security?' he asked. 'Don't they have guards?'

Slightly ahead of us, the younger guy turned and held up a wallet with a badge.

'You're shitting me,' I said.

'Nah, it's legit,' the older man said.

We followed the flashlight beam across the cracked pavement, then cut through more dry grass and came to what must have been the indoor pool. Behind the building, across a ravine, I saw the old hospital, its windows dark and broken.

We ducked through a side door, the top half closed by plywood. Gravel slid under my feet, probably from the roof. Stars and moonlight shone through it. The beam lit up lane lines dangling over a debris-littered basin. Rainwater pooled still and dark on the far side, in what had been the deep end.

On the other side of the pool I saw the red ember of a cigar glowing like a slowly blinking eye. 'Y'all bring those two along over here,' the smoker called.

We walked along the side, past exit doors boarded over. The air smelled swampy. Of dead things that had recently been alive. The water couldn't have been more than a few feet deep, but it looked bottomless. Shapes rose above the surface, half-submerged, half-dissolved, like carcasses or ruins: slatted deck chairs, old bottles, rotting buoys, anything that could be thrown, tipped, or rolled.

He had two of the old slatted deck chairs at the edge of a ten-foot drop, above the cluttered basin. They made us sit with our backs to the stinking hole, and they used plastic zip ties to bind our wrists. Just a nudge was all it would take to send us over, headfirst and helpless all the way down.

Then they would have to haul us out of there I told myself. And that meant they'd have to wade into all that gunk themselves, which they certainly weren't going to be eager to do when the time came. But maybe they were used to it.

The younger man used a lighter to start a bonfire on the tiles a few feet away. The paper flared quickly, the flames licking across the lacquered planks of a bench some previous visitor had busted up. In the firelight the room seemed both to shrink and expand, the near parts coming nearer, the opposite end withdrawing to such a great distance that when I glanced over my shoulder the shadows seemed to swallow everything.

The fire lit the face of the man who had been smoking. When the paper was burning on its own he tossed his cigar end into the water. I heard it hiss below. 'Looks like you left your camera behind.'

'It's good to finally see you in person.'

He chuckled. But I didn't like the sound. Teddy was quiet. 'Quite a coincidence, isn't it, meeting here tonight?' Damon asked.

'Aren't you going to introduce me to your associates?'

Beside me Teddy now laughed, and I felt a spreading chill, wishing that I hadn't heard that sound.

A pause. 'You think this is funny, motherfucker?' Damon wanted to know.

The older of the two men who'd been handling us came around to stand loose limbed by Teddy's chair, his palm cupped over my brother's shoulder.

Teddy didn't seem to register the presence of the man at his side, the killer's touch. 'You're so incredibly weak. I can smell the weakness on you.'

I spoke quickly. 'This is the guy I took the pictures of,' I told him.

132

I asked myself if Lavinia once again had set us up, if Campbell was anywhere near this place tonight. Plus, I couldn't tell whether Teddy remembered those pictures I'd taken, whether he realized who Damon was. And yet through my fear and dismay I felt a pulse of wonder: for the first time since before the shooting, my brother had for a moment sounded like my brother again.

The older man still had one hand on Teddy's shoulder, the shotgun in his other. He began to push Teddy over experimentally, finding the pivot point where the front chair leg lifted off the ground. Teddy didn't take his eyes from Damon. He was grinning, more alive than I'd seen him for months.

Hoping to draw their attention, I said, 'You must be anxious to find out who betrayed you. Who told me about your meetings with Campbell. You must realize that the same person told me to come here tonight. You have a meeting planned? You expecting another visitor?'

A moment lapsed before Damon looked at me. When he did, his face was dreamy, abstracted. This was his true anger I saw, total absorption in the pleasures of his rage, when he became merely an observer to what was about to happen. I saw that he was more dangerous than I'd supposed.

'I know who betrayed me. Jamil Robinson. Jamil, now, he ain't no longer in this world, so I don't have much need for your information.'

'It wasn't Jamil who betrayed you. He wasn't the person who called and told me to crash your little reunion. I can see how you might think that, because it was what Nikki Matson wanted you to think, but you're wrong. I'm the only one who knows who really called me, and I'm not going to tell you.'

'Nah, see, that ain't gonna fly. Teasing, holding the milk bone in my face and yanking it back, that ain't right. That's the way to get your hand bit.' Damon beckoned, and the younger of the two men came over from the fire.

'You had Jamil killed,' I went on, pressing my luck. 'He wasn't yet my client when I took those pictures, only later, at the end, and only thanks to Nikki sending that false press release to the KTVU News, blowing smoke up your ass.'

'Nikki Matson would sell out a client for a steak sandwich on rye bread.' This, from Teddy.

Damon's face twisted; then he chuckled. 'I hear you're some kind of a retard these days. Don't know how I feel about killing no retard.'

'Put the gun to your own head and pull the trigger,' Teddy said. 'That's the only way to find out.'

Damon raised the handgun and pointed it between Teddy's eyes, my brother staring back at him. Damon glanced at me. 'So this gonna be the second time you had your brother's brains on your face. Hope the bullet *takes* this time. I hate to see a good job done bad.'

Teddy just stared at him, the heavy gaze of a man you don't want to fight, because no matter how many times you hit him he'll get back up to his feet, prepared to slug away, if too little, too late.

'Damon!' a voice called from the other end of the pool, and without a word Damon raised his aim and fired into the darkness, the sound momentarily deafening me. I'd seen him alter his aim, yet I couldn't help squeezing my eyes shut.

'Police! Throw down your weapons!'

I opened my eyes. Damon was hunkered down, with Teddy and me as shields. His gun barrel passed my face once, then again. His sidekicks lay on the tiles.

'See?' Teddy said. 'What did I tell you? He's finished.' I looked and saw he was gloating. Was this part of his pathology, an inability to recognize danger? Had his survival released him from fear? Or was it that now, longing for death, he no longer feared it?

Whatever it was, he seemed as unfathomable to me as he'd always been, an indication that the brother I knew was still in there, fighting through the fog.

'It's Campbell!' the voice called. 'I was just fucking with you. I'm coming down to your end now.'

Damon persisted in scanning the darkness through the space between Teddy and me, then stood. Campbell came along the pool edge in his patrol uniform. Even now, wearing his regulation blues, he carried himself like a man in a six-hundred-dollar suit, his shoulders back, a subtle swagger to his athletic stroll.

Damon again halfway raised the gun, suspicious. 'This the end? They got the place surrounded? They send you in to negotiate? 'Cause you know, man, they ain't taking me alive.'

'Nah. I'm fucking with you. They got me on patrol duty. I'm patrolling.' He looked around.

Damon raised the gun a little higher. 'Then what the fuck you doing here? This ain't Oakland.'

'Relax. I got a call about some trespassers up here at Oak Knoll. I'll bet these two are them.' He nodded at Teddy and me. 'Looks like you managed to detain them without a struggle. Makes my job easy.'

'What job might that be?'

'Why, to arrest them, of course. Take them off your hands.'

'They ain't even here,' Damon explained. 'You ain't never seen them.'

Campbell considered this, then shook his head. 'No. We aren't going to play it like that.'

'What I hear is you telling me no. That's *all* I've been hearing from you lately.'

'Your real friends are the ones who say no when you need to hear it.' I had to admire the way Campbell was staying cool, but I wasn't certain Damon was into life lessons.

Meanwhile, the two guys on the floor had stood up. The younger one brushed off his clothes, then accepted the gun from Damon.

'Don't worry,' Campbell said. 'I got plans for these two. They're not getting off the hook. By the time I'm through, we'll know what they know, and you won't have to worry about it coming back on you.'

'You listen to me. Nobody else but you could have stopped me from shooting that retard. Nobody. You hear that? But something always comes back.'

'Send one of them to unlock the gate,' Campbell told him, nodding at the pair of goons. 'I'm taking care of it now.'

Campbell gave my car keys to the younger guy and told him to ditch the car in Oakland, neither too close to our apartment nor too far away. 'That way when they find it they won't know what to think if these two haven't turned up. Maybe they went to dinner; maybe the car got jacked. So don't leave prints, but don't wipe it down, either.'

Then he told them to put us in the trunk of his unmarked car. Teddy resisted and offered a moment of struggle as the trunk was opened. He managed to jerk away briefly in a frenzied spasm. In an instant I was knocked down with a punch to the jaw while Teddy took the shotgun butt slammed into his chest. He slumped and was levered in. Damon and Campbell went on chatting with apparent unconcern. I was on my feet again almost immediately, head spinning. Now the younger one had his handgun out. Gesturing me in, he lowered the trunk decisively just as I yanked back my hand.

A moment later we were moving, jostling against each other in what felt like a moving coffin. We bumped and rolled over potholed roads inside the hospital grounds. Then the pavement hammered beneath us as we headed onto the freeway.

'Leo,' Teddy said hoarsely. 'I think this guy might just kill us.'

'Like Damon was going to let us go?'

'The fucking psychopaths I understand, and always did much better than normal people. But a cop, someone who thinks he's above the law . . .' He didn't finish the thought and didn't have to.

We were quiet then for a while. Listening to the highway noise, trying to figure out where Campbell was taking us. At least that's what I was doing. I don't know what thoughts were running through Teddy's head, or how his mind worked anymore. After what had happened back there at the pool, I understood that I didn't know the first thing about him.

Eventually I realized that I was making sense of the almost imperceptible clues and could visualize our progress northward through the I-80 interchange toward Berkeley. Exiting the freeway, we turned once, again, then a third time. Shit. I was lost. We drove on and on, bumping over potholes, turning, stopping, rolling through intersections. I dropped into a nightmarish sleep, then was jarred awake by the loud exhaust pops of a motorcycle in the next lane.

At last we stopped, and I felt the driver's side door open. When Campbell lifted the trunk I saw the faintest tinge of dawn at the horizon, but the orange glow of the city still lit the clouds. 'Get out,' he instructed, and we did. Me first, then Teddy, my brother moving stiffly, haltingly, with a stunned, startled look that made me think he didn't remember what had happened.

My knees were weak. We were in our own neighborhood, at the stub end of a street that had been cut off by the freeway, fenced on three sides, with some kind of electrical shed on the ivy-covered slope beneath us. The Rabbit was parked on the far side of the cul-de-sac.

'Get out of here,' Campbell said. His face was ashen. From his exhaustion I understood how precarious our fate had been. I wondered if I was the one who'd put him so far out on whatever limb he was on. I didn't think so, not entirely, but I was there with him, and it would only take the slightest stumble for us both to fall.

I took Teddy's arm and turned him, and we began walking as fast as he could manage, his limp now more prominent than it had been in months. We were about four blocks from home. The sky was growing brighter by the minute. I was supposed to be in court in about two hours.

'It was her,' Campbell called behind us. Startled, I glanced back. He stood just where we'd left him. 'She tipped you off again. Just try to tell me she didn't.'

Teddy paused, but I made him keep walking.

Chapter Fifteen

I'd like to say that I rose to the occasion, that the pressure of the situation brought out my best performance, but it was all I could do to get myself shaved, showered, and out the door in a suit.

Teddy was in bed, and I hoped he'd stay there. I'd had to support most of his weight as we walked from the elevator to our door, his right leg almost as useless as it had been at the very beginning of his rehabilitation. He was out of his head, making no sense, asking insistent questions in a voice like a drunkard's about a file he seemed to think I'd borrowed from him.

Jeanie came into court just before nine and dropped into her seat at the defense table with a loud exhalation. Scarsdale was between us. 'I thought we were going to walk through your opening,' she said, leaning back to speak past him. 'I've been trying to call you.'

'I must have lost my phone.'

'Walking in here, I was wondering what the hell I'd do if you didn't show. So tell me you're ready to go.'

'Ready as I'll be.'

Before she could say anything more the bailiff commanded us all to rise, and the judge entered. Our chance at conversation washed away like water down a drain. This was the chance I'd been looking forward to ever since the day I decided to go to law school. And I felt like I'd already lost the case.

The judge dealt summarily with a few issues, then called in the jury and instructed them briefly that what they were about to hear was not evidence, that the opening statements were offered by the lawyers for no other reason than to guide their understanding of the case. After this, Mooney stood up and delivered one of the best openings I'd heard, an objective but carefully crafted summary of the evidence. When he spoke of what he expected Erica's testimony to be it was so quiet that I heard the swish of his trousers and the scuff of his shoes. The eyes of the jurors never left his face. Neither did Cassidy Akida's.

When he finished, I did something I'd promised myself I would never do. I rose from my chair and told the judge that I was deferring my opening statement until after the close of the state's evidence. Scarsdale didn't stir, but Jeanie made a noise in her throat.

Judge Conroy peered over at me, then turned to the jury. 'Ladies and gentlemen, a little explanation is in order. The state has just finished its opening statement, and in the normal course of things the defense would now give its version of the facts. However, the defense has the option, after hearing the prosecution's opening, of deferring its opening statement until after the close of the state's evidence.

'The purpose of the opening statement is to aid the jury in its understanding of the evidence that is about to be presented. As I explained a moment ago, what the lawyers say is not evidence. In no way should you hold it against Mr Scarsdale that his lawyer has decided to let the prosecution present its own version of the facts without similarly attempting to preview the evidence the defense expects to elicit. The defendant, of course, is under no obligation to present any evidence whatsoever, or indeed, to present a defense. You must presume Mr Scarsdale to be innocent and you must not accept the prosecution's version simply because Mr Maxwell has decided not to speak at this time.'

The judge nodded to Mooney. 'The state may call its first witness.'

Mooney rose. 'The state calls Erica Lawler.'

The first surprise. I'd expected him to build up to the girl's testimony, to set the stage, but his style was to be exceedingly direct; at all points he sought the quickest path to his goal. Erica's eyes sagged, and her face was pale. Though a victim's advocate walked right beside her, the girl seemed somehow beyond her reach.

As the pair arranged themselves in the witness box, Jeanie passed me a sheet of paper folded in half. Her note said, 'If you were working on that other case instead of preparing for this one, we need to talk.'

Scarsdale, meanwhile, was oblivious to me, to Jeanie, to everything in the courtroom but Erica. A few jurors glanced in our direction. I was conscious of Erica's family on the other side of the aisle behind the prosecutor's table. The uncle was there. Tomorrow or the next day I'd get my shot at him.

Standing at the podium, Mooney began the examination conventionally enough, asking her name, how old she was, where she went to school. Under his questioning she seemed to come to life, seeking his approval. They had obviously established a rapport.

But once they'd moved past the preliminaries the life went out of her voice, and I remembered how unconvincing her story had seemed when I first heard it. For the prosecution there was no getting around the fact that she'd recounted the same facts over and over, and that each retelling had accumulated catch phrases, moments where I sensed that repetition had muddied truth.

Mooney worked his way slowly but deliberately to the topic of Scarsdale's daughter, Erica's best friend.

'Did you ever stay over at Angela's house?'

'Yes.'

'When, most recently, did you stay at Angela's?'

'Last summer,' she said. 'June.'

'June what, if you remember?'

On the night of the alleged crime, Erica had helped herself to a bottle of vodka from home. The two girls had mixed the Stoli with fruit punch.

'Weren't you afraid that your parents would miss the vodka?'

'I took it after a party they had for my dad's work. They didn't know.'

Angela's mother went to bed early. They started drinking around ten o'clock. Angela went to bed around eleven thirty. Erica stayed up watching a movie by herself.

When she opened her eyes the movie was over and

Marty Scarsdale was there with her on the couch. Her shirt was unbuttoned and her pants were down. Angela's bedroom was right off the TV room. All Erica could think was that she had to endure it as quietly as possible, that if she made the slightest noise, Angela or her mother would wake up and blame her for what was happening. Mooney did not spare her the details. He made her describe everything Scarsdale did to her, everything she'd felt.

She went home the next morning and didn't tell anyone. Then she found out she was pregnant – or felt certain she was. Her uncle was staying with them that winter. He was the one who dropped her off before her activities, picked her up, and drove her home. Her parents were distracted by their jobs and not getting along. One day in the car with him she started to cry. When he asked her what was wrong, she told him a lie about a boy at a party. She begged her uncle for help, pleading with him to keep her secret.

She asked him to take her to get an abortion, and he did. That evening, however, she broke down and told her mother the truth. The next day her mother drove her to the police station, where she was interviewed by the detective. This was the taped interview

Scarsdale had been watching during his breakdown at the motel.

Mooney finished sooner than I expected, without exploring Erica's story as thoroughly as I'd guessed he would.

We'd known from the beginning that Jeanie would cross-examine her. You do not send a male attorney up to cross-examine a young female victim of sexual assault. In a competent cross it is the attorney who testifies, not the witness; the witness is merely a prompt, a voice repeating yes.

'Isn't it fair to say that you drank more alcohol the night of June seventeenth than on any other night in your life?' Jeanie asked.

'Yes.'

'You and Angela, you girls finished the bottle?'

'No. There was some left. Angela poured it down the drain.'

And so on, with Jeanie seemingly trying to show that Erica had drunk so much she could have no idea whether anything had happened later or not.

Except that wasn't really where Jeanie was going. We had a few cards to play, and this was the first. That bottle of vodka hadn't come from Erica's father's party, as she'd testified. Car had obtained the liquor store invoice, spoken with the caterers, and confirmed that no hard liquor had been served at that party – only wine and beer.

Almost as soon as Jeanie started to push, Erica folded, admitting that she'd lied. 'Was that because someone bought it for you, and you didn't want to say who?' Jeanie asked. Erica said yes.

Jeanie went on to question her about her uncle, establishing that for a period of several months she'd spent more time with him than with any other person, that they'd been alone together each afternoon in the house and often eaten dinner alone, that her parents were preoccupied and sometimes didn't come home until seven or eight o'clock. This morning, during Mooney's direct examination, all had seemed lost. Now the cracks in the DA's case were starting to show. I felt the same dirty elation I'd felt when I'd kicked Scarsdale. On the topic of the assault, Erica admitted to Jeanie that her memory of the rape was hazy. Here that was all she admitted. We were a long way from proving she'd invented the assault, but the first seed of doubt had been planted.

Jeanie turned from the podium. 'One last question. Would you like to tell the jurors who bought that vodka for you?'

148

A long pause. 'Do I have to?' Erica finally said.

Jeanie looked at her for a moment, then looked pensively at the jury, held the gaze of a man in the front row, and shook her head.

The judge might have chosen to ask the question again, but he didn't. Instead, he asked if the state had any redirect. This was Mooney's opportunity. 'No redirect, your honor.'

Like many crucial questions in criminal trials, the question of who bought the vodka for Erica was destined never to be asked, at least not of Erica.

We broke for lunch.

The detective, Razlo, was still in his thirties, young, and ambitious. He answered Cassidy Akida's questions with a look of intense concentration, his eyebrows in motion. He wasn't just some cop on the stand, his expression seemed to say. He was a genuine intellectual. It was going to be up to me to make him pay for wanting everyone to see how smart he was.

He was led through a workmanlike tour of the investigation, beginning with Erica's mother's call, then the interviews with Erica in which she'd described the rape, followed by the arrest of Scarsdale. Cassidy's direct took less than an hour. An open-and-shut case.

Yet Razlo had skimmed over Erica's visit to the abortion clinic, hardly mentioning it. I was up from my chair almost before Cassidy sat down.

'Detective Razlo, more than six weeks elapsed between the date of the alleged rape and the date when Erica first reported it, correct?'

'That's about right. Early August to mid-September.'

'During the course of your investigation, did you locate any physical evidence?'

'I'm afraid not.' He smiled as if indulging a child.

'So without physical evidence, the results of your investigation were based solely on what Erica told you?'

'Yes. That's basically right.'

'You must have done some investigation to confirm her version of events.'

'She was an entirely credible witness, and she'd been through hell.'

'You must have confirmed that she had an abortion, at least.'

He didn't answer. In his eyes I saw a brief glint of every investigator's worst fear, the colossal blunder exposed for the first time on the witness stand. Then his confidence visibly returned.

'Did you ask her the name of the clinic?'

'It was the Foothill Plaza Medical Clinic in Santa Rosa.'

'You must have sent them a subpoena.'

'I didn't see the need.'

I looked at him sharply.

'No,' he said. 'I didn't send a subpoena.'

'She came to you immediately after she'd had the abortion, correct?'

'I don't know about immediately. The next morning. She was still weak. The uncle told me that he took her there. He sat in the waiting room. He drove her home. There was no doubt in my mind that she'd been pregnant and that she'd chosen to terminate her pregnancy, which is her constitutional right to choose.'

'Her uncle – Nate Blair – told you that he'd gone with her?'

'Yes.' He wet his lips.

'You interviewed him?'

'Not a formal interview. I wanted to find out if he knew anything. He didn't. He was trying to help the girl. A little misguided, maybe, keeping the parents in the dark. They weren't very happy about that, under-standably, but at bottom this was a well-intentioned individual.'

151

'Do you know if it's possible to run a paternity test on an aborted fetus?'

'I don't know. I suppose it's possible. Anything's possible these days.'

'You didn't try to do that, though, did you?'

He shrugged. 'You can come in after the fact and invent all sorts of things you say I should have done. I ran my investigation based on the actual evidence in this case. There was absolutely no reason to question Erica's story.'

'Wouldn't the aborted fetus have been physical evidence?'

'In what sense?'

'Wouldn't that have either confirmed or contradicted your suspicion that Martin Scarsdale committed this crime?'

'It wasn't a suspicion. She told me your client raped her.' He pronounced each word separately, his expression righteous and indignant. 'I don't know how many times I have to say it. Here was a thirteen-year-old girl telling the truth.'

'Didn't this physical evidence potentially exist at a time during your investigation when, if you'd acted promptly, you might have obtained it?'

Cassidy stood. 'Objection. Calls for speculation.'

The judge said, 'I'll allow the question.'

Razlo shook his head. 'It would have told me what I already knew. Erica had already described to me in graphic detail how she became pregnant when Martin Scarsdale raped her.'

'But if you'd obtained that physical evidence when you had the chance, you'd be able to tell us to a medical certainty who the father of Erica Lawler's child was, wouldn't you?'

'I *know* who the father was.'

'If you'd run a paternity test, and the result came back that my client wasn't the father, that would have changed your investigation, wouldn't it?'

'The girl knew better than anyone who the father was.'

'Precisely. However, sitting here right now, you can't tell us to a medical certainty, can you?'

'She'd only been raped by the one guy.'

'Did you ask her how many guys she'd had sex with?'

Cassidy was up again. 'No,' Razlo pronounced with extra emphasis.

The judge motioned Cassidy down impatiently. I shot the jury an indignant glance. Don't glare at me, was the message. I'm asking simple factual questions.

153

I'm not the one making things up under oath.

'So, in fact, you have no idea whether she'd had a boyfriend with whom she'd been having sex, do you?'

'As far as I know, the first time she had sex with anyone was when your client raped her. For the rest of her life, that will always be her first time.'

'You're simply making that up, though, aren't you?'

He didn't answer. He looked like he wanted to hit me, and he probably did. I asked the judge to order Razlo to answer the question I'd asked, and in a bored voice he did, instructing the court reporter to read it back first.

'I don't know for certain whether she'd had sex with anyone else.'

Again I asked the judge to order him to answer the question. Again the judge ordered the question read back. This time Razlo gave in and answered yes, admitting that he'd made up the bit about her losing her virginity to Scarsdale.

'Did you ever send a subpoena for any documents the clinic might have?'

'No need.'

'So you never obtained any evidence that might

have existed at the clinic that could help you confirm your guess about the identity of the father?'

'I never sent a subpoena,' he said, fear suddenly making itself visible again. I could see him wondering if she'd put the father's name on some form she filled out. If I could see it, the jury could, too.

'These are records we obtained from the clinic,' I told him. 'We sent our own subpoena and got a packet back in the mail, simple as that.' Off to my left I saw Cassidy start to rise, then sit again without speaking. 'You've never seen this document before?'

He studied the paper I handed him. 'That's correct. I've never seen this.'

'This document is the payment receipt for a procedure on September 10, 2001, at the Foothill Plaza Medical Clinic in Santa Rosa. Correct?'

He agreed.

'The procedure was an abortion, and the patient was Erica Lawler.'

'It says "termination of pregnancy."'

'Does that mean something other than an abortion to you?' I waited, then went on. 'Now, during your investigation, did you ever determine who paid for this procedure?'

'Like I told you, we never saw these documents. She told me who the father was.'

'Did Erica Lawler have money of her own to pay for this procedure?'

He saw a chance to stick me and with obvious relish he took it, looking directly at the jury. 'I don't know what kind of allowance her parents gave her. When I was a kid I got ten bucks a week. But a lot of kids get more these days. Or maybe she had savings bonds, who knows.'

We had to take a long detour then, establishing once again that he hadn't asked her about her allowance, her finances, or whether she had savings bonds, ending with him being forced to admit, once again, that he was making things up.

Finally I got back on track. 'Whether she'd paid for the abortion, or how she might have paid for it, wasn't something you were interested in, was it, Detective?'

'No.' He gave the jury a look as if to say, Can you believe this guy?

On their faces I saw disdain, impatience, sympathy, interest. At least a few of them were with me. But only a few.

'So who paid for the abortion, Detective?'

He looked at me stupidly, and I nodded toward

the document in front of him. Aloud he read, 'Nathan Blair, with a credit card, according to this exhibit. Her uncle.'

In a similar fashion I led him through a few more exhibits, laying them before him like a surgeon setting out his instruments, establishing with each one that he had not seen it, had not requested it, that on the whole he'd done nothing to verify Erica's story. It was starting to go more quickly, Razlo agreeing to what he had no choice but to agree to.

I put the final exhibit in front of him. 'Looking at this document, there's a place down at the bottom there where she has to write who brought her to the clinic and who's going to bring her home. Tell me what it says.'

'"My friend Nate."'

'That would be her uncle, Nathan Blair. You don't think it's odd that she wrote "my friend" rather than "my uncle" in that blank?'

He looked bored. 'You'd have to ask her.'

'You didn't ask her, though, did you?'

'Same answer as the others. She told me in graphic detail how your client raped her during a sleepover with his daughter. After I heard that, I didn't need to ask any questions about the uncle or anyone else.'

'You didn't ask her uncle Nate, for instance, why he took his thirteen-year-old niece, this child, to get an abortion without informing her parents what she was doing, trying to hide from them the fact that she'd ever been pregnant?'

'No. I didn't ask him that.'

'And you didn't ask him why he paid for that abortion with his own money when he was unemployed and supposedly so broke that he had to live with his sister and brother-in-law, spending his time as nanny to their teenage daughter.'

'No.'

'And in fact you couldn't have asked him that because you didn't know that he'd paid, did you? Because you didn't get the records from the abortion clinic.'

'Asked and answered,' Mooney droned from his seat without rising.

'And you didn't ask her why she'd put on the form where she's supposed to identify the person who drove her there, the person who's going to drive her home and make sure she's safe, why she called her uncle Nate "her friend." You didn't ask her that, did you, Detective?'

'Even if I'd known that, I don't see how it's important.'

158

'Did you ask her what feelings she had for her uncle?'

'No,' he said with distaste.

'Did you ask her if she was in love with Nathan Blair?'

'It's not my job to make stuff up. I look at the evidence, the facts.'

'Ah.' I began gathering the exhibits together. 'Some of the facts, you mean.' I put them on the clerk's table. 'Nothing further.'

The judge ordered court adjourned until morning, giving Mooney the evening to decide whether to redirect Razlo or call Nate Blair to the stand.

Around seven that evening, while I was going over my notes for my deferred opening, the phone rang. I glanced at the caller ID. It was Debra Walker, a woman whose son Jeremy, my client, had been shot to death the previous summer. I'd been avoiding her calls all week, but knew she'd keep dialing my number until I picked up or called her back. 'This is Leo.'

'I was beginning to think that phone of yours was broke.'

'It's the person who's supposed to answer it that's the problem.'

'But this time you picked up.'

'I know what a determined woman you are.'

She sighed heavily into the phone. 'Tamara, she still asks for Jeremy every morning. It's gotten now like she knows the answer beforehand, but every day she asks.'

Jeremy and I had met as visitors at the rehab center where Teddy was staying, relearning how to talk, walk, feed himself. His wife, Tamara, was also a patient; around the same time Teddy got shot in the head, a virus had attacked her brain. When Jeremy needed a lawyer for a marijuana arrest I got the case thrown out. A year and a half ago, while Tamara and Teddy were still in the rehab center, Jeremy had been shot walking to work at the post office.

'I haven't forgotten. It's just that there's nothing I can do about it.'

'We'll see. I got a favor to ask, but I don't want to ask it over the phone. If you're going to turn me down, I want you to do it to my face.'

I was sure I knew what the favor would be, to help her find her son's killer. 'I can't meet you this week. I'm in trial. Next week my schedule should be more open. Why don't you call during business hours and make an appointment, and I'll be happy to see you here in the office.'

160

'Nah, I don't want that. Better you and Teddy come for Sunday dinner. Got to fill the table just to feel like myself, even if I'm too old to be cooking for a crowd every week. And this way we can kill two birds with one stone. I know your brother won't object to putting a smile on Tamara's face.'

The virus that had ravaged her daughter-in-law's ability to form memories had left her beauty hauntingly intact.

'Mrs Walker, whatever it is, I don't think I can help you.'

'You be here for dinner and we'll see.'

Chapter Sixteen

On Friday morning the prosecution rested without either redirecting Razlo or calling Erica back to the stand. I was surprised by this decision but not overly so. Mooney thus far had declined to engage my theory of the case, questioning his witnesses as if I hadn't said a word, as if I'd proceeded since deferring my opening statement with further silence.

A less experienced lawyer would have called Nate Blair to the stand to refute my accusations. Mooney's decision to rest his case without calling him was a risky move. If I didn't put Blair up, the jury wouldn't hear from him. In an ordinary case, Mooney's apparent reluctance to call him might in itself support a reasonable doubt, given that the state, not the defense, has the burden of proof. But Mooney apparently was calculating that reasonable doubt wasn't going to win an acquittal for my client here. I agreed with him.

The judge addressed the jury. 'You'll remember that I spoke to you at the beginning of this case about Mr Maxwell's decision to defer his opening statement until after the close of the prosecution's evidence. The state has rested. So Mr Maxwell will have the opportunity to deliver that statement now. You are to remember that the statements of counsel are not evidence . . .' He gave them a shortened version of the jury instruction he'd read prior to Mooney's opening last week.

My task was delicate. I needed to make it look like the state had something to hide in not calling Blair; at the same time, I couldn't promise much. The surest way to lose would be to forecast testimony I couldn't deliver. 'The prosecution has just closed its case,' I said as I took the podium. 'That means that the DA will put up no more witnesses, except in rebuttal of witnesses put up by the defense. The state will not be calling Nathan Blair.

'You've heard the judge's instructions on the burden of proof. The defense has no obligation to put forward any evidence, to produce any witness. Mr Scarsdale is entitled, right now, to rely on the presumption of innocence and have the evidence go to the jury as you've heard it. Without the testimony of Mr Blair.

'In just a few hours I think you're going to understand the state's reasons for not wanting you to hear from Mr Blair. Mr Scarsdale intends to call two witnesses. The first one will be Mr Blair.

'Let me just briefly sum up what you've heard about Nathan Blair's involvement in the life of Erica Lawler, his thirteen-year-old niece. First, you've heard that Mr Blair, when he lost his job as a teacher for whatever reason, also lost his apartment, and so came to live with his sister, Erica's mother, and her family. You've heard that Erica's parents were preoccupied with their work, and that they were grateful to have someone around to drive Erica to school and to her extracurricular activities, to pick her up, to spend time with her at home in the afternoon before her parents returned, sometimes eating dinner with her alone when they didn't get back until as late as seven or eight in the evening. You've heard that Erica, this impressionable young girl, spent more time with her uncle than with any other person in her life.

'You've heard about the bottle of vodka that somebody bought Erica, and you saw the look on her face when my colleague asked her who. And you've heard that at some point, most likely in June of last year, Erica Lawler became pregnant, and Uncle Nate found out about it. Without telling her parents, he drove her in secret to an abortion clinic in Marin County and paid for the procedure that ended her pregnancy. Paid for it with money he seemingly didn't have.

'Why would he do these things? That's the question you have to ask yourselves. He's not going to get up on the witness stand and admit to being the father of the child he paid to abort. He's not going to admit to having a sexual relationship with Erica, under her parents' noses and in their own house. He's not going to admit to raping the teenaged daughter of the only sister he has ever known. And so you're going to have to do something difficult. You're going to have to use your intuition and your knowledge of human nature. You're going to have to watch his reactions and decide what, if anything, you believe Nate Blair is hiding, and what he stands to gain or lose by his testimony today.'

It was a fairly objectionable opening statement. Mooney might have stood up at any of a half-dozen points and shut me down, but he didn't. He sat with his elbows on the table before him, making unhurried notes on a legal pad, continuing his strategy of pretending that the defense didn't exist. If the strategy was meant to rattle me, it worked. The longer I went on speaking, the more disturbed I was by the stillness from the other side of the courtroom. It was as if I were so far gone in error that he didn't need to point it out.

He was right. With every word I was aware that I was doing something that couldn't be undone, smearing the character of an innocent man with accusations that would taint him in ways that neither he nor I could foresee. We were in a court of law, and the accusations I was making were privileged by the forum, perhaps even mandatory according to the ethics of my profession. Those ethics dictated that I mount the strongest possible defense of my client no matter the consequences to others, yet my hands shook and my voice kept catching. I felt a wave of nausea gathering far off, like the surge that comes before the storm. Again and again I swallowed it.

'The second witness you'll hear from is an expert witness, a professional in the field of child psychology. You'll learn her qualifications, along with her expert opinion on how, why, and under what circumstances kids invent allegations of sexual abuse. If you accept that opinion, you may rely on her knowledge in coming to the verdict I'm confident you'll reach in this case.'

I'd skipped over several subheadings in my notes; glancing down, I decided not to backtrack. What was important was to get Blair on the stand and do what needed to be done before I lost my nerve. I wrapped up quickly, saying nothing about whether Scarsdale would testify, preserving for Jeanie, Scarsdale, and the jury the illusion that there was a choice to be made, not knowing myself what I would do at the moment of truth.

'The defense calls Nathan Blair,' I said when court resumed.

Blair was thirty-five years old, with a baby's fat stubby-fingered hands, a baby's face, and strangely pale eyes that when they fixed on me gave me a sense that either he or I was falling. His voice broke like a fourteen-year-old's as he swore to tell the truth. The courtroom was silent, the jurors attentive, primed by me to expect scandal.

'You may proceed, Mr Maxwell.'

'Your Honor, I'd like to invoke the rule.' I was asking the judge to allow me to treat Blair as a hostile witness. Ordinarily, the party calling the witness must ask open-ended questions, but if the judge allowed my request I would be permitted to put words in his mouth.

'The state objects,' Mooney said, stirring himself at last. 'Mr Blair is Mr Maxwell's witness, and I'm sure he'll be quite willing to answer any questions that the defense puts to him, without the need for leading examination.'

'Overruled. Mr Maxwell, you may lead the witness. I will allow the state the same latitude on cross-examination, of course.'

I came around into the well of the court and spread my notes along the far edge of the counsel table, so that I could glance at them if needed. 'Mr Blair, you're aware that Erica brought a bottle of vodka to her friend Angela Scarsdale's house on the night she says she was sexually assaulted?'

Blair squinted and looked at Mooney, but there was no help for him there. So he was going to be one of those witnesses, I thought, the kind that have trouble with the English language. I knew how to deal with them.

'You don't want to answer that question?'

'I'm aware that she brought it, yeah.'

'You were the one who drove her to Angela's house that night, isn't that right?'

'I think so.'

'You saying you weren't?'

'No. I think so. Yes.'

'You saying you don't remember?'

'No, I remember.'

'There's no uncertainty about it, is there? You drove her. And you knew when you dropped her off that she had that bottle of vodka in her bag.'

Again he looked at Mooney, this time with an edge of panic in his gaze. Was it possible that Mooney hadn't prepared him for this line of questioning? I stepped between Blair and Mooney, making it obvious to both Blair and the jury what I was doing. 'Mr Blair, what conversations have you had with the district attorney about your testimony in this case?'

'I gave a statement.'

'That was to the police. I'm talking about the prosecutor. Have you met with Mr Mooney, or Ms Akida, or anyone else from their office?'

'Ms Akida.'

'What did Ms Akida tell you to say today?'

Mooney rose. 'Objection. She didn't tell him to say anything. She told him to tell the truth.'

'You're not testifying, Mr Mooney,' the judge said. 'He can answer the question.'

'She told me to tell the truth,' Blair said.

I heard a juror laugh, just a small sound at the back of the throat, likely inadvertent, but it was all I needed, permission to press the attack. 'What did Cassidy Akida tell you about testifying in this case?'

'She said I wouldn't have to.'

I realized what had happened. I'd called their bluff. Mooney hadn't thought that I would put Blair on the stand, and so they hadn't bothered to prepare him. In the guise of glancing at my notes, I looked at Cassidy Akida. She was stone-faced, ashen. She'd screwed up.

'Let me ask you the question again. When you dropped Erica off at her friend Angela's, you knew she had the bottle of vodka in her bag, correct?'

'I didn't *know* it.'

'You didn't know it? Did you *not* know it?'

'That's right. I didn't know it. I knew that she had it, but I didn't know that she had it with her. I mean, I figured.'

'And you knew that because you were the one who gave it to her, right?'

'Am I the one on trial?'

'You knew that she had the bottle of vodka because you were the one who'd given it to her.'

'I guess.' He corrected himself hurriedly. 'Yes, I gave it to her.'

'Did she ask you to buy the vodka for her?'

'Yes. A few days before the sleepover.'

'Did you buy that vodka with your own money?'

'She gave me money. I don't know where she got it. From her friend, maybe.'

'What were your finances like at this time?'

Mooney might have objected but didn't. Probably he sensed what I did, that the jury wanted to hear from Blair, and that the lawyer who stood in the way of his testimony was going to be blamed for any answers he did not give. 'Not too good,' he said.

'Did you have *any* income?'

He shook his head. No doubt he saw now where this was going, if he hadn't seen it before. He looked like a man who'd just been hit in the back with a sledge-hammer.

'Savings?'

'No, not really.'

'Did you tell either of Erica's parents that she asked you to buy her alcohol?'

'Of course not. Claire, my sister, she would have killed me. I figured if they don't get it from me, they're going to get it somewhere. They're just going to go up to some bum on the street. Who knows what might happen? Girls get taken advantage of.'

I let that comment pass for now. 'Did you tell either of Erica's parents after the fact that you'd bought her the alcohol, or did you keep it a secret?'

'Well, that would have gotten Erica in trouble. I didn't want that. She trusted me. I didn't want to betray that trust. See, this was a point in my life when I didn't have a lot going for me, as you pointed out. Erica would talk to me about things she didn't feel comfortable talking to her parents about. That was important to me. Made me feel like I was useful to someone.'

'Would it be fair to say that your relationship with Erica was the most interesting thing in your life during the summer of two thousand and one?'

His face looked wan, as if I'd hit him with that hammer again. I waited for the objection, and again it didn't come, although I heard Mooney shift his feet as if preparing to stand. 'Interesting, I don't know. I don't know if that's the word I'd use. It was important to me.'

'Can you tell the jury anything that was more interesting to you, or that you thought of as more important that summer?'

'Getting back on my feet. Getting a job, I guess.'

'So you must have been sending out applications left and right, doing whatever you could to get out from under your sister's roof and back on your own.' I was off script now, doing my best to hang him with his own rope.

173

'Yeah. You know. Here and there.'

'Name one company you applied to, or one application you submitted.'

Again the stunned look. He shook his head. 'I can't think of any. But I was applying to places.'

'You've got a job now, don't you.'

'Yes.'

'A good job. The best you've ever had.'

'Yes.'

'You don't want to lose it.'

'Hell, no.'

'You know that it's a crime to provide alcohol to minors.'

'Like I said, they were going to get it one way or another.'

'On what other occasions have you provided Erica with alcohol?'

'Just a few times.'

'A few times you went to the liquor store or the grocery and bought alcoholic beverages for her and her friends?'

'That's right. Only a few times.'

'Did you ever drink with her?'

'If I was having something she'd ask for a sip. In the evenings.'

I was going on instinct now, doubling down with each question. I couldn't understand why the guy kept giving me the answers I wanted. 'And sometimes you'd make her a drink of her own, wouldn't you?'

'Maybe once or twice. Always very weak.'

'Do you know if Erica drank before you came to live with her?'

He just looked at me.

'You don't know if Erica ever had a drink before the first one you gave her, correct?'

'That's right. I don't know one way or the other.'

'Were her parents home on those occasions when you made her drinks?'

'Sometimes. They were usually upstairs. We'd be watching a movie or something downstairs.'

'And you were also drinking on these occasions, correct?'

'Yeah, I never made her one unless I was having one.'

'Did she ever get sick after drinking with you?'

'Once,' he said. He sat as still as a statue.

Responding to something I saw in his eyes, I moved a step closer. 'Since the events of that summer, have you joined Alcoholics Anonymous or any other addiction support group?'

He frowned. 'I don't think I should have to answer that question.'

Mooney stood. 'Objection. Relevance. Calls for improper character evidence.'

'Sustained,' the judge said in a voice that suggested he would have sustained the same objection ten questions ago if only Mooney had made it. But Mooney had been like a man watching a slow-motion crash, expecting at every moment that Blair would turn away from the disaster he was steering into.

The cross was going better than I'd dreamed, all my doubts and self-disgust swept away in the thrill of the hunt.

'And one day you learned that Erica was pregnant, didn't you.'

'She told me.'

'Did you learn before she told you?'

'No, of course not.'

I had to be cautious now. I had to remember he was an innocent man, and that sooner or later he'd have to oppose me.

'Do you know if she told anyone else before she told you?'

'I don't know that.'

'To your knowledge did she have any friend in

whom she confided that she would have told about it?'

'Look, I didn't get the sense that she told anybody. I don't think she even meant to tell me, even. It just came out. We were in the car, I was driving her someplace, and suddenly she started crying. I pulled over and asked her what was the matter, and she told me.'

'Did she say who the father was?'

He hesitated. 'No,' he said finally. 'I didn't know that until they arrested him.' He glanced quickly at Scarsdale. He was finally getting angry.

'Did you ask her who the father was?'

'Of course I did.'

'And the question was offensive to her, wasn't it?'

He shook his head, a long slow shake. 'She wouldn't tell me. I should have known by the way she was acting that it was something like this, that she'd been raped. But no one wants to believe that. She wanted to get an abortion, she said. She didn't want me to tell her parents. I should have told them, but I wanted to help her.'

'You were afraid your sister would blame you.'

'No. I don't think she would have blamed me. She knows I wouldn't do something like this, what you're suggesting. It's outrageous. This whole thing is outrageous.'

'You did what she asked you to do, correct? You took her to get an abortion.'

'Yes,' he said.

'Without telling her parents that she was pregnant or that she'd made this choice.'

'That's right. It was wrong of me but I only wanted to help her.'

'And you paid for this procedure with your own money. Money you didn't have.'

'That's right.'

'And if Erica herself hadn't told her mother later that night, no one would ever have found out about it. Isn't that right?'

'I suppose. But no one can keep a thing like that secret. Thank god she didn't. I just wish she'd trusted me enough to tell me everything.'

'And two weeks later you moved out of her parents' house.'

'That's right.'

'Erica's mother told you that you were no longer welcome to stay there, didn't she?'

'Yes. They were pretty pissed off at me, and they had every right to be.'

'Just to be clear, you never told her parents or the police that you'd bought Erica vodka?'

178

'No, I never told them that.'

'What else didn't you tell them?'

He just looked at me. I held his gaze. Then finally I flinched. I felt sick to my stomach, the nausea catching me so forcefully that sweat beaded my upper lip. I swallowed, then swallowed again. 'Your witness,' I said to Mooney.

He held three fingers in the air as he walked to the podium. 'Three questions, Mr Blair. Only three. Then, I hope, this will be over. First, did you ever have sexual relations with Erica Lawler?'

'No,' he said. 'Never.' His relief at finally being asked the question was like a dam breaking. My own throat ached. I couldn't seem to breathe.

'Second question. Did you ever know your niece to lie about anything?'

'No, she's always been honest to a fault. She went through my stuff once, after I moved in. She waited about a day. Then she broke down and told me what she'd done. It's not like I cared, but she couldn't stand having a secret like that. Last year, a group of girls cheated on a cross-country race, hid in the woods and jumped out on the second lap. The others kept quiet but she told. They gave her hell for that, but Erica, she always does the right thing. She's really amazing that way. If she says Mr. Scarsdale did it, then he did. I don't think she could live with herself otherwise.'

'Third question. How do you feel right now? Are you afraid?'

I was on my feet at once. 'Objection.'

'Sustained,' the judge droned, but Nate Blair didn't need to say anything. He sat on the witness stand, his hands in his lap, tears running down his face. A pathetic figure.

The judge looked at the clock, sighed, then released the jurors for the weekend. Court would reconvene on Monday, when Jeanie would put on our expert witness; we'd decided previously that it would be wise to give the jury a change of pace after my hatchet job on Blair.

All I could think about was getting home to the TV and a six-pack of beer.

Chapter Seventeen

On Sunday at noon Teddy and I presented ourselves at Debra Walker's door. She lived in a three-bedroom house in a pleasant East Oakland neighborhood. I glimpsed a garden in the back, the red of tomatoes.

Tamara answered the door. In the six months since I'd seen her, her beauty, which had been so fresh when she and Teddy were together in rehab, had dulled. The light in her eyes had dimmed, the edge of expectancy faded, creating a face of grief that lacked only the haggardness. The loss had been steadily working its effects, and she was the only one who could not perceive it.

She was about five feet eight inches tall, slim, with high cheekbones and dark curls. She wore jeans and a blouse with frills at the neck and sleeves; I guessed that her mother-in-law picked out her clothes.

'Remember me?' Teddy asked.

'Oh, yes,' she said. But her smile was empty as she stepped back to let us in.

Teddy looked her up and down, made a pistol out of thumb and forefinger and shot himself in the head.

'You and Teddy were in rehab together,' I explained.

'Oh, I'm terrible with names.'

'You got your memory book on you?' Teddy demanded.

She brought it shyly from her back pocket, a little composition book. He took it from her, scrawled a note, and handed it back.

She only glanced at the note, gave a start, then shoved the notebook into her pocket. In the backyard four men were playing horseshoes on the other side of the garden, while three more leaned against the back fence. All were middle-aged or older. We joined the watchers, exchanging nods. The breeze was cool but the sun scorched my arms. There was a heavy air of ritual, as if the same players had been pitching the same horseshoes for the same small audience every Sunday afternoon for years.

We watched one game, played as a team against the winners and lost, and then Tamara came to the door and called us in. One of the men blessed the meal, the signal for Mrs Walker to begin serving up heaping portions of ham and mashed potatoes with gravy and green beans onto heavy white plates.

Teddy had eyes only for Tamara, glance after speculative glance. I saw Mrs Walker notice. Maybe I'd been hasty to think she'd invited us because she wanted something from me. I remembered what she'd said about Tamara still asking every morning about her murdered husband, as if for her he died each day again.

After the meal the men went back out to their horseshoes while the two women carried the dishes into the kitchen. Mrs Walker suggested that Tamara and Teddy watch TV, which they went off to do, as requested, while she carefully wiped the table. When she was finished she pushed aside her rag and sat across from me.

She studied the wrinkled backs of her hands. 'I got a bone to pick.'

I went for flattery. 'You can pick me clean after that wonderful dinner.'

She shook her head. 'Uh-huh. You're the fly in the ointment.'

'I try not to be. I try to stay aloft.'

Her voice swelled. 'All this time he's been working

Jeremy's case like a dog with a bone. But now he's done. Patrol duty. They're gonna close the file.'

It took me a moment to understand. 'Campbell was the detective on Jeremy's case?'

'He's the only one who cared. Now he's done. Those pictures you took, the department put him out on patrol and it looks like that's where he's going to stay. Now what do you have to say for yourself?'

I shook my head. 'I was set up, Mrs Walker. I haven't yet figured out why, but I was. All I know is that I saw what I saw, and those pictures show what they show. I didn't come here to argue with you in your home, but Campbell is a rotten cop.'

'Rotten, says who?'

'Says me. Other cops. Says my dead client who got set up by Campbell for murder and killed in jail because it seemed like he was the one who tipped me off. You really think Campbell was going to find Jeremy's killer after all this time?'

'He was going to find them if it took him the rest of his life. He had a feeling about this case. That's what he told me. A feeling. He cared. That's more than you can say for the rest of them.'

'If he cared before, he'll care now. It shouldn't matter whether he wears a uniform or a suit to work.'

'That's not good enough. You can't just throw up your hands.' She spoke with the moral weight of a woman who had lived all her life as a patch of high ground in the flood. 'You've got to make this right.'

'And how am I supposed to do that?'

She gazed at me for a moment. Then her shoulders sagged and her eyes dropped. 'For the life of me, I don't know.'

Her sudden defeat was a terrible thing to see. Pity wasn't compatible with the dignity she radiated. She'd lost a son, been left as the caretaker of a disabled daughter-in-law, and undoubtedly knew as every victim knows that finding her son's killer wouldn't bring Jeremy back, but she clung to an idealized hope.

'I don't have any connections,' I told her. 'Cops despise defense lawyers. Absolutely despise them. I ask one for a favor he'll spit in my eye. I wish I could help you, but that's how it is.'

She just nodded, her face settling into an outward placidity, the face of one who endures. She looked so tired.

From the other room came the sounds of the television, a low laugh from Teddy, then Tamara's answering giggle. It reminded me of an engine coughing to life, rusty but alive. 'Now there's a sound I haven't heard in months,' Mrs Walker said, pleased.

I suddenly heard myself offer, 'There's this private investigator Teddy used to work with. I can have a talk with him, call in a favor, ask him to look into things. He still has sources in the department. He can at least let you know if Campbell was working the file like he said.' Even as I spoke I feared I might not be able to deliver. If there is a golden rule of lawyering, it is never to promise. Yet that's what I did that day, sitting in this kind woman's dining room while nearby my brother and Tamara could be heard laughing at the TV. I promised her that I'd do what I could to find Jeremy's killer. This didn't cost me anything, but it made me feel more human.

In the car on our drive home Teddy lounged with his elbow out the window. He looked happy, almost normal, if I could forget how he'd been before, the fierce, formidable intelligence that was gone and would never return.

On Monday morning Jeanie examined our expert witness, who testified that children occasionally did invent allegations of sexual abuse. Her testimony took about an hour. She was polished, she was professional, but she was completely irrelevant. If the jurors hadn't made up their minds by now, nothing she said could sway them.

Mooney's cross-examination of her was perfunctory. He established in a few brisk questions that she'd never met Erica Lawler, never talked to her, that her testimony was purely hypothetical and academic and had nothing whatsoever to do with the actual facts of this case. Beside me Jeanie rolled a pencil between her thumb and forefinger. The expert had been my idea. At the end of Mooney's cross, Jeanie lifted her shoulders and let them fall, sighing.

'Any more witnesses?' the judge asked after our expert had stepped down. There could only be one. I glanced over at Scarsdale. He nodded at me. *Yes*, he mouthed. Jeanie, sitting on his other side, avoided my gaze. Last night I'd finally told her about his confession. She'd taken the news without reaction. It was my problem, not hers, her silence seemed to say; clearly she didn't want anything to do with this decision. My call. I could feel the courtroom waiting. If I didn't know what I knew, if he hadn't confessed, I'd have no choice but to put him on. Without something more, we were going to lose the case.

'The defense rests,' I said, half rising. I waited for

Scarsdale to make a stink, to insist on testifying, but he just let out a breath and seemed to collapse into himself, becoming once more the nonpresence he'd been throughout.

'The state would like to put on two rebuttal witnesses,' Mooney said. 'I don't have them here right now. I'm afraid we were expecting the defense case to take a bit longer.'

Sensing opportunity, I rose. 'Your Honor, the district attorney just made a highly improper comment regarding my client's decision not to testify. The state has failed to prove its case, and Mr Scarsdale has the constitutional right to remain silent. The defense moves for a mistrial based on Mr Mooney's violation of my client's Fifth Amendment rights through what he just said.'

'You're the one who made that connection,' the judge said. 'Motion denied. We'll break for lunch.'

In the afternoon, Cassidy Akida examined Erica's therapist, who told the courtroom about the trauma Erica had described over numerous sessions, rebutting my accusation that she'd lied. I objected again and again, the judge almost always siding with me, no doubt because he didn't want to risk creating an issue for appeal. In truth, her testimony was devastating.

Then Erica's teacher rounded out the session by testifying about her honest character. By the end of the day I felt worn to the bone.

Near the end of Mooney's closing argument Tuesday morning, he ratcheted himself up to a register I hadn't seen before, his cheeks flushed with indignation. 'This man, this guilty man, had the temerity to accuse a person whom he knows to be innocent, and he deserves your contempt,' he concluded, standing right beside Scarsdale. 'He raped a child, committed the most reprehensible and incomprehensible crime most of us have ever been forced to imagine. You've done a great service here, but it's still not complete. I urge you to take your time, consider all the facts, and give this family the closure they deserve by reaching a unanimous verdict of guilty on all counts.'

My own closing argument was more measured. 'Think how it would feel to be falsely accused of a crime as terrible as this one,' I told them. 'Think of the fear you would feel now. That fear speaks to the responsibility you all hold in your hands. A responsibility to follow the law, to give Mr Scarsdale the benefit of your presumption of innocence and to hold the state to its burden of proof. You can't let the severity of these accusations influence you. The judge will instruct you that you have to decide on the facts with your heads, not your hearts. Life doesn't always come wrapped up in a neat little package. There are no easy answers. It's human nature to want to accept the ready explanation that allows us to stop thinking of what disturbs and angers us, but the desire for closure is not part of the instructions the judge will give you. You have the facts, and you have the law. There is nothing else. And the facts are riddled with holes.

'We may never know what happened in this case. We may never know who the father of Erica's child was, or whether she was having a relationship with her uncle, whether he was abusing her. We all want answers in life. We all want closure after traumatic events, but in many situations we have no choice but to live with uncertainty. This is one of those times.' I went on to list all the evidence against Nate Blair, taking a softer tone than I had when he was on the stand.

The instructions took the better part of two hours, the judge reading them aloud, the lawyers following along listlessly at our tables. The jurors slumped, blinking. Then they went home without a chance to deliberate Tuesday night.

On Wednesday morning we didn't have to wait

long. We were in the courtroom, debating whether to stay or go, when there came a loud knock on the jury-room door. A moment later the judge came out, and the courtroom clerk took the verdict form from the foreperson and read it. Guilty on all counts. Scarsdale's head sank to his hands.

Sitting beside him as the verdict was read, I felt a relief that was indistinguishable from shame. During law school I'd planned to become a public defender, and my abandoned notion had left its residue. The more unpopular the client, the more my back stiffened – or so I'd believed until Scarsdale, which is when that layer of illusions about myself dropped away.

He was guilty, and so it was a shameful relief when he was remanded into custody, then led through the back doors of the courtroom. After his sentencing in a few weeks, he would sleep in the reception ward of San Quentin.

Jeanie assured me that I'd done a fine job, the best I could have done. She had her car there but I didn't want to be with anyone. I wanted to walk. That was my privilege. I was allowed to walk out of the courtroom into the open air. I went the long way around the lake, my briefcase strap digging into my shoulder.

Chapter Eighteen

I stopped for lunch and a beer at a Vietnamese restaurant on Grand Avenue. At that time of day it was empty, the manager at a nearby table going over his books. It was a good place to hide from Teddy, from Jeanie, from the office and the apartment, all the familiar faces that today would seem like sources of rebuke. I tried not to think of Scarsdale.

My promise to Mrs Walker weighed on me. Unlike Marty Scarsdale, Debra Walker's son Jeremy had been innocent, gunned down in the street for no reason. The idea of his innocence disturbed me more and more. Finally I broke down and left a message for Car. 'You can't say I didn't warn you,' he said when he phoned back.

'You never said I'd end up on the evening news, if that's what you mean.' I explained how I hadn't issued that press release and hadn't given the photos to the press, that I'd been set up by Nikki Matson.

He was unsympathetic. 'When you've been in this business as long as I have, you know when a tip's too good to be true. I told you then and I'm telling you now. Maybe next time you'll listen.'

'I was hoping to ask you for another favor. Only this time it's not for me, it's for Teddy.'

'Let's get this straight. I worked for Teddy because he won cases. He took what I gave him and he got results. You and me, we don't have the same kind of relationship. If Teddy needs a favor, let Teddy ask.'

'It might help his love life,' I said. 'Get him out of the office. You wouldn't mind that, would you?' I'd had the sense lately that Car and Jeanie were on the skids, and that Teddy was the problem.

'You call that a life?'

'I'll buy you a drink.'

He bought his own drinks, he said, but he told me to meet him at Frankie's in South San Francisco.

When I got there I saw Car in a red vinyl booth at the back, one leg up on the bench beside him. When he saw me walk in he looked away. I ordered a bottle of beer and another vodka tonic for him.

'Suppose you heard about the verdict by now,' I said as I set the drink down in front of him.

'I heard they didn't keep you waiting.'

'Guy must have wanted to go to prison. He fucked his whole case. Came out and confessed to me. Can you believe that? After he told me he did it, I couldn't very well put him on the stand, could I?'

'You shouldn't tell me that. Case is done. I don't need to hear it.'

'What did he want a lawyer for, if he was going to tell me the truth?'

Car stabbed at his drink with a swizzle stick. 'Jeanie, she's a great lawyer, but she'll rep anything that comes through the door. When Teddy handed me a jacket I always knew if I pushed hard enough, something would crack. You can't learn that. It's instinct. Jeanie, I love her, but she don't get it.'

I watched him, wondering how long he'd been here drinking. 'So you don't think I could have won it?'

'Not you. And not Jeanie. Maybe Teddy.'

'So Teddy could have won it.'

'The only person who could have told you that was Teddy, and he's gone,' said Car. 'Gone but not forgotten.' He drained the rest of his drink and reached for the fresh one I'd bought.

'You and Jeanie on the splits?'

'Fuck off. What do you want from me?'

'I got a case; that's all. A good one. Favor for a friend.'

'Friend of yours or Teddy's?'

'Remember when he was in rehab?'

'Sure. I visited. Once was all I could take, though.'

'There was a girl there. Her name was Tamara.'

'I remember a girl.'

'She's one you would definitely remember. She had a virus. It doesn't look like there's anything wrong with her, but she's got a short-term memory of about half a minute. No joke. You'll be talking to her. Then she'll give you this blank look and say "Hi, I'm Tamara." Then you have to start all over again.' I explained about her husband being killed and how Mrs Walker, her mother-in-law, had contacted me. 'Turns out Campbell was the detective on the case, and she thinks he was making progress, even after all this time. She seems to think that no one else is going to pick up the file now that he's on patrol.'

'She's probably right,' Car said. 'Been a year?'

'More.'

'Then I doubt anyone's going to give it even a look. They'll just be waiting for a tip, hoping to get lucky. Or not. But that's how it usually goes. Let's say someone gets picked up for something else; they've got information they want to trade. That's the only way a case breaks when you've got no suspects and no witnesses.'

'You've still got a few contacts in the department.'

'Oakland PD? A few. More than I've got over here. Ever since Teddy and Santorez, the well kind of went dry on this side of the bay. What do you want?'

'Get a look at the file. See if she was right, if Campbell was pushing it. Maybe see how far he got, if there were any suspects. Maybe even drum up interest. See if you can't get them to take a look at it again.'

'They'll laugh. Why should I care? Why do you care? You've got no dog in this fight. This isn't a case. Unless you're planning to rep the killer if they find him. I don't think you're that desperate for business, are you?'

'Look, Campbell was dirty. We both know that.'

'Doesn't mean he wasn't a good detective.'

'Maybe that's what it is. This business with the tip, me being set up. The way I was thinking about it before, it was like – someone's trying to knock off Damon, or else trying to expose this dirty cop. One of Damon's guys, a business rival.' A feeling kept me from telling him about Lavinia. 'Now I'm wondering if maybe

Campbell was the target. Maybe it had to do with one of the investigations he was running.'

'Like he was making it too hot for someone and they wanted to cool things down?'

'This is just me thinking. But ever since Mrs Walker told me about Campbell working her son's case – or at least making her think he was working it – there's been this nagging thought in the back of my mind. I mean what other cases isn't he working because he's down on patrol?'

'You could ask the man.'

'Forget that. He's got his own agenda. Mine is simple. Someone used me and I want to know why. And maybe in the process we can do something for Mrs Walker and Tamara. Jeremy was my client. I got him off on a marijuana charge. I guess it made his mom overestimate my powers.'

'But I don't.' He rattled the ice in his glass. 'You're a prick. You know that? I don't have time for this. I got no shortage of paying work. Every lawyer in town calling me. Take my choice.'

'So you'll do it.'

'For your brother's sake. I get the feeling he has his eye out for this Tamara.'

'They seem to understand each other.'

'The blind leading the blind.'

'That's about how it is.'

He looked up. 'And if that little business works out you might have Teddy off your hands.'

I flushed. 'And I'd be off his. He's got to figure out how to live on his own. He's the same Teddy deep down, whatever you say. He may not even realize it, but it's killing him, living with me like this.'

'Yeah, I can see how it would.' Car let his leg slide to the floor and stood up. 'I'll sniff around. There may be nothing there. Cops aren't exactly keen to tell me things, like I said. But I've still got a few angles left, a few markers I can call. I'll tell them Mrs Walker hired me, that might help.'

He mussed my hair. 'Give Teddy my best.'

I lay awake most of the night listening to Teddy's snores through the wall, in bed but not trying to sleep, hands folded behind my head, eyes on the ceiling, mind running through the events of the trial. I took inventory, trying to decide how at fault I was, what I hadn't done that I should have done, what I'd said in front of the jury that was wrong. At key moments, sure, I'd been caught flat-footed. Maybe I shouldn't have reserved my opening, but that was always a judgment call, especially when so much depended on what I could get the witnesses to say.

He should have pled guilty, is what it came down to; we shouldn't have gone to trial. I could blame the client, but the truth was he probably would have pled guilty if I hadn't pushed him, and he would have gotten a sentence half as long as the one he'd get now.

In the morning Jeanie didn't come to see me right away, but after an hour or so she appeared in front of my desk. 'Look, a client like that, there's nothing you can do. They'll always find a way to hang themselves. You've just got to put it behind you and move on.'

'Okay.'

She had a file under her arm. 'Here.' She smacked it down, a thin misdemeanor file, a DUI. 'I want you to step back for a while, focus on DUIs. I want you to defend nothing but drunk drivers until you can do it in your sleep. Then the next time you step up to felonies you'll be ready.'

'Come on. It's not that I wasn't ready this time. From the start you knew that Scarsdale was a loser and you dumped him on me.'

'If you'd been ready, you would have seen it for the loser it was and pleaded him out in five minutes. I wasn't getting anywhere with him. I thought maybe you could, and then you let him go to trial with a case you couldn't win. Better, at least, to make that mistake like this, with someone who's guilty.'

'Well, he was guilty, all right. We both know I did everything I could have done.'

'There's *always* something you could do better. The minute you start thinking, "Oh well, he was guilty anyway," you're done.'

'Sure,' I said. I knew she was playing with me, trying to make like she'd set me up for some kind of a test that I'd failed. We both knew it wasn't that simple, but she was the boss – and that made me the one left standing when the music stopped.

With Car working on Campbell and his open cases, I decided to find out what I could about Lavinia Perry. It was easy to confirm the basics: in five minutes I had a printout listing all of her addresses for the last twenty years, her debt history, her employers, even her fishing license; I was able to confirm that she was married to Detective Campbell and that they hadn't divorced. There was a long list of cases in which she'd appeared as a testifying witness, and a civil lawsuit filed against her in federal court. But it had been thrown out without her having to give any testimony, a run-of-the-mill problem for any urban cop.

I decided to pay a visit to Nikki Matson.

Her office was in a rehabbed Victorian not far from the courthouse. It looked like she rented out the bottom floor, which had shabby curtains on the windows and a side porch full of junk. Across the street was a liquor store. An unmarked car sat double-parked as if watching the place.

The front door opened directly into a reception room. Nikki's secretary was a wizened black woman. An oxygen tank stood on a dolly beside her chair, the mask and hoses draped over the handles.

'I don't have an appointment, but I was hoping to see Nikki.'

'You don't have . . .' she began, then began to cough – a dry metallic sound.

I came around the desk and helped her adjust the mask, tucking in bits of her stiff, white hair. Then I turned the cock of the oxygen tank as she sucked.

'I can't let you in without an appointment,' she finally said.

'I hope you don't mind me saying this, but you don't seem to be in any condition to be working.'

'You call this work, all the hoodlums that come

through here?' She took the mask from my hand. Then in a low voice, 'I'll let the bitch know you're here. What name should I say?'

'Leo Maxwell.'

'She isn't taking new clients, and she doesn't pay referral fees. Just so you know.'

She got to her feet, holding on to her mask until the last second as she swayed away like a swimmer clinging to a rope. Then she went with short, quick steps across the reception area and through a door, activating the lock with a key fob she wore on a rubber band around her wrist.

I began to worry as soon as she was gone. There might have been another fifteen feet of hallway on the other side of that door before she reached her destination.

Just as I was getting ready to call someone she came back with a sheet of yellow notepaper in hand.

'She won't see me?'

'Yeah, she won't see you. She's in there with that client.'

I felt myself go stiff, a film of sweat breaking out on my brow. 'Damon.'

'That's the one. You know what she calls him? A community activist.' She dropped into her chair and jammed the oxygen mask over her nose again.

I came around the desk and rested my hand on the cock of the tank, then gave it an extra half turn. She looked up at me, her eyes startled but not censorious. 'It won't last,' she said in a whisper, her eyes locked with mine. I took my hand from the valve but she didn't turn it back to its previous level. She just sat there breathing. After a moment I gave it another half turn, and she drank it in, an actual, real breath for the first time since I'd come in, tears filming her eyes.

'He's got a man inside, in Santa Rita,' I whispered. 'Probably another client of hers. I figure she's the one who carried the message. I want his name.'

She shook her head. 'I don't know nothing.'

I stared hard at her, then twisted the valve, cutting off the flow of oxygen. No more Mr Nice Guy. Her face grew more and more ashen as she strained to withhold the cough, but at last it tore itself from her. Now she stared hard back at me as her fingers scrabbled for the valve.

'Someone who was in last week, someone she went to see when there was no good reason to see him. He murdered my client, Jamil Robinson. Your boss set it up, making her as good as an accomplice. Just give me a name. I'll keep you out of it. Spell it on the table with your finger if you don't want to say it aloud.'

She gathered her hand into a fist, crooking her index finger. But instead of tracing a name she pushed the sheet of yellow notepaper my way, then reached up and turned the oxygen on all the way. From somewhere she'd produced a book of matches. She held it, looking at me levelly, then made a striking motion with her hands; I lunged forward, but it was only a feint. She produced a roaring sound with her tongue against her teeth, the sound of an accelerant taking flame.

I wondered if she'd always been crazy or if working for Nikki Matson had made her that way. I grabbed the piece of notepaper and got out of there, her metallic coughs echoing behind me.

Chapter Nineteen

On the sheet was an address and a time: 2300 Crestwood Boulevard, 8:00 PM. Nikki's home in the hills, on a dead end off Skyline Boulevard, high above the flatlands. You couldn't have walked the boundaries of her lot without a climbing rope and harness; cables and pylons held the structure in place. I wondered what perverse impulse had inspired a three-hundred-pound woman to live on a thin shelf of steel and glass suspended from a crumbling mountainside.

She had money; that was certain, more than I would have supposed, even for one of the city's most successful underworld lawyers. The place was lit inside and out by floodlights. I wondered whom she was afraid of. With clients like hers, I guess I would have been uneasy, too. Her Lincoln was in the driveway. There were no other cars, but that didn't mean she was alone. I figured that if Damon wanted to see me again, he knew where I lived; he didn't need to lure me here.

There was a security camera at the door. I pressed the buzzer, and after a pause the lock clicked open. Nikki met me in the slate-floored front hall. On the wall above a thick rug was a picture of riders in red jackets and their striding, hungry dogs. 'Come out to the balcony!' she boomed. 'We can talk there. What are you drinking?'

I followed her through the living room, which was entirely white – from the marble floor to the couches – and out to the balcony. 'A beer, if you've got it.' The house was a box with a living room, kitchen, office, and bedroom, maybe six hundred square feet.

'You can have gin or vodka,' she said. 'I only keep white liquor. No beer.'

'Whatever you're having.'

The balcony was small but jutted out into empty space to spectacular effect. Oakland, San Francisco, and the bay all were laid out beneath us. I never got tired of that view, but at the moment, at least, Nikki seemed immune to it. She brought me vodka on ice, a drinker's drink. We sat in aluminum chairs, troubling in their lightness above all that empty space.

'I can offer you one twenty a year, not a penny more.'

It was a third higher than her last offer. 'Sure. Maybe that's just what I need. A change of employers, a mentor with her finger on the pulse. And six months from now, a bullet in the head.'

'That's good,' she said. 'Very good. Maybe you do have a future in the courtroom, even if I doubt it, from what I've heard. Don't worry, Leo. Everyone loses. Some of us more than others, but everyone now and then.'

'You're not really offering me a job, even if I were stupid enough to take it. You and I both know what you want.'

'What *I* want.'

'What your client wants.'

She inclined her head, giving me the blankest of smiles, letting me understand that we both knew we were talking about Damon.

'I met him the other night,' I went on. 'He really doesn't have much impulse control, does he? It seemed clinical to me, but I'm not a psychiatrist. You might want to get an expert to work up a diagnosis.'

'Some impulses are worth controlling. Some aren't.' She straightened her leg, letting her foot rest near my ankle.

209

'You know what impulses I'm talking about. The murderous kind. He held my brother and me at gunpoint and would have killed us. I suppose sooner or later you'd have seen the pictures, once they sorted out the jurisdictional question.'

'What jurisdictional question?' She seemed to pay no attention, as if she were only marking time before she made her move. She had poise; I had to give her that. I was beginning to realize how much of what she showed to the world was an act.

'Whether to prosecute him in state or federal court for murder,' I said, forcing myself to go on. 'It was federal land. Up at the old VA hospital. I got a tip that he and Campbell were meeting up there and I went and there he was.'

'Corpus delicti.'

'Watch your mouth.'

'You know what I mean. You're just out of law school. Tell me they're still teaching the Latin. You'd have to show me a body before anything you're saying makes sense. It's murder you're talking about, and as far as I can see, no one's dead. You see, Leo, I'm really not interested in hypothetical questions. I limit myself to facts.'

'I'm sure it would have been very interesting to you

if you'd been there. It probably would have turned you on, a little fear, the promise of blood. After all, you never see him in the act. You come in afterward and clean up, then frame some chump for it. Like Jamil. You set him up pretty nicely for that murder.'

'Come back to me when you've got that hole in your head.'

'I'd rather find a way to prevent that. That's why I'm here.'

'If I'm not going to pay you for your services, what am I to pay you for?'

'Security. Yours and mine. You're just as much in the soup with Damon as I am, and maybe more. I know you're the one who gave those pictures to the TV station and issued that phony statement. I may be Damon's target now, but I can be convincing when I need to be. I kept my mouth shut the other night, but there's no guarantee I won't talk next time he gets hold of me. How far do you think he trusts you?'

'Anything is negotiable, but you can't guarantee your own silence. When someone really wants you to talk, you'll talk. No, I think I prefer it my way. You say what you want and I deny it.'

'The guarantee is two people with the same problem and the same solution. Your client has more enemies than he can count. He's wondering who set him up, making his lists and checking them twice. It wasn't Jamil who hired me. Damon knows that, but he had Jamil strung up anyway, for appearances. You probably carried the order to Damon's man inside, whether you knew it or not. Probably you pretended not to know, but he's no dummy; he won't believe he has you fooled. It seems like you're pretty high above it all up here, but at night you can hear the gunshots if you listen. And when Damon turns against you, when he begins to suspect you, when he finally decides that you're more risk than use to him, all the locks in the world won't keep him from coming through that door. If he thinks you betrayed him, you're done.'

She seemed amused. 'And where would he get that idea? From you, I suppose.'

'He's on a hair trigger is all. He gets an idea in his head, from whatever source; he doesn't second-guess. He just picks up a gun and does what he has to do. How many others can there be with the knowledge and opportunity to sell him out? You were Jamil's lawyer. You had a copy of the pictures. It looks bad enough on its own. But then there's the fact that sooner or later you *will* betray him, at least from his point of view –

212

because he's on a downward spiral and at some point you're going to want to get off the ride.'

'You're barking up the wrong tree, my friend, if you think threatening me will get you anywhere.' She settled lower in her chair with her drink. 'I learned something about myself a long time ago. However far anyone else is willing go, I can go further. There's no absolute limit on what I might do, or how much I can hurt you, and I won't feel a damn thing one way or another about it, and I won't play by any of the rules you seem to believe in. No, Leo, you don't want to play the game my way. You'll find out pretty soon how little stomach you have for it.'

'Your practice can't revolve around Damon's crew forever. A man like that, he can't go around pretending to be a businessman much longer, not when the whole world knows half the drugs in Oakland go through him. What happens when the money runs out? You walk away? You really think so?'

She contemplated me for a moment, sipping her drink. 'You're a cocky kid. Too cocky. I don't think you have anything for me. I think you're bluffing.'

'You're on his list, whether you admit it or not. My guess is that you know more than you'd like to know about how Jamil ended up hung to death in his cell at Santa Rita. How much is a disloyal lawyer worth?'

'Obviously that depends on the lawyer. How much are *you* worth?'

'What I really had in mind was an exchange. Maybe we could just talk it through together.'

'Fine. You start.'

'There's who hired me, which is the question you asked me last time we met. And then there's why, which happens to be the answer I want to know.'

'I think you'll find that *who* is a very good question in our line of work. If you're arguing about why, you've already given too much ground. Stick to who.'

'I happen to find why more interesting.'

'Then you're on the wrong side of the bar. I thought you must have learned how to be ruthless from your brother, but maybe you're truly a sap. If that's the case, then it would be a waste of my time to go on protecting you. You can't protect a sap from himself.'

I let her comment about protecting me pass, but it gave me an ominous intimation, a chill that was deeper than the growing chill of the evening. Maybe Campbell had saved our lives that night, or maybe he'd just been playing his part in a larger piece of theater. It'd seemed real enough, but I had a vision of how it might have been worked, Campbell and Damon the actors on stage, Nikki in the background pulling the ropes and working the lights, making sure that when I fell there'd be a net to catch me, just off the ground.

But that would mean that Lavinia was in league with Campbell and had been from the start, playing a deeper game than I'd suspected. I didn't believe in conspiracies, at least not the kind that required the conspirators to be smarter than I was. At bottom, most conspiracies were founded on stupidity, not cleverness. A clever conspirator doesn't conspire; he works alone.

'Let's start with Campbell,' I said.

'What about him?'

'Campbell and Damon. They grow up in the same neighborhood, boyhood friends, all that stuff. One grows up to be a cop; his pal ends up on the other side. Against all odds, the friendship survives. Do I have it right?'

'Like I told you, I don't deal in hypothetical questions.'

'There are two Campbells, the way I see it. Two possibilities. The way things appear now – the way someone wants them to appear – is that Campbell and Damon are the same thing, except that Campbell has a badge and Damon doesn't. A dirty cop and the dirt he rolled in.'

'All cops are dirty. You ought to know that,' she said. 'Or maybe you haven't learned your catechism. Every word that comes out of a cop's mouth is a lie, and all of our clients are innocent. It's either a frame-up or a cock-up.' She held up her glass, and after a moment I realized that she expected me to refill it. I rose, took it from her, went to the bar just inside the door, poured a hefty dose of vodka over ice, and brought it back. I hadn't touched mine.

'A frame-up, then. I'm not asking you to reveal your client's secrets – but did Campbell plant that gun on Jamil?'

'I think revealing client secrets is exactly what you're asking me to do. Assuming that I had a client who figured in this discussion.' She'd turned her chair to face the bay. I smelled eucalyptus, heard the screech of a BART train braking into MacArthur Station. Then from farther off came a rapid *pop-pop-pop*, like a noise heard at the edge of sleep.

'Maybe I'm naïve, but I don't see how someone so corrupt could have risen so high in the police department. Or why he would jeopardize what he's earned.' I could play naïve if that's what she wanted.

She snorted. Her second drink was nearly gone. 'You're young. You still care why people do the things they do. In a few years you'll understand that the why doesn't matter. He wanted this so he went and did that. Uh-uh. Neat little motives don't explain a thing. Christ, you'd have to be a cop to believe that.'

'What I'm saying is he didn't get to be a detective by looking out for his friends. That must have come later, after he'd already become what he was. He must have been good at his job once. He must have believed in it. I don't see how he got from there to planting a murder weapon on an innocent man.'

'Try boredom. There's not much in this life that boredom doesn't explain.'

Maybe it was as simple as that. 'Fair enough. But someone obviously was sitting on this, waiting for their moment. Why did Campbell have to be brought down now? That's the question we have to answer.'

'That's just another way of asking who. And *we* don't have to answer anything.'

'Not another way of asking. A better way.' I went on quickly. 'You want me to put my cards on the table? Here they are. I know who came to me, but I don't know who's behind that person. I want to know the identity of the person pulling the strings as much as you do.' I thought of the voice on the phone pretending to be Jamil, a voice that might have been the voice of a white man trying to sound black.

'And you think I can enlighten you – and that I would even if I could. If I knew anything, what would I need you for?'

'I thought you don't like hypotheticals.'

'Fine. What do I need you for, Leo?'

'There's knowing and then there's knowing. I'm ninety-five percent certain this person came to me because of a case Campbell was investigating. I have a feeling that you have a pretty good idea how Campbell spent his days. I bet you could give me a short list. But you need insulation. You need to keep pretending not to know what happened, and you need to keep blaming Jamil and me. But you also need to be ready for when Damon realizes that Jamil didn't set him up, and that the folks who put his face on the evening news are still out there.'

'What I could do and what I will do for you are different things. I've done more than I should, more than any prudent person would. If it weren't for me you'd be dead. I said, No, the kid's just a sap. He's being played and he doesn't even know it. Don't prove me wrong. I like you, Leo, despite my better instincts. I don't want to see anything happen to you, but then again it wouldn't bother me much. My advice is to back off, go home, be there in the morning to make sure your brother remembers to wipe his ass.'

'I'm your insurance policy, Nikki. I'm not asking you to be disloyal. I've already given you more than you can give me. We're not trading names; we both know that. I'm asking about Campbell, not Damon. Just tell me what everyone in the police department knows. What was he working on before he got sent down to patrol?'

Her face turned toward me in the darkness. There was a new sobriety in her posture, all the arrogance and condescension drained away; for a moment she seemed to look at me with a shared humanity. 'I don't know where you got the idea that he was a crooked cop.'

'Isn't that obvious?'

She didn't say anything, then in her regular conceited tone answered, 'Of course. They're all crooked, all on the take. It's just the ones that get caught who give the department a bad name.' She edged her chair forward and laid a heavy, damp hand on my thigh. Her breath had a floral, alcoholic scent. I was intimately aware of the bulk of her, all that flesh and blood.

219

Her voice was low, without hope or expectation. 'You'll need to move your car somewhere more discreet if you're going to stay tonight. Don't think that what I'm offering you is insignificant. If you prefer to leave, I understand, but when you walk out that front door, you'll be without my protection. Bedroom on the left, street door on the right, the same way you came in. You decide.'

She rose and went in. From the other side of the house I heard a tub begin to fill. I had gotten as much as I was going to get from her, at least without giving more than I was prepared to give. Still, I didn't leave for a moment, but sat taking in the view. I'd begun to pity her and was trying to understand why. Her warning made me fear what the night might hold.

When the water stopped I roused myself and went quickly through the house and outside.

I was picked up as soon as I turned onto Skyline, with a pair of headlights blazing from my mirror. I mashed on the gas, but he kept a foot or so off my back bumper, a big V8 truck or a Hummer, the high beams at eye level, lighting up the dashboard bright as day.

Nikki's parting warning hadn't been an idle one. Even now she must be chin-deep in her bath, both knowing and not knowing what was happening out here on the road. My pursuer didn't try to get ahead. Whenever I slowed, he rammed me, the higher bumper riding over the rear end of the Rabbit with a screech of tearing metal. Each time he hit, he accelerated; it was like falling, that helpless sensation you get in the pit of your bowels. My tires squealed as I struggled to keep from fishtailing, but each time he backed off as we came to a curve. He was experimenting, I realized, getting a feel for how to push me off the road without losing control and following me. Each push lasted a little bit longer, left me swerving a little closer to the edge. There were plenty of long drops.

My only advantage was that even in the dark, I knew every twist and turn. I'd ridden Skyline on my bike dozens of times, and could fly down any number of steep, winding descents back to the flatlands without crashing. The Rabbit's lower center of gravity and narrower wheelbase would give me at least a fighting chance of staying ahead on the way down. Or so I hoped.

I knew the road I was looking for: it was called Thorndale, and it was the steepest, most winding route down from the heights of Skyline that I knew, with at least three hairpin curves. In several places no room existed for two cars to pass, and at every turn there was another driveway. At night, they would be impossible to tell from the road itself.

The trick was making the first turn off Skyline onto a street called Elverton, which wasn't steep and merely wound along the contour of the slope for half a mile or so, past the top levels of the kinds of houses that were common up here, with the garages on top and the living quarters beneath them.

The curves were what saved me. He didn't know when they were coming, and I knew just how much I had to slow down to get around each one without skidding. The road began to drop and I gained ground. In the next few curves he managed only a few nudges, but I was near the edge of control already. We had to go back uphill before Elverton met Thorndale, and as we reached the top he caught me again, slamming me so hard that my head whiplashed. 'Fuck you, fuck you, fuck you!' I shouted.

Now the road took a ninety-degree turn, then a precipitous hairpin. If I could open up some distance between the first and second set of turns, I ought to be able to lose him in the warren of twisting roads above Mountain Boulevard.

I took the first ninety-degree turn hard, straightening

in the downhill curve. With no choice but to slow for the hairpin, I scraped the guardrail but kept on the road. For the first time during the last several minutes, the demonic headlights fell away. Risking a glance in the rearview mirror, I saw him backing up; he'd had to do a three-point turn. I came out of the S-curve, killed the lights so he wouldn't have my taillights to guide him, and floored it. If he caught me on this straightaway, I was dead.

He held back just enough. That section of the narrow road winds slightly between a steep bank on one side and tall eucalyptus on the other, so that at no point can you be sure that another curve isn't just around the bend. I reached the second set of curves ahead of him. These were gentler, but he had no way of knowing that. I was at the advantage now, and in full control; I rode the gas all the way down, lifting my foot slightly at the start of each curve, then pressing hard on the pedal as soon as I found my line around the corner.

At Sobrante I took a sharp right, his lights no longer in my mirror. I was on Thornhill now, and more or less out of danger of plunging off the mountain. My only clear glimpse of the vehicle had been when he'd stopped to make that three-point turn, a big black pickup with dual tires in back, the kind you see pulling eighty-foot yachts or horse trailers.

No doubt he knew where I lived. Meaning I was actually no safer now than I had been a moment ago. Still, I felt the animal aftertaste of fear, the escape from immediate danger that's the only relief a hunted creature knows.

Just above Mountain Boulevard, I stopped to check the car. My door wouldn't open. Neither would the passenger door. I had to lie on the passenger seat and kick the driver's side door with both feet before it gave way, and after that it wouldn't stay closed. I don't know how I made it home without being stopped as a drunk driver. I thought about calling the police, but I feared it'd been Campbell at the wheel of that truck. I needed sleep, then a chance to think.

I wasn't going to get it.

Chapter Twenty

They came through the front door at 4:31 AM.

I'd been asleep for maybe two and a half hours. I'd gotten home just past twelve and found Teddy pacing the darkened apartment. 'Where were you?' he cried. Then he did something that surprised me more than anything: he grabbed me and wrapped me in a sour-smelling hug.

He'd come home from dinner with Jeanie and found me gone. I'd left him a note about my plan to go to Nikki's, but when I didn't turn up, he'd assumed the worst.

Nothing could have been more startling to me than the pacing worry that had evidently consumed him since finding my note. He'd not put the doggie bag from the restaurant in the fridge, hadn't turned on any lights other than the one in the hall. When I was fifteen, sixteen, Teddy never seemed to notice the hours I kept. That would have meant revealing that he cared about me, totally out of character for the old Teddy.

The new Teddy, by contrast, was reduced to nail-biting anxiety and worry when I failed to come home within an hour of the time I had promised. The new Teddy expected me to call if I'd promised to call, and if I didn't, he couldn't think of anything else but where I might be, what might have happened. I'd become the fulcrum around which his world revolved.

By the time I made him understand that I was okay, I was too wired to sleep. We made popcorn and started to watch a movie, then stopped it because Teddy couldn't follow a conversation with the TV on. I told him everything that had happened, everything I'd done. I'd never seen him look so helpless as when I told him about the truck following me when I left Nikki's and that wild chase down from the Oakland Hills.

'Nikki didn't give me anything,' I told him. 'All I can hope is that Car turns up what I need. He's supposed to be checking with his sources at the Oakland PD.'

'What about this other cop?' Teddy asked. 'The one who's married to Campbell? Can't you ask her for help?'

'Every time I talk to her I want to believe her. She's too slippery. I've got to have some way to pin her down.'

'So was it Campbell or Damon?'

I could only shake my head. 'Don't forget the one who called me pretending to be Jamil, the one who's in with Lavinia – Sgt Perry – in all this. The worst part is I don't even know who tried to kill me – or when they're going to try again.'

We went to bed without resolving anything, not seeing the way forward any more clearly than we had two hours ago. Then at 4:31 AM the police broke through the door.

I thought it was an earthquake, and it took me a moment to realize that the tremors I felt weren't the building shaking but my heart thudding in my chest. I heard Teddy shouting something and jumped to my feet. My own first instinct was to run. Then men were in my room yelling, 'Police!' and "Get down!"

I dropped facedown, and a boot pressed down on the center of my naked back. My arms were wrenched behind me, my cheek pressed into the carpet, my wrists handcuffed so tightly that my thumbs sparked with pins and needles. Teddy was quiet now, though I could hear him letting out small gasps. By turning my head,

I could just glimpse him through the crack between the door and the jamb, occupying a similar position in his own room.

'You know your rights, Leo. I don't have to read them to you and I'm not going to bother.' I listened to this unfamiliar soft voice speaking from the doorway like he owned the place.

It was impossible to believe he was in my bedroom where just moments ago I'd been asleep. 'What am I being arrested for?'

'What do you think?' said the detective. It was a white man's voice, the kind that could hush a crowd, make everyone strain to hear him.

'Indecent exposure. How about you let me put on a shirt and some pants?'

'Want the boys to get them from the closet? Or maybe the dresser?'

'My clothes should be right beside the bed. I don't want you opening anything without a warrant.'

'Don't worry,' he assured me. 'We'll get one.'

An officer pulled me to my feet. Another patted down my pants, then slung them with my T-shirt over my handcuffs. Teddy wasn't cuffed. They had him up now, too. He was sitting on the bed, a cop standing guard before him. He shot me an anxious look but they hurried me past his open door.

'You're coming with us,' said the voice behind me. 'It's just a few questions. Shouldn't take more than fifteen to twenty years.'

I finally got a look at him. He was tall, thick, and heavy and still more or less in shape. It surprised me that a voice so soft should come from a man that large. His face was all bones and sun-tightened creases and eyes that never smiled. The tough-guy effect was undone by the ears, which were too large.

It was a short ride to headquarters down by Jack London Square. From the parking garage they took me up the elevator to homicide and put me in an interview room. I'd been in such a room once before, in San Francisco. I was faced now with the same dilemma I'd faced then, whether to say anything, and if so, how much, knowing that the smart play is always to keep silent. At the same time the only way for an innocent man to prove it is to talk.

After twenty minutes the door opened and Detective Campbell walked in. I wasn't surprised to see him, but I was surprised to see him wearing a suit. 'I thought you looked better in uniform,' I said.

'Detective Kristofferson asked me to keep you company while he finishes some paperwork.' He leaned on the corner of the table beside me.

'You're just hanging around, looking for someone to talk to?' I felt cold and jittery. My hands were still cuffed behind me.

'Early bird gets the worm.' He motioned for me to turn so that he could take the handcuffs off. 'Hello, worm.'

I flexed my wrists, trying to bring the feeling back in my hands. 'Or maybe you didn't get to sleep last night.'

'My head hits the pillow I go right out. Six hours later, I'm wide awake, ready to go. Total refreshment. You can't get that quality of sleep without peace of mind. If you're worrying, you got stress, something eating at you, you'll toss and turn all night. Me, I get a crick in my neck sometimes from lying in the same position, not moving a muscle.'

'So you're not on patrol anymore.'

'That's right. You went too far, Leo. I don't know when you first crossed the line, but when a defense lawyer manufactures evidence in a criminal case, law enforcement has to act. Instead of arresting you right away, the department did what cops do. It saw two black men having a conversation and inferred a conspiracy to commit murder. That's the racism of the system, Leo, what I've been working against all my career. Instead of coming to me, asking for my side, they gave you the chance to frame an innocent man for what your client did.'

'I tried to frame someone? You mean Damon?'

'Damon Watson is a businessman and a respected member of this community.'

'You were there. You saw what happened. If it wasn't for you he would have killed me and my brother.'

'By your brother I take it you mean Teddy Maxwell. Truth: if someone hadn't gunned him down he'd be in prison now for manufacturing evidence. So I hope you had a good night's rest, because it's the last sound sleep you'll get for a while. Tonight you'll be in Santa Rita. If you're smart you'll cop a quick plea, spend the next twenty years with your dad in San Quentin.'

'Someone tried to kill me last night. Damon was going to kill me last week. You were there,' I repeated, my eyes searching for the camera, even as I knew the recording system must not be turned on.

'You'll be nice and safe in the custody of the county until we get it all sorted out.' He stood to go.

I thought of Jamil hung to death in his cell. If they

couldn't get me on the outside, couldn't make it look like an accident, well, maybe a young lawyer facing a lengthy prison term might do something rash and desperate. A twisted sheet, my knotted pant legs. Or maybe just a sudden shank in the back.

'What am I here for? No one's told me why I'm here.'

He paused at the door. 'Here's a tip. It comes a little late to help you, but maybe you can pass it on. If you don't ask right away, we think you know. I've got nothing against stating the obvious. We might as well have the cards on the table. Since you ask, you've been arrested for the murder of Nikki Matson.'

He went out, locking the door behind him.

When Kristofferson finally came he didn't say a word. He just dropped a nine-by-twelve envelope on the desk. 'I want my lawyer,' I told him. I'd decided that my chances of getting out today were slim to none. I lacked too many facts, and had nothing to gain and everything to lose by talking.

'I'm not asking you to say anything. Just look at those pictures,' he said in his murmuring voice. 'There isn't anybody in this world that doesn't want to get a look at a mess like that. Most of us are just too embarrassed to admit it. Ease your curiosity. I put the photos in front of you; you looked at them. That's all the report's gonna say. Even an innocent man wants to know what he's up against.'

His voice was soothing, hypnotic. It made me want to do what he said. And in truth I wanted to see the pictures. I needed to know what had happened to Nikki after I left her house.

I lifted the brads of the envelope and pulled out a stack of glossy prints showing Nikki carved up in her bath. She was naked and immodestly posed, her landscape of flesh on full display; the killer's last act had been to drain the tub. I saw the red inner wall of her larynx, the yellow globules of fat under her half-severed breast, blue intestines hideously bulging, layers of skin and muscle sectioned and on view. I tried to visualize the blade that had made those cuts but could not, tried to picture the hand that had wielded the blade, the arm that drove it in. But I could not picture the hand or the arm, or the eyes that had watched them at work.

I could see Nikki, though. She'd had a few seconds at most. She hadn't managed to get up, or if she had, she'd fallen right back into the tub. She would have had time to see blood spattering the ceiling, walls, sink, floor, mirror, every surface, a wild spray, as if someone had pressed his palm over the nozzle of a hose. She would have seen her attacker's face and no doubt recognized it.

Looking at the pictures, the blood on the walls and ceiling, I realized the killer would have come out of Nikki's house soaked with gore. His hair, clothes, and shoes would have been sodden with it, warm on his skin at first but cooling in the night air, a sticky mess. Realizing this, I knew they couldn't pin it on me. They'd tow my car and wonder at its condition, but they'd find no traces of Nikki Matson's blood on the seats or carpet. They'd analyze my clothes and shoes, and the results would clear me. They'd be able to keep me in until Monday, when I'd have to be arraigned. Then for lack of evidence they'd have to cut me loose, or so I told myself.

Even given the best scenario, I was going to spend the weekend in jail.

I put the pictures back in the envelope. My hands felt clumsy. I had to assume that at some point this weekend, whoever had come for Jamil would come for me. 'I said I want to call my lawyer,' I told Kristofferson. 'Now.'

* * *

I spent several hours in a holding cell at the police station. Around 10:00 AM, manacled and dressed in orange, I was escorted to the parking garage and into a waiting mesh-caged van.

I tried to keep my fear at bay. I'd often wondered what it was like on the other side, I told myself. From now on, I would know. Also, I reasoned, I'd been handed a prime opportunity to investigate Jamil's death. Any witnesses were probably still in Santa Rita. Of course the killer was probably here as well, and possibly on the lookout for me. I had the advantage of being forewarned, but I had no illusions about my ability to defend myself from an unexpected attack.

I was a murder suspect, and after being booked I was placed in a high-security unit in C Pod with more than a hundred other inmates, two to a cell, the same one Jamil had been in. I was relieved not to be in the lower security dormitory units, those feeding grounds for the various street factions, long rows of bunk beds housing dozens of inmates, all locked together through the long, long night.

The pod was a two-level enclosure, with a half ring of cells on the top tier and another half ring on the bottom, the two tiers curving around a large open space with fixed tables, vending machines, and a TV ringed by benches, all watched over from a guard station behind Plexiglas. I was put on the upper tier; inside, my cellmate sat on his bunk, elbows on his knees, reading. Then he looked up and I saw the pinched, small mouth, the hollow, stubbled cheeks. It was my client Marty Scarsdale.

'You've got to be kidding me,' I said, so demoralized I wanted to weep.

He was dressed in a padded beige getup like a giant pita roll. With no sleeves or pant legs, this ill-fitting, inflexible garment was designed to present no possibilities for self-strangulation. Inmates classified as high risk for suicide were forced to wear it, a policy that reminded me of the medieval treatment for mental illness, which was simply to lock the insane in a darkened room.

He stared at me, his gaze uncomprehending; then his eyes blazed. 'What the hell are you doing here?'

'A sick joke.' Somehow, after he'd walked out the back of the courtroom between two deputies, I'd imagined I'd never have to see him again – though of course I'd known that I couldn't avoid appearing at his sentencing hearing.

'What did you do? Kill somebody?'

'You're not supposed to ask people what they're in for. You try to kill yourself?'

He slid back on his bunk, folding the bulky fabric around his legs. 'They're going to send me to prison. You're the one who told me what happens to guys like me there.'

'I never actually told you. I left it to your imagination. If you tried to kill yourself, it doesn't look like you did a very good job.'

His Adam's apple twitched. 'You wouldn't really care if I did kill myself, would you?'

'Maybe you're new to this, but you're not supposed to confess to your lawyer. You're supposed to lie to me, feed me a line of halfway plausible bullshit so I can lead you through the dance.'

'You didn't even ask if I wanted to testify or what I was going to say if I did.'

'The only point of testifying would have been if you were going to say you didn't do it. If you're going to lie to the jury, you've got to lie to me, and you've got to be halfway convincing about it. Yeah, you're going to prison. I don't feel great about that, but I'm not the one who raped that girl.'

They probably wouldn't lock him up as long as they were going to lock me up if Kristofferson managed to pin Nikki's murder on my back. The thing was, I couldn't let myself believe there was any real chance of that. It made me feel stronger to pick on someone even weaker than I was. But tearing down Scarsdale only made me feel better for about a minute. Then I felt worse.

I left him and went to look for the telephone. The upper tier had phones on the outer wall between every fourth cell. These didn't accept change; rather, inmates called collect through a 1-800 service that charged exorbitantly to the recipients. The expense – often exceeding a dollar per minute – meant that the phones weren't in great demand, despite ease of access, so I didn't have to wait long. I hadn't gotten hold of Jeanie earlier. Again this time she didn't pick up.

I called Teddy. I'd spoken to him earlier, when I hadn't been able to reach Jeanie. I'd asked him to keep trying to track her down. He'd sounded confused and disoriented, as if he didn't remember what had happened and didn't know where I was. The usual strategy was to bluff his way through confusion, hoping he'd eventually catch the thread. That wasn't good enough now; I needed him to understand, to remember, and to plan, all things he was no longer any good at, especially after a shock like last night. Stress and anxiety had the effect of working against all the progress he'd made.

'Did you manage to get hold of Jeanie?' I asked when he picked up.

'Oh, yeah. I saw her last night. We had fingers at – at the doormat.'

'You had dinner at the restaurant?'

'Sorry. I'm not thinking straight. It's hard . . . I'm tired.'

'Don't worry about it. You remember me calling before?'

'Yeah, I remember,' he said. But I could tell that he didn't.

'Last night the police came. They woke us up, and they took me away. I'm in jail now, Teddy. That's why you had to accept the charges. I'm calling collect from jail. I need you to find Jeanie for me and ask her to come here to see me. I'm at Santa Rita Jail. Can you write that down for me? Can you make a note?'

'I don't know. Hands are kind of – quaky. Shit!' he cried, and I knew that he'd burned or cut himself. He groaned, nine parts frustration and one part pain.

'Teddy, you still there?'

His voice shook. 'Leo, I'm here.'

'What are you supposed to do, Teddy? What did I just ask you to do?'

'Find Jeanie.'

'Okay. Hang up and do that right now. If you can't get her, try Car. He might know where she is.' I hesitated. 'And when you talk to Car, ask him if he's made any progress on that thing he was going to check.'

'What thing?'

'Just ask him. Tell him Leo wants to know if he's made any progress.' All the calls from jail were recorded. I couldn't say anything more.

'Okay,' Teddy said.

'You can do this,' I told him. 'It's all a frame-up, and I should be out by Monday. You just need to hold it together until then.'

He had already hung up.

Chapter Twenty-One

I sat at one of the fixed circular tables in clear view of the guard station, flipping through a week-old newspaper. I didn't want to spend more time in my housing unit than I had to. The cell interiors were among the least visible places in the pod.

Any corrections environment was going to have a rigid authority structure. Here in the high-security unit, filled with gang members serving sentences of a few years and murderers awaiting trial, the population was more stable than elsewhere in Santa Rita. It seemed to me that whatever had happened to Jamil, it couldn't have happened without the blessing of whoever was in charge.

The pod was one-third black, one-third Latino, and the rest whites and Asians, invisible boundaries criss-crossing every square foot. The eyes of the white guys were on me from the start. I used to think that being a defense lawyer would cut in my favor if I ended up inside, but that was before Scarsdale. My most recent client was every penal institution's lowest form of life, and I was guilty by association.

I'd been pretending to read the same page for the twentieth time when the sounds of the conversations around me grew quieter. I heard stifled laughter, looked up, and saw a powerfully built man with stringy red hair and a beard.

'Hey, buddy,' he said gently. He was standing several paces away, but with that tone of voice he might as well have been sitting in my lap.

I didn't say anything.

'If you're not my buddy, you don't get to be my friend,' he went on.

'Whatever you say.' I pretended to go back to my newspaper, but he stayed put.

'Don't worry. I didn't come over to stomp you.'

'That's a relief,' I said, watching him over the paper.

He looked me over, then shook his head. 'Nah, man, I don't see it.'

'See what?'

'You don't look like no kind of badass woman-slicing motherfucker. You look like a little lost bird.

I hear you used to be a lawyer.'

'Still am,' I said. 'Only just now I'm not taking any new cases.'

'There isn't anyone in here with any love for lawyers, especially one who can't keep himself or his kiddie rapist client out of jail.'

I lowered the paper and his eyes drilled through me.

'Now, there are exceptions to that rule. For instance, there's one of Nikki Matson's clients in here. That would be Peabo over there. Normally, a white guy like you would have protection, but the rest of us figure, hey, you wanted to play by their rules outside, well, you might as well play by the same rules in here.'

I wondered if he'd come over to warn me, or to scare me, or just to take the measure of what he could get. I followed his glance and saw two black men playing cards, one with cornrows and a teenager's build, the other in his forties, with freckled skin, prison muscles and tattoos, a black do-rag on his head. They slapped down card after card in a fast-paced game of War.

'The older one or the younger one?'

'The older one. Even that kid could handle you, though.'

'Maybe he's glad to be rid of her. Maybe he owed her some fees.'

243

The guy gave a laugh, his voice insinuating. 'Man like Peabo, he don't always know what he's feeling, only how he's going to act. Maybe Nikki was the kind of lawyer that needed to get killed. All Peabo knows is you killed one of his.'

The longer I looked at Peabo, the deeper my heart sank. He didn't look up even once. 'Does it make a difference that I didn't kill her?'

'You saying it don't mean anything in here, any more than it's going to mean to the DA. Unless you can give them a name and bring him in here to take the heat off you? Maybe you're innocent, maybe not, but before you get out of here, you got to talk Peabo into forgiving your ass.'

'Is that what happened to Jamil Robinson? He couldn't convince him?'

Instead of answering he just smiled. Then he turned and walked away toward a group of men at a table across the room, half of them doing push-ups and other calisthenics, the other half sitting on the tables looking at me.

After that, to my shame, I found myself sticking close to Scarsdale. He had a week's more experience in this place than I did. The crucial thing was not to be alone, it seemed to me, to have someone to watch over my shoulder. The two of us were the pariahs, and neither of us had any choice but to trust the other.

That evening in the chow line I'd just turned from the serving counter to follow Scarsdale to one of the fixed tables. Not far from us was a group of the white guys who'd been watching me earlier. As we walked past them, one of them sucker-punched me in the back of the head.

At least that's what I figured must have happened. All I knew was that my vision went dark and my tray clattered as I fell. I braced for the kicks that were sure to follow, but none came. The guy who'd hit me simply kept walking out of the mess hall and back to the pod.

If the deputies had seen what happened, they gave no sign. After a silence, everyone went back to eating. One of the inmates who worked in the kitchen brought a mop, but wouldn't meet my eye as he moved the mop in slow circles around my crouching form.

I went on to the table where Scarsdale sat alone. 'You see it happen?' I asked. My voice sounded strange in my ears.

He nodded, chewing, not looking up.

'You had any trouble with that guy?'

He shrugged. 'They call him Chopper.'

I could only hope that Chopper had hurt his hand.

I felt like throwing up. I waited until he'd finished eating, then we went back to the pod next door. Every step sent shooting pains up my neck. At the back of my head I felt a sliding heat.

The rest of the evening until lockdown I stayed close to the guard station, pretending to read the same week-old paper until it was time to be secured in my cell.

My mattress was a thin foam pad over the metal shelf of the bunk. With every movement, my neck twinged and my head throbbed. So did my thoughts, which kept returning obsessively to the punch. I'd never been a fighter, and the insult was a continuing shock; my thoughts fizzed and overflowed with it. I could tell Scarsdale wasn't asleep on the bunk beneath me, but neither of us spoke.

My thoughts ran ahead to tomorrow. I wondered if Jeanie would visit, and how I could keep safe during the daylight hours. The showers might be avoided, but I'd have to mingle with the other inmates during chow and yard call. I could get a pass to the infirmary if I needed one and avoid the chow line, possibly, but it would only be temporary and wasn't much of a plan.

For a while there were noises: talking, joking, the

sounds of radios and portable TVs. Most of the cells spilled light onto the tier, but ours was dark.

There were no catcalls, no torment; it wasn't like the movies. It was as if the rest of the inmates had chosen not to witness our existence, knowing we wouldn't be here long.

'You going to ask for protective custody?' Scarsdale finally asked, his voice low.

It hadn't occurred to me that it could be so simple. 'Then what happens? They came after me because I'm your lawyer.'

'I thought you didn't give a shit about me.'

It was tempting to do what he said. In the morning, first thing when the guard came around, I could make the request. My whole body ached for sleep, but my heart was still racing, my muscles tense and jumpy. 'If I saved my own ass and you turned up hung in your cell, I'd have to look for another line of work. My last client who died, it happened on this tier.'

'You mean the one who hung himself.'

'He didn't, though. He was murdered. Probably by Peabo.' If Nikki Matson was Peabo's lawyer, it made him the natural suspect for Jamil's murder.

'I wasn't here then. They brought me up here after the conviction.'

'Obviously someone saw something. Even those who didn't see must know.' I yawned. Maybe in a few minutes I'd be ready to sleep.

'It figures,' Scarsdale told me. 'I understand now.'

'What?'

'The only time a client becomes important to you is when he's dead.'

Maybe it was just that my living clients always seemed to work against me. I could have told him this, but I was too exhausted to argue. Even so, I couldn't sleep.

Toward morning I slept for an hour or so. When the lights outside came on at six I found that I couldn't sit up or turn my head. I had to slide sideways off the bunk and drop to the floor.

When the cell doors were opened a deputy brought Scarsdale an orange smock and sweat pants to put on. 'How'd he try it?' I asked while the deputy, whose name was Espinoza, waited for Scarsdale to surrender his padding.

The deputy snorted. 'No actual attempt. Only a comment.'

'A cry for help?'

'We helped him.'

'I think he learned his lesson.'

'I sure hope so. The paperwork we got to fill out . . .' Espinoza shrugged. 'Still, it's less than if he actually did it. If he says he wants to kill himself and then he does it, the family can sue the county, hold it liable. That's how messed up things are. It happened once; now all the suicidals got to wear the sack.'

'I guess Jamil Robinson didn't give you any warning.'

Espinoza took the outfit from Scarsdale. 'I ain't supposed to be talking to you,' he said and walked down the tier.

After breakfast came yard call. It was a bright, clear morning, already hot here in Dublin, shielded from Oakland's fog by the coastal hills. Scarsdale and I kept in motion, walking brisk laps around the edge of the field while other inmates did exercises in scattered groups, one inmate always standing guard while the others did their push-ups, crunches, and presses.

When we came in an hour later I told Scarsdale I was going back to our housing unit to lie down for a while. I should call Teddy, I knew, see if he'd managed to find Jeanie, but my imagination was beginning to run, my fears overwhelming me. I could die in here tomorrow. If I survived, I might end up in prison. Me being in Nikki's house, plus a plausible motive was all that a skillful prosecutor would need to convict me. She'd as good as killed Jamil, and she'd put out that false press release, setting me in Damon's crosshairs.

I'd been lying on my bunk for half an hour, trying to make myself get up and go call, when I heard an explosion of shouts. I looked down from the tier and saw a man run stumbling across the open space below. Another lay on the floor. Not far away, a black guy stood his ground against half a dozen white attackers. Next the redhead who'd talked to me yesterday waded into the scrum and knocked the man down with one punch. The others then closed in, kicking him in the torso and head.

I saw Peabo coming along the tier. Noticing me notice him, he shouted something. The fighting drowned out his voice.

Tear gas billowed. I thought I saw something in Peabo's hand. A glint of metal. He closed in on me like a fielder with a runner picked off. The steps on the other side of the tier were blocked. I made an instinctive move toward the false safety of my cell, then stopped myself, rushed back to the rail, looked over, looked back at Peabo, then swung a leg over and let myself drop.

The shock sent a jolt up my spine and I pitched

forward onto the hard cement, jamming my wrists and kneecaps, the tear gas blinding me, a feeling like someone wringing out each lung between strong hands. I rose but was knocked down, which seemed to deafen me. Someone else kicked me in the ribs. I started to rise again, but suddenly the deputies were there. They wore gas masks and swung batons.

I came face-to-face with one of them. He blinked behind the visor of his gas mask and I recognized Espinoza as he raised his arm and brought the baton down, down, down. There seemed to be no impact, but then all was silence, my skull felt cold as ice, and the world swam to the side and went out of focus.

I woke up shackled to a gurney. Every time I breathed, I started to choke. Whenever I moved my eyes there was a sensation like a ball bearing shooting along the rim of my skull, and my knee was a block of cement.

In the prison hospital I was placed in a bed next to Peabo. 'Crazy bitch,' he said when he saw I was awake. Like me, he was shackled hands and feet. A ragged line of blood seeped through the bandage on his head.

I didn't say anything. The ward was crowded, the beds filled.

Peabo's voice was thick tongued and full of gravel. 'Wasn't no call the way you did Nikki. From what I hear, she was cut real bad. Should have done it clean. Should have left that woman looking like herself.'

'I didn't kill her. Why would I? I look like Jack the Ripper to you?' His torso was bare, wrapped in elastic bandages. His eye was swollen shut, his lip split. He didn't speak like a stone-cold murderer and he didn't look the part, either. He looked beaten, like a man whose only ambition is to walk away from the fight. He grunted.

'What happened to you?' I asked, my tone neutral.

'After you jumped? Shit. Those deputies came up when they finished below, cleaned us out the upper tier. They were pissed off big-time. Two of them caught me up at the top of the stairs, whaled on me for a while, then tossed me down. But I've been hurt worse. I'll stay in bed for a while, a little rest. Ain't nothing I've been wanting more than a little rest.'

'Damon and Campbell have been sending a lot of work your way.'

'I wasn't about to stick you. You done jumped off that rail for nothing.'

'Not jumping didn't seem to help you any. I'd say

I even came out ahead, putting aside whatever you were hoping to stab me with.'

'I wasn't going to stick you,' he insisted.

I didn't reply.

'You don't believe me.'

Again I didn't respond.

'I knew your daddy,' Peabo said after another pause. 'We was both in the Q.'

'That's probably not the best reason not to kill me you could think of.'

Very few people knew who my father was or that he was in prison. For years, Teddy had been working to get him out.

Finally I spoke again. 'I haven't seen my father in over nineteen years. From what I've heard, he hasn't exactly been on a character improvement plan.'

Peabo seemed to radiate disapproval. In the two years since I'd allowed myself to believe my father might be innocent of my mother's murder, I still hadn't visited him. Teddy, though, had gone, getting Jeanie to drive him there. Some paralyzing dread was holding me back. For the past year, I'd worked to get the Innocence Project and other non-profit organizations to look at the case, but none had agreed to take it on. Teddy had represented my father himself, but I thought he needed a lawyer who wasn't his son.

Finally he said, 'You think because your daddy's white and I'm black we couldn't have no friendship inside? Is that what you're saying?'

'Friendship is just a funny word for it.'

'He helped a partner of mine, a younger guy who got a bad deal. Most jailhouse lawyers – most *white* ones – they wouldn't help a brother, but your dad didn't care about skin color. Got my friend out, too. Filed a brief with the state Supreme Court and he won. Shit, you should be proud; your pop the best jailhouse lawyer in California.'

It was the first I'd heard of this. Our father had been an attorney, albeit an unsuccessful one, before his arrest and conviction. His practice had consisted of petty plaintiff's litigation, personal injury, insurance defense.

I'd preferred to believe we had nothing in common with him, that Teddy and I were sui generis. Now I also was wrongly accused. Thrown together with a man who'd known and seemed to respect him, I couldn't avoid understanding how my father must have suffered. And I couldn't avoid thinking of the monstrous mistake I'd made in cutting all ties with him, a mistake I still hadn't had the courage to face. I felt again as if I had to vomit.

At the same time, I didn't want to talk about my father with this man who'd tried to kill me. 'Did you see what happened to my cellmate?'

'He in here somewhere. Got his nose broke, and a nasty crack on the head, but, far as I know, he'll live.'

That was good news. I hadn't lost another client. 'Was he what started it?'

'Black guy taking a swing at him was what started it. Guess he figured it was open season, but he guessed wrong. Them white boys was all over him. Taking care of their own. It's almost enough to turn me cynical.'

'So how did Campbell and Damon figure you were going to get away with doing me the way you did Jamil?'

'Man, why do you keep talking to me about Jamil?'

'He was my client. I just want to know which rule he's supposed to have broken. For my own piece of mind. You see, I got a little sideways on this one. Nikki was part of it. She set me and Jamil up, made it look like we crossed your boss. That was my fault. Now I can't stop thinking that Jamil's the one who paid the consequences. You're not the one who gave the order. You're just a soldier.'

He'd turned his head away from me. 'That boy went out of this world a tormented spirit. He couldn't hack it in here. Couldn't do the time. Nothing anybody could have done for him. It's been bothering me, that I didn't do nothing for him.'

'Sure you did. You gave him a hand up before he took a swing.'

He shook his head. 'You're wrong. I ain't done that.'

'Who killed him then, if you didn't?'

'If I had to guess, it was Chopper. The one who slugged you. They was cellmates. But I haven't wanted to think about it too hard. Because if that's how it went down, we got to make a reprisal, but there ain't enough of us inside to do that. All the best old soldiers in prison, and these kids, the best you can say is they ain't afraid of nothing.'

'Not Jamil, though.'

He shook his head. 'No, you're right about that. That boy was afraid of his own shadow.'

'Someone set him up.'

'Someone told the cops to check his ride for a gun, if that's what you mean. No doubt about it.'

'I'm not looking to rat you out to save my own skin.

Because they can't pin Nikki's murder on me. There's the simple, obvious fact that whoever killed her would have left bloody footprints to his own front door. Which lets me out. So help me understand. What did Jamil do that he shouldn't have done?'

Peabo took a deep breath, let out a sigh. 'Man, me and everyone else told him to get rid of that gun.'

'What do you mean, get rid of it?'

'You do a job; you ditch the gun. Ain't nothing would have happened to him if he hadn't kept driving around with it. That made him vulnerable, but Jamil, he was a weak link.'

'You mean he couldn't do the time?'

'You could say that. Among other things. It was his fear, man. He wasn't no killer. It was eating him up inside. A little fear's a good thing, in my mind, long as you don't let it control you. But he couldn't keep it in.'

At last I heard what he was telling me. 'You're saying he did the shooting. The one the gun was tied to.'

'Course he did. Jamil do anything anyone tell him. Don't start cryin' on me. You must have known your client was guilty.'

So there had been no planted gun, no frame-up, no conspiracy. Jamil had been guilty all along. Everything

I'd wanted to believe about him was a lie, as no doubt he'd have told me if I'd let him give his side of the story the day I visited him here. Lavinia had put down the bait, and I'd obligingly swallowed it.

I kept on thinking. 'So Damon turned in his own man and arranged for you to kill him in here.'

'Damon? Nah, he want to kill a man, he'll do it. I told you, it wasn't me. If Jamil didn't hang himself, the only one who could have done it was that Chopper. It wasn't Damon's thing.'

'Then whose was it? Campbell's?'

'You're talking about the only clean cop in Oakland.'

'How about Lavinia Perry?'

'I don't know no Lavinia Perry,' Peabo said.

He turned away from me and pretended to sleep.

258

Chapter Twenty-Two

After two nights in the infirmary, I was transported downtown with a busload of other prisoners to the county courthouse, where I experienced the chaos of Monday morning arraignments from the other side.

Jeanie was there, and had worked out a deal with Cassidy Akida. Instead of arraigning me, Cassidy announced the decision of the district attorney's office not to charge me for the murder of Nikki Matson. I was processed out and released. They could always arrest me again, but Jeanie didn't think it likely, not unless new information came to light. 'It'll make a good war story someday,' she said as she drove me home.

I felt humiliated and abashed, angry and exhausted. I needed to sweat out the experience on my bike, I thought, then take a shower. I felt infected with the taint and the stink of Santa Rita. 'I don't want to talk about it,' was all I said to Jeanie.

'I'm here if you change your mind,' she said as she dropped me off. 'Just know that.' Her solicitude unnerved me, completing my sense of failure. I couldn't get out of the Prius fast enough. Still woozy from the knock on the head, I ought to have gone straight to bed, but I needed the open road. I went upstairs and changed into my biking things.

'I'm home,' I called to Teddy, who was in the bathroom. 'I'm going out for a ride.'

'Okay,' was all he said. No welcome home, no how are you? Just that.

The apartment bore all the usual signs of his habitation, but it was in better shape than I might have supposed. In my absence no disasters had struck, no fires or floods, no accidents requiring a trip to the emergency room. It was more or less clean, if disorderly, Teddy's physical surroundings reflecting the functional disorder of his brain. The stereo was playing full blast, green lights shooting across the equalizer, but no sound came from the speakers. Teddy, not remembering how to turn it off, had simply pulled out the speaker wires. In the laundry hamper I found our unopened mail.

I made it as far as the front door, my bike on my shoulder and my biking shoes on my feet. As I looked out at the street my legs began to feel weak; the trees seemed to swim in the heat waves rising off the blacktop. I felt a wave of dizziness. It was a joke that I'd thought I was physically up to it. Not to mention that whoever had tried to run me off the road three nights ago was still out there. Just because I'd survived the weekend didn't mean I was safe.

My knee hurt from the fall at the jail, I told myself as I turned away from the double glass doors and wheeled my bike onto the elevator. That was why I wasn't going out. I knew better, though. They'd gotten to me.

When I came back in, Teddy didn't ask me why I'd changed my mind. I took off my biking gear, throwing the clothes in the hamper even though I hadn't sweated in them, and took a shower.

When I got out he was in the kitchen getting ready to make a sandwich, consulting the sheet tacked to the wall. The carafe of the coffee maker was filled with orange juice, I noticed; in the microwave I found watery ice cube trays. I took comfort in the familiar task of rectifying my brother's cognitive mistakes, my anxiety eased by his dependence on me.

'I guess you heard all about it,' I said.

'Heard about what?'

'Nikki's dead.'

'Nikki . . .'

'Nikki Matson. The lawyer. The one I was visiting the other night before they arrested me.' Though I hadn't been ready for a conversation with Jeanie, I wanted to discuss it with him. I felt an unreasonable frustration. I needed a reaction more like he'd shown that night, interest and sympathy in what happened to me, gratitude for my return.

'Someone chased you,' he said. But it was as if the events we were speaking about weren't real to him. Only the task he'd this minute begun was real. He'd taken out a slice of bread but now was off track, staring down at the mustard jar and the meat, a butter knife in his hand. The knife was for the mustard, but as I watched he used it clumsily to slit open the deli bag of meat. Talking to me meant he didn't have enough concentration left over to make his sandwich.

'Whoever was chasing me, I think he went back up there and killed Nikki.' I wanted his attention; I wanted to tell him what Peabo had said about Campbell being the only clean cop in Oakland, and his reaction when I'd mentioned Lavinia's name. But Teddy had his own preoccupations. He opened the jar and spread mustard on bread, then spread mayo on the other side of the same slice. Then he draped meat across the bread and studied the result with a frown. Not right, but not completely wrong.

'Aren't you glad I'm not going to be charged with murder?' I asked.

'Real glad, Leo.' Teddy didn't look up, still studying the sandwich.

Teddy had always been a creature of routine. Now that I'd returned, normalcy was reestablished. For him, at least, it was as if there'd been no interruption. Or maybe his weekend alone had made more of a difference than I supposed; maybe he was beginning to realize that he could manage his own life.

I asked him if there were any messages, and he took out his memory book and studied it. 'Oh yeah,' he said. 'Car called. He wants you to call him back.'

I was too depressed to call Car. I turned my phone off and spent the rest of the day on the couch with the TV on, rousing myself every now and then to get another beer. Teddy's pistol lay on the side table in easy reach. If he saw it there he didn't say anything. He puttered around the apartment, then went out for his weekly odyssey on the AC Transit bus to his rehabilitation group.

We shared a delivery pizza for dinner. I was on the couch again, dozing around midnight, when I heard the distinct click of the pistol's hammer and felt the weight of someone sitting at the foot of the couch. When I opened my eyes all I saw was the gun. Then the face behind it came into focus, and I recognized Car.

He uncocked it, flipped the cylinder out, sighted down the empty barrel, then snapped the cylinder back into place and set the pistol on the coffee table. 'Bang. You're dead. Shot with your own gun.'

Allowing myself to breathe, I sat up. 'Car. Jesus.'

'You'd think someone was trying to kill you, keeping a pistol lying around like that.'

'Someone is.' And I told him what had happened after I left Nikki's.

He listened impassively, his face betraying neither belief nor disbelief. Every once in a while his eyelid twitched as if in amusement. Finally he said, 'Well, if that's the case, you're making it easy. Passing out drunk on the couch with a gun practically in your hand. Where's Teddy? Sleeping?'

'I guess.'

He moved his foot and knocked over several empty

beer bottles on the floor. They went rolling and clattering in different directions. 'Shit, Leo, you are truly a mess.'

'What are you doing here?'

'I've been leaving messages all weekend. I thought you wanted my help on this thing. I got tired of waiting for you to call back.'

'They arrested me for Nikki's murder. I spent the weekend in jail. You must know that.'

'Well, you're out now.' He kicked a bottle as it came rolling back. 'So how was it? You get it in the ass?'

'I wish I knew what your problem was,' I said, but in fact, I was just going through the motions. I was almost glad to be hassled, I realized, as if the events of the weekend were just a series of ordinary misfortunes.

'Come on. Get up,' he urged. 'This place smells like ass. I'll buy you that drink I owe you.'

What I wanted most was to crawl into bed and stay there for about three days, but my curiosity got the better of me. It was so unusual of Car to make any overtures that I figured he must have found something good, and that the glint of it had somehow rubbed off on me.

We walked over to Grand Avenue and the Alley, a dive with ramshackle wood paneling. Near the main bar was a piano covered in Plexiglas with microphones around the perimeter where people could sit and sing their requests. When no one cared to sing, the gravel-voiced piano man took the floor.

We sat in one of the uncomfortable booths as far from the piano as we could get, where the volume was just right for not being overheard.

'You remember that Jeremy Walker business you asked me to look into? That wild-goose chase? Well, I may have found your goose.' Car downed half his vodka tonic in one swallow and wiped his mouth. 'So it turns out your buddy Campbell isn't too popular these days. At least in some circles. My guy was happy to talk, but he's going to have my nutsack if I repeat anything.'

'I'm listening.'

'You asked about your client who got gunned down walking to work at the post office over a year ago. Well, my guy says that Campbell was working the case pretty hard. Evidently he'd just picked it up again recently. When he was looking through the file, one thing stuck out. Campbell had written up a warrant for the cell phone records and pulled the CAD printouts for another police officer.'

'Campbell was investigating this cop for Jeremy's murder?'

'Ex-cop now. He resigned last year. Sgt Christopher Lucas. White guy. Narcotics. And here's the good part. Guess who Lucas was fucking at the time of his resignation.'

'Campbell's wife. Sgt Lavinia Perry.'

'Hey there.' It was like we were playing basketball and I'd made a lucky shot. He lifted his drink to me, finished it, and signaled to the waitress, who ignored him. 'Maybe you knew him. He had this dog that went everywhere with him, big thing like a bear. Violated just about every department regulation.'

I thought of Trigger, the dog Lavinia had when I walked with her on the Berkeley Pier.

'Also, he was cited twice for carrying a knife on duty. Big fucking thing he used to wear under his vest in back.'

I just nodded.

Car went on, 'Like I said, Campbell's not too popular. You don't go after another cop on a murder case, even if he is fucking your wife. And if you do, you don't handle the case yourself. You give the file to the FBI and let them run with it.'

Car went to the bar for another drink. He was in a celebratory mood. As soon as he was gone, the waitress came. I ordered another round, figuring that he'd put away as many vodka tonics as I set in front of him tonight.

When he came back I shoved the extra drink across the table. 'I picked up some other rumors,' he said. 'Looks like the feds may be looking into the possibility that certain cops have been moving in on the drug trade, trying to set themselves up as suppliers. My source couldn't say whether Lucas was one of them.'

'What about Lavinia?'

'He didn't tell me it couldn't be her.'

'Say Lucas was one of these rotten cops. And Lavinia was in on it, since she was sleeping with him. And Campbell found out. And he was trying to make a connection to the murder of my client last year.'

'I don't suppose you can carve off a piece of the drug trade for yourself without killing a few dealers along the way,' Car said. 'It would look at first like the dealers were killing themselves off, tit for tat. The kinds of murders that solve themselves. Just wait, and next week this week's shooter goes down.'

'Only problem with that theory is that Jeremy wasn't in the drug trade.'

Car shrugged. Thinking of what Campbell had said in the interview room, what Peabo had said about Campbell being just about the only clean cop in

Oakland, I went on, 'Maybe there's a war going on and the rest of the department is content to let it look like the dealers are killing each other off. But Campbell didn't like the murders of black men being treated like they don't count. It didn't matter to him that the dead men were drug dealers. He'd want whoever is responsible brought to justice. Especially if it was a white ex-cop.'

'Maybe.' But his flat voice made clear that I'd gone further into the realm of speculation than he was willing to follow.

It was plausible – maybe – but it didn't explain any of what had happened next. There was no connection I could think of between a rogue cop moving in on Oakland's drug trade, Jeremy getting gunned down on his way to work a year ago, and the deaths of Nikki and Jamil. I couldn't think of a single reason why someone I hadn't even met might want me dead.

Unless he thought I knew more than I did, or that Jamil or Nikki had told me more than they did before they were killed. That would be the ultimate irony, I thought, being targeted for knowledge I'd never acquired.

Thinking of the picture Kristofferson had shown me, Nikki's body in the bath, I was instantly gripped by fear. My only security lay in finding the truth, finding Lucas. 'I don't suppose we know where this guy is, this ex-cop Lucas.'

'Like I told you, he resigned last year, and he hasn't been heard from since. It's a safe bet he isn't too far away, though, if all these guesses you're making are right.'

'And probably the only person in the department who really wants to find him is Campbell.'

'There may be an attitude in the department that this guy, Lucas, if the rumor about the federal investigation is true, is doing the cops' work for them, what they'd be doing if they didn't have one arm tied behind their backs. They figure he'll get what's coming to him before long.' Car shrugged again.

'So the only person who could possibly help me get out of this jam is the man whom I've irremediably pissed off.'

'That's one way to put it.'

I stared unhappily down at the table. I found myself wishing it were Damon who was trying to kill me rather than, perhaps, an ex-cop with a trail of bodies behind him. When I considered the two of them side by side, I could almost accept Campbell's description of Damon as a prominent businessman, an important member of the community.

Car changed the subject. 'There's something else I've been meaning to bring up.' It was as if he'd been working himself up to something. 'I heard about this place that's going to come up for rent, up in the hills. Real quiet place, kind of like Teddy's old house in the woods, only not so far out. On the bus line. Friend of mine is looking for someone long-term. He's a good guy, great landlord. Real hands-on.'

'I own my place. We're doing fine on the mortgage. What do I need an apartment for?'

'I wasn't thinking about you.'

I kept my voice calm. 'I can't afford the rent on a second place.'

'Teddy gets a disability check, doesn't he? It wouldn't be that much.'

'Well, he isn't ready. I was gone three days, in jail three days, and when I came back, it was no pretty picture. In fact, it was a miracle that he didn't burn the whole building down.'

'Tell me one thing you do for him that he couldn't be doing for himself.'

'Clean up his shit every day.'

'So he's a pig, so what? Jeanie thinks he's backsliding.'

'So why isn't Jeanie talking to me about this?'

'I don't know. Maybe she thinks you're pissed at

her. Maybe she's pissed at you. That's between you and her. She didn't want me to say anything, but I'm saying it. Your brother's a good friend of mine.'

'So where were you all those months he was there in the rehab center? When he was relearning how to talk, how to walk, how to dress himself, when he was figuring out that he wasn't going to be a lawyer anymore. Where were you?'

Car didn't rise to the bait. 'He wouldn't have wanted me to see him like that.'

'You weren't there then, you're not there now, yet you sit in front of me claiming I'm not helping him. Go ahead and tell me whatever you think you have to tell me, but let's get one thing straight. Teddy's my brother, and you're a guy who used to work for him, and who was fucking his wife behind his back.'

Car's face went stony. Without even realizing that such a thing was possible, I'd hurt him badly. I felt bad, but not too bad. I'd been wanting to say that to him for a long time, and it felt good to get it off my chest.

There was a lull in the conversations around us, people looking up and glancing our way.

Car's voice was sharp. 'In the beginning it was like he had an ambition to get better, like he thought he was going to be a lawyer again if he worked hard enough.

Now he doesn't seem to care. That's what bothers me. That's what I wanted to talk to you about.'

'How's he going to get better? There's no getting back to where he was.'

'What's he going to do with his life if he doesn't try?'

'You can't practice law with a hole in your head. He can't even make a sandwich.'

'What's the alternative? He sits at home on the couch? That isn't a life. At least to Teddy, it wouldn't be. It's a goddamn waste, is what it is. Everyone's got to have something to live for, and Teddy, he lived for being a lawyer.'

'I'm not arguing with you,' I said. 'But that's all over.'

'So you keep insisting.' Car took out his wallet and dropped money on the table. 'I've said my piece. I'm out.'

I caught the waitress's eye. She brought me another beer.

Chapter Twenty-Three

In the morning I called Mrs Walker and asked her if I could look through Jeremy's old things. I needed to retrace Campbell's steps in investigating his death over a year ago. If there were a connection to Sgt Lucas, I hoped to find it among Jeremy's possessions.

Mrs Walker told me to come right over, and suggested that I bring Teddy. The TV was still going, but he wasn't watching it. I found him sitting on his bed, one shoe on, one off, hands on his knees. 'Teddy,' I said, and when he didn't respond I said his name again. He started to stand, then realized he had only one shoe on. 'I'm going over to Mrs Walker's to look through Jeremy's things.'

He sniffed himself, nodded, and stood. 'I'll come.'

My car was in no condition for the streets; we had to call a cab. As we rode I kept glancing at Teddy. Car's interference – really, Jeanie's – still rankled me. I resented the implication that I found it convenient to keep Teddy with me, purposeless and dependent. True, his disability payments helped with the mortgage, and we lived more cheaply together than we could apart. And I knew that Car was right, that one of these days one of us had to broach the subject of Teddy living on his own, but Car's notion that Teddy could somehow practice law again was a fantasy.

Again Mrs Walker's house was filled with the smell of rich food, and again the table was laid. As before, Tamara was polite, as if with a stranger whose status she couldn't puzzle out. Teddy talked constantly, messing up more than usual, dropping food in his lap, while she listened intently, pretending to understand.

He was trying to tell her about the early days of his practice, when half his clients were cases where the public defender's office had declared a conflict of interest – junkies, whores, and thieves. Teddy was a born raconteur, and his stories had a great effect on me growing up. When he was telling them he'd give me his attention in a way he did at no other time, and listening I'd feel as if I were resurfacing into the sunshine from the underwater world where I spent most of my adolescence.

The story he was attempting to piece together now was one I'd heard many times. It was the story of two of his early clients, a prostitute and a junkie-slash-car thief.

'Our tale begins with a crime of public indecency in the third-floor bathroom at the Hall of Justice,' Teddy liked to begin, whenever he used to tell it. 'Angela Esmerelda and Billy Ray Rey, two of my clients whose court hearings were scheduled the same morning, found themselves in what might be called a compromising position, that is, if either had any moral dignity to compromise. Because they don't latch the stall door behind them it keeps banging Billy Ray in the ass. Word has it that the officers waiting to testify heard the thunking from the hall.'

Here, he'd pause and assume a tone of utmost seriousness. 'And that, believe it or not, was the beginning of one of this city's great love affairs.'

However, what came out now was this: 'I had these clients when I was a lawyer. She was a toaster' – he meant hooker – 'and he used to steal cars for this Russian chop suey.' Russian chop shop, he meant.

'I'd like to try that,' Tamara said, listening intently.

Teddy gave a little nod of concentration and went on, his brow furrowed with the effort of translating the story he remembered into the speech he was now capable of, speech that barely allowed him to say what he meant, let alone imply something without saying it. 'I'm trying to think of their names,' is how he began now. 'They got arrested for fucking in the courthouse bathroom.'

Tamara blinked. She didn't look away from his face.

I had no appetite for hearing my brother stumble his way through a story that could only sound sordid, stripped of the high drama he used to give it. I turned to Mrs Walker. 'Let me help you clear the table.'

I helped her with the dishes, and then she took me into a bedroom that served as home office and storage room, with a desk and computer, and boxes stacked on every other available surface. 'It's their things, Jeremy's and Tamara's,' she said, indicating the cartons with a despairing gesture. 'I keep telling myself that one of these days I'm going to put it all in order – but it's just too hard.'

She showed me the boxes that contained Jeremy's papers, then left me with them. From the other room I heard Teddy's low voice, and snatches of Tamara's laughter. Then I didn't hear their voices anymore.

I went through box after box of bills, school papers, pictures, all the junk that accumulates during a life.

It was tedious, depressing work, and it left me feeling like the desecrator of a grave, sitting cross-legged on the floor with so much stuff spread around me.

I missed it the first time and found it only because I dropped a stack of papers as I was putting them back into their box. It was a pocket folder like kids carry homework in. Inside I found a police review board complaint form that Jeremy had filled out halfway but not finished, and behind that a computer printout statement, single-spaced.

I'm writing this to inform you what I witnessed on May 29, 2001. I was walking to work when I see this van pull up and stop outside a house near Fifty-Ninth and Bancroft. A bunch of guys with guns jump out. They kick down the door and start shooting. One of them, I don't remember his name, I know works for Damon Watson, who runs a crew that is very active in this neighborhood. They have been attacking drug dealers and robbing them. They solicit 'donations' from people who feel they have no choice but to pay up.

I ran around the corner. There I saw an unmarked police car. As I'm about to go up to it the white detective at the wheel sees me coming and drives away. I recognized him as a narcotics detective who arrested me a year ago and violated my rights. His name is Christopher Lucas.

I think the people of Oakland deserve better than to have white police officers sit by and watch while black men kill each other.

It wasn't signed or sworn. It was simply hearsay and, as such, it wasn't worth anything more than the paper it was printed on. But we weren't in court, and it told me everything I needed to know about why Jeremy Walker was dead.

I made the connection only now that Lucas had been the arresting detective on Jeremy's case. I'd cross-examined him during a suppression hearing. His report, like thousands of others, listed so-called furtive movements as the reason justifying his stop of Jeremy, who'd been walking home from work. When I'd cross-examined Lucas, he'd been unable to say what that furtive movement was, acting as if the hearing were a waste of his time. The dog, Trigger, had also been involved. Lucas claimed that the animal had reacted to Jeremy, justifying a search for drugs. I'd succeeded then in establishing that Trigger wasn't an official police dog and had no training. Disgusted by Lucas's attitude, the judge had suppressed the marijuana from evidence and thrown out the charges.

If the rumors were true about Lucas crossing to the wrong side of the law, he'd need muscle, firepower. That might be where Damon fit in.

From the other room I heard a piano. I went back out into the other room. Mrs Walker was playing a hymn.

I was about to ask where Teddy and Tamara were when I heard a sound of pleasure from behind a closed door at the end of the hall, then Teddy's voice, and another moan from Tamara.

Mrs Walker came to the end of one hymn and immediately began another, her hand rising to turn the page. 'Find what you're looking for?'

My cheeks burned. I was too stunned to answer. She went on playing, but her music couldn't mask the sounds from the room.

After a moment I moved closer to the piano, trying to follow her lead. 'Did Jeremy ever tell you about seeing something on his way to work in the morning? A shooting?'

'He probably would have figured that was one of the things I didn't need to know.'

'Did Campbell or anyone else ever look through those boxes?'

'No.'

'So you never heard of a Sgt Lucas?' Jeremy's case hadn't gone to trial; Mrs Walker hadn't been present at the suppression hearing, and so would have had no occasion then to learn the name of the detective who'd arrested her son.

'Don't know why I should. I don't have doings with the police myself.'

'How about Lavinia Perry?'

She lifted her hands and the music stopped. From the other room came Teddy's loud groan. My cheeks heated again, but the look on Mrs Walker's face was far away, her abstraction genuine. 'Why, I just dreamed about that child. It's so odd that you would mention her name now, after all these years. She was the first one, the girl my Jeremy wanted to marry. This was back when they were in high school. He broke her heart.'

'I've never been so embarrassed,' I said to Teddy on the bus on the way home.

He didn't respond. It was loud. Maybe he didn't hear. We were surrounded by a bunch of kids heading home from Skyline High. My head was pounding.

'You can't just do that.' I'd known that sexual inappropriateness could be a symptom of brain damage, but this was the first I'd seen of it.

Teddy was looking out the window. He resembled nothing so much as a kid who'd just eaten too much candy, and was both satisfied with himself and about to be sick.

I tried again. 'Look, you can't have sex with a girl who doesn't know who you are from one moment to the next. I'm talking as your lawyer here. I don't even think Tamara is legally capable of giving her consent.'

'Oh, she consented. I've never seen consent like that.'

'The walls are thin. The woman's seventy years old.'

Teddy didn't have anything to say to that, but I knew what he could have said – that he was only taking what was offered, and that Mrs Walker wasn't going to accuse him of anything. When we were leaving, she'd said, 'We'll see you on Sunday. We leave for church at nine AM.'

'Okay,' Teddy had told her. I knew then that the bargain was sealed, and that Mrs Walker would make sure Teddy lived up to his end.

'She thinks you're going to marry her daughter-in-law,' I told him. 'She's old school. That's what it means to traditional people when you go to bed with a girl. She thinks you're going to take Tamara off her hands.'

His face went through a series of contortions. Finally he said, 'I don't have a problem with that.'

'You do whatever you want to do.' I turned to the window. It seemed to me that I'd been teetering on the edge of exhaustion for a long time, ever since Teddy was shot, and now I was sliding over the edge. I didn't have the energy to do anything but lay my head against the grimy seat back and watch the streets slide by. My life was veering out of control, or rather I'd never had it under control. I'd been like a child making believe that I could steer the vehicle I was riding in. A city bus. Goddamn it.

At home there was a message from Jeanie, asking when I'd be back at work. There was a hearing coming up in one of the DUIs she'd dropped on my desk. She was right, I realized. It was high time that I stopped worrying about dead clients and started paying attention to the live ones, while I still had the chance.

Chapter Twenty-Four

I sat at my desk and turned on my computer with the relief of a drunk in sight of home and free to collapse. This was an illusion, of course. There was still a rogue ex-cop out there who wanted to kill me, and a woman who wanted Teddy, who was dependent on me, to marry her brain-damaged daughter-in-law. My desk was heaped with files, my inbox choked with e-mails, the message indicator on my phone blinking a staccato pulse. Yet here at least a semblance of control was possible: all it took was sitting at my desk until the work was done.

I kept the door closed. I didn't want to be disturbed. I went through the cases one by one, checking the court's orders against my calendar, making sure that all the dates were noted correctly. Then I wrote brief memos to file, summarizing the status of the case, what had been done and what remained, the investigation that needed to be conducted, the names of witnesses, holes that I'd previously spotted in the DA's evidence.

I was tired of criminal law. Lord, was I tired of it. Was it too much to ask to be able to sleep at night, safe in my bed and secure in my conscience?

Before Jeanie left she knocked on my door. 'Hey.'

'Hey.'

'Let's talk. Tomorrow. Tonight I'm too pooped.'

'I'm going to pull a late night, but I should be here by eight thirty, tops.'

She seemed about to give me some warning, then just nodded and went out, pulling the door closed even though I was the last one left in the office.

She was going to get rid of me, I figured. I didn't blame her and I didn't blame myself. I'd done what I'd had to do, what it seemed to me was my duty toward my clients. It was just that death had stayed one step ahead.

By midnight I had the cases in a state where another lawyer could easily take them over if Jeanie decided to fire me, if Lucas succeeded in killing me, or if I decided that it was time to walk away and start over, buy a motorcycle and take a trip down through

Mexico and South America like I used to fantasize about. Or maybe do it on a bicycle, see how it felt to be in the kind of shape where you can pedal all day and not be tired, eat two dinners, rise in the morning, and do it again.

I'd given up work and was looking on Craigslist for a used motorcycle, plotting the route I would take down through Baja California. I had my feet up on the desk and I was drinking a beer from the office fridge. The ringing of my phone broke a silence that seemed to have gone on longer than I'd lived.

I was surprised to hear Car's voice. 'I thought you didn't go into the office anymore,' he said. 'I called your place, but Teddy said you were out.'

'You know about motorcycles?'

'You thinking about buying one?'

'Maybe.'

'Funny thing. A man seriously considers buying a bike, then doesn't go through with it, he won't ever again be the man he was before the idea came into his head. It diminishes a person to think about himself on a motorcycle and then say no. Afterward he'll always have that question in the back of his mind, that what if. It's like corrosion on the soul.'

'You got a bike?'

287

'I don't need to put a thing like that between my legs to prove I'm a man.'

'So it's damned if I do, damned if I don't.'

'I'm just saying, if you don't feel masculine enough, motorcycle's a pretty good purchase.'

'Why you calling me, Car?'

'Little update on what we talked about the other night.'

'Talk to Teddy about Teddy. It's none of my business where he lives.'

'The other thing. Your little problem. I had another talk with my guy in the Oakland PD. He called me, actually. Seems there's an addendum to that dirty laundry he wasn't supposed to be airing. So I twist his arm again, and he tells me that your friend Sgt Perry hasn't shown up for her shifts the last three days. They sent someone to her house. She wasn't there. Official line is she's taking an unscheduled leave, but if she comes back they're going to fire her ass.'

'*If* she comes back?'

'Let's just say that he expressed a certain skepticism of the official line.'

'Shit.' I remembered the pictures of Nikki Matson. The thought of Lavinia having been dealt with in similar fashion was unbearable.

'You think something happened to her?' Car asked.

'Yeah. Don't you?'

'She was into something, and Campbell was into her. Isn't that what you think? So now she's gone. *Adios*. Down to Mexico.'

'Find her,' I said. 'Can't you find her? Can you do that?'

'I don't know if I can. I don't know if I even would want to.'

'You want to,' I told him. 'Otherwise you wouldn't have called.'

'I want to get paid, is what I want. How do I get paid on this? There's no case.'

'When I get paid you get paid.'

'You need a case to get paid. There's no case. Where's the client?'

'Jeremy was gunned down in cold blood to keep him from telling anyone he saw Lucas orchestrating an assault by a bunch of thugs in broad daylight on a drug dealer's house. How's that for a case?'

'What, like a civil case?' The spirit seemed to drain from his voice.

'Sure. Wrongful death. Civil rights.' Why go on defending criminals, I thought, when I could make a contingency fee working for the truth rather than against it. 'She's definitely a witness. Call it our precomplaint investigation.'

'You got a client for this complaint you're going to file?'

'I got my dead client's mother. And Jeremy's widow. You find Sgt Perry, we meet with her, get her to talk to us, convince her to give us a statement.'

'I get paid up front.'

'Then don't take the job. You've got your pick. You don't have to work for me.'

A pause. 'I'll put a couple of hours into it. If I don't find her, I don't find her. I'm not going to spend a whole week on this. Someone like her, a cop, she ought to know how to stay hidden. And if she doesn't, well, I'm not going to lie to you. There's probably someone out there who wants to find her more than me.'

'You'll find her.'

Chapter Twenty-Five

With Jeremy's handwritten statement in hand, I decided that I finally had enough information to merit an approach to Campbell. In the morning I called the police department and left a message on his voice mail, telling him I wanted to speak with him regarding Jeremy Walker. 'I'm mystified,' he said when he called me back. 'Unless you're calling to talk about Nikki Matson, I don't think we've got any business.'

'Kristofferson showed me the pictures,' I said. 'The person who cut Nikki up would have come out of there with so much blood on him you'd have found it behind his ears. He's probably still got it on him.'

'Then I guess we don't have business.'

'Jeremy Walker was my client. I know Chris Lucas killed him, and I think I can help you prove it. Just hear me out; that's all I'm asking.'

Campbell paused so long that I thought he'd hung up. Finally he said, 'I'll be at your office in five minutes. We'll drive.'

I was waiting on the curb. Campbell leaned across to open the passenger door but didn't say anything. I had no proof he was an honest cop, as Peabo had said, but I got in beside him. For all I knew, Campbell might have killed Nikki. I'd come to think there must be an innocent explanation for his meetings with Damon, or at least one that didn't involve a conspiracy to frame Jamil and have him murdered in jail. Still, I wouldn't have bet my life on it.

We didn't speak for a minute as he worked his way through traffic. Then Campbell seemed to choose his words carefully. 'So do you know something connecting Chris Lucas and Jeremy Walker or is that just a shot in the dark?'

'Not as much as the US attorney knows. What about you?'

'Oh, I know Chris real well.'

'When I was in jail I met a guy who knew you. Guy by the name of Peabo. One of Damon's men. He seemed to think you were just about the last honest cop in Oakland. And that got me thinking maybe we've both been fooled.'

'My wife asked you to take those pictures, didn't she?'

'She told me she was Jamil Robinson's sister, and you and Damon were trying to frame him for murder. Then I got a call from someone pretending to be Jamil. I figure that was Lucas.'

He sighed. 'When was the last time you saw her?'

'Week and a half ago. I went out and found her during one of her evening shifts with the vice squad. The next day, she came by my place. We drove to the Berkeley Pier, had a chat.'

Campbell was heading up into the hills where he'd met Damon, where I'd taken the pictures. He drove without glancing around and wasn't interested, it seemed, in the proof I'd discovered, supposedly the point of our conversation. If I were wrong about him, if he were dirty, I'd find out soon enough. If that moment came, I needed to be ready.

I didn't actually know that the feds were investigating Lucas, whom I'd never met. Maybe I'd been right the first time, and the meeting I'd photographed was precisely what I and the city's white power structure had assumed, a criminal conspiracy. Maybe Campbell was some rogue cop trying to seize control of the city's drug trade. Every fact I'd discovered certainly fit that conclusion.

If so, the only way to save myself was to dive out of the car, roll, and come up running.

Campbell turned into the lot beneath the trees and parked. There were no other cars. 'Let's walk. You go ahead of me. Up the trail. You know the way.'

'What are you going to do? Shoot me in the back?' I tried to make it a joke – but it didn't come out that way.

'I need some air; that's all. Need to exercise my legs. I got to think how to play this, and when I think, I got to move. And until I've thought this through I'm not letting you out of sight.'

I went up the trail ahead of him. Despite Jeremy's connection to Campbell's wife, and her connection to Lucas's scheme, Campbell hadn't removed himself from the investigation. Maybe he didn't trust anyone else to care about murdered drug dealers and police corruption, or maybe he wanted to leave a way out for Lavinia and for himself. Again I had the sense of a man pulled in conflicting directions by unwholesome pressures, destined to snap in the direction of whatever force yanked the strongest.

After ten minutes of steady climbing we came out onto the ridge trail. 'That view,' Campbell said.

I wasn't interested in the view.

'Now why don't you tell me what you were so eager to tell me,' he proposed.

'It wasn't about money, not at the beginning,' I said, still breathing hard from the climb, sweating in the warm sun, feeling that everything depended on showing him that I understood his intentions. 'Not for you. It was about sharing information, letting Damon's crew do what the police couldn't do because of people like me, lawyers looking over your shoulders.'

He stood facing me, a few feet of trail between us, surrounded by the silence of the wind and the birds in the trees. 'You're gunning to bring me down.'

I shook my head. 'Then someone decided that the cops who tipped off Damon's crew should share the take. Lucas was probably the one who came up with the idea of putting the drugs back on the street. By then you were out. And ever since then you've been trying to stop them.'

'You seem to have all the answers. Doesn't sound like you've got proof.'

'I've got this statement Jeremy Walker wrote.' I took out a photocopy of what I'd found. After reading it he folded it carefully and put it in his pocket.

'I suppose you told someone you were meeting me.'

I felt another wave of fear so palpable that he must have seen it. 'You're no killer.'

His nostril twitched. 'People surprise themselves. And others.'

'I know that you're not completely clean in all this, but I also know you got out before it became mercenary.'

'You said you last saw my wife a week and a half ago. That's a lie. I'm not a violent man but I swear by god I'm not a cop right now.' He enunciated each word separately. 'Tell me where she is.'

'If I knew I would tell you.'

He studied me. 'No, I don't think you would. But I could make you tell me. I know the ways, Leo. I could leave you without a scratch on you, not a bruise. Or if it went too far, I could make sure they never find you. I could put you in a place you'd never get out of. Last weekend was just a taste.'

Fear clawed at me. My collar was damp, my eyes misted. I knew by the look in his eyes that he was right, that he could make me tell anything, make me say anything. 'She used me, but that doesn't mean she trusted me. She could be running. Either with Lucas, or from him. Or from the police.'

'Do you even know that she's alive?'

'My investigator's looking for her.'

'And what then, if he finds her?'

'I want to try to bring her in, sit her down, get a statement. Lucas ought to pay for Jeremy's murder. The city ought to pay. But even if I didn't represent the family, I've got to find this guy. Because sooner or later he's going to come after me.'

'That's right,' Campbell said. 'You're the man who knew too much.'

He stood poised for – something. I could almost believe that he might have murdered Nikki and tried to kill me, except I couldn't imagine him using a knife.

Then his limbs loosened, and the crisis passed, and he moved to a bench beside the trail and sat down on it. He looked exhausted, as if he'd aged thirty years since I'd last seen him here. 'They found her car a block and a half from her condo, not in a place where she'd ever park it. Like someone left it there.'

'Which one, the Bronco?'

'She's only got the one car.' He looked up at me.

'When I met her she was driving a blue Pontiac convertible.' I explained how she'd knocked me off the road – deliberately, it seemed.

'Where did she get the money for a car like that?'

I didn't say anything. The answer was obvious: she'd gotten it from Lucas, and Damon, and the scores they made.

Campbell rose without another word and started back down the trail almost at a run. I hesitated, remembering my fear of him a moment before. Now he seemed to have forgotten me, but I followed him. When I arrived breathless at the base of the trail he was already in his car. I got in on the passenger side. He flicked the computer screen. 'There we go. Blue Pontiac, impounded three days ago in San Francisco.'

He snapped the laptop shut. The tires spat gravel as he cranked the wheel and pressed the gas. 'Three days,' he said, keeping up a hard beat on the wheel with the side of his fist. 'Three goddamn days.'

His skill on the downhills made me think that he couldn't have been the driver who followed me the night of Nikki's death. He treated the freeway like a private course, curving around other cars as if they were motionless, breezing through the express lane onto the Bay Bridge, the city seeming to rise to meet us. The impound lot was down under the 101 next to the Hall of Justice, where Teddy had won verdict after verdict in his prime.

Campbell badged the overweight cop at the gate and gave him the description of the car. After searching through a printout he pointed Campbell toward the far end of the lot.

When we got out I found the scratch my bike pedal had made on the side of the Pontiac's hood. Campbell peered through the windows, but there was nothing to see, the interior shaded by the freeway above us. He went to the trunk and pulled out a flashlight and a slim-jim, took a quick look around, then slipped the tool between the window and the doorframe and popped the lock.

I'd noticed the odor when we first got out of the car. I'd written it off to the location under the freeway or the usual city smells of sewers and garbage cans, but it wasn't that. When the door opened, the foul air, a sickening sweet stink of rotting food with an overtone of rust, made me take a step back.

'Blood,' Campbell said, shining a light on the driver's seat, which was covered with darkish stains. He wiped the seat with a tissue. It came away dry. But these stains were not the source of the smell. Campbell reached down and popped the trunk.

I remembered a story about a body going undiscovered in a van in this same impound lot for months.

The stink wafted forward to meet us as we went back on either side of the car. I felt a retch bubbling up, and hysteria mixed with the deepest dread. Not another one, I thought. Not Lavinia. It took me a second to see that the trunk was empty.

The absence of a body hardly mattered. The contents were there. Black blood was congealed on the carpet, coating the underside of the lid as if sprayed there, gumming up the lock, giving off a stink like rotten meat.

Campbell stepped back. 'Oh my lord,' he said. 'Oh, baby.' He looked away, then raised the flashlight and clicked it on. The beam picked out an object in the mess. I recognized the little nickel-plated revolver. He went back to his car for rubber gloves and fished it out. 'It's been fired,' he said. 'Only once.'

I caught the implication. No little twenty-two had made a mess like this. Whatever'd been done to the person whose blood was in that trunk, it'd been done with a knife.

Campbell started to tuck the gun away into an evidence bag, then stopped himself and tossed it back into the ghastly recesses, slammed the trunk, and wadded the evidence bag and the rubber gloves away.

We got back in his car, Campbell breathing erratically. 'We don't know that's her blood,' I began, but he cut me off.

'Don't fuck with me. Same person who did Nikki did that.'

I hesitated. 'I hear Lucas used to carry a knife.'

He drove back to the gate and rolled down his window. 'You got an inventory form on that car?' he asked the cop at the shack. 'Doors are locked.'

'Doesn't look like they've searched it,' the man told him after consulting his paperwork.

'Well, don't bother. There's nothing in it. It's been picked clean. It's not the car I was looking for. Thanks anyway.'

He turned onto Bryant, driving without urgency and seemingly without destination. He turned, then turned again, stopped. 'I've got to get out of this car,' he wheezed. 'Need to breathe.'

He left the car double-parked.

Again, after a hesitation, I followed him. He stalked up South Park Street, a tree-lined enclave in that postindustrial neighborhood. Stopping at a bench, he grabbed the back of it and bent like a jogger stretching, spat on the ground between his feet, then retched. Nothing came. He spat again, the sweat glistening on his face.

'I knew it was going to happen,' he said, breathing like he'd just sprinted here from the impound yard. 'It had to end this way.'

I just stood there beside him, able to offer nothing, feeling responsible, wanting to be away from him, to be home, to put it all behind me – except I couldn't. Lucas was still out there, and I might be next on his list.

'It's my fault,' he finally said, looking up at me with haunted eyes. 'It was my idea, using Damon and his business. I used to call him up and say, we got so-and-so at this location, but he ain't breaking no laws that *we* can see. Drug dealers. I'd make a call like that, and he'd go in all military and take what there was to be took.'

He paused, spat again, still breathing hard, like an engine racing after an accident.

'I'm the one who brought Lucas in. Score had to keep getting bigger every time. Got so Lucas would have Damon hit the dealers rather than make the arrest, even when he could make a righteous bust. And if Lucas thought any of Damon's crew was holding out, well, he could always arrange a month or two in Santa Rita.'

'And by then Lavinia had left you for him.'

He spat on the ground between his feet again. I came around to stand on the other side of the bench.

'You have to promise me that you'll call me first if you find him,' he said, looking up, his gaze made of clear, hard anger. 'You don't call the police. You call me. I want to be the one who brings him in.'

'I understand.'

He closed his eyes and nodded. Then we went back to the car and he drove me back across the bay to my office.

Chapter Twenty-Six

I didn't sleep that night, but by morning I knew what I wanted to do. I called Mrs Walker and asked if she and Tamara would meet me at my office. Whatever else happened, I owed her an explanation. 'You asked me to look into Jeremy's death and the police investigation,' I said to her in the conference room that afternoon. 'I think I know what happened, but I can't prove it.'

I summarized what I'd found, telling her that Jeremy had witnessed an attack by Damon's men on an East Oakland drug house, and that he'd been able to place a crooked narcotics officer, Chris Lucas, on the scene. He'd intended to file a citizen complaint but evidently he'd spoken with the wrong person about it, and before he could finish the complaint Lucas had shot him dead.

'I want to sue Lucas and the city for wrongful death,' I told her. 'This is a huge scandal, and in a matter of weeks or months it's going to break wide open. With luck I think I can get the proof I need before that happens.'

I'd prepared a new retainer form, one with my name alone. 'You don't pay me anything unless I get a settlement for you,' I explained. 'Then we take our expenses off the top and split the rest, sixty for you and forty for me.'

She seemed about to sign, then squinted up at me. 'Make it even splits. Third for you, third for Tamara, third for me.'

I didn't try to bargain, but simply made the change, and she signed for herself and for Tamara. She and Teddy were at the window, with him leaning close to her, talking a blue streak of nonsense, something about the gondola drivers in Lake Merritt, Tamara half-listening, standoffish.

The more I saw of her the more it seemed to me that behind her protective wall lay an intact core of self that had somehow survived catastrophic illness, and that she was beginning to reassert herself. Her confusion seemed both an act and not. If she didn't remember who Teddy was, she unmistakably knew him and intuited the contours of their relationship. She couldn't make plans or form intentions, but she'd become adept at assessing the texture of the moment she was in.

When they left, Teddy went with them, not because Tamara asked him to but because she seemed to assume that they'd arrived together and together was how they would leave.

Jeanie came into my office. 'Who was that?'

'Debra and Tamara Walker. I just signed them up.' I handed her the retainer form. 'Don't worry. Your name isn't on it. They're not your clients. Only mine.' Seeing the anger in her face, I quickly looked away. 'You said you didn't want anything to do with this case, remember?'

'What case?'

'Those pictures I took, the guy that died in jail. He wasn't the only one. Mrs Walker's son Jeremy, Tamara's husband, was murdered by a crooked narcotics officer, the same person who set me up. I once represented Jeremy Walker and now I'm going to represent his family against the city. A civil suit. Wrongful death.'

'You know how expensive those cases can be?'

'I'm not asking you for any money. That's why I had

them sign a separate retainer.' I hadn't thought how I'd pay for the commitment I'd just made to them, but that was a problem for another day. First I needed the proof; first I needed Lavinia.

'Did Teddy leave with them?'

'Teddy and Tamara were in the same group at the rehab center. That's how I met her and her mother. Jeremy, too, for that matter.'

'Ah.' She turned, seemingly about to go. But first she paused. 'By the way, have you talked to Car? I haven't been able to reach him. You wouldn't know what he's working on, would you?'

'I might.'

She nodded. 'You're an asshole,' she said and walked out.

Car didn't answer his phone, didn't return my messages. That was hardly unusual, but I found Jeanie's worry infectious. I reminded myself that he knew how to take care of himself, that he'd been in dangerous situations before and no one had gotten the drop on him yet.

I went home around six. Teddy wasn't there. He must still have been at Tamara's. Finally, around eleven, my cell phone rang. It was Car. 'I was starting to worry about you,' I said, and I told him briefly about the police finding the Pontiac, leaving out the part about Campbell and me. 'Looks like someone got cut up in the trunk,' I told him. 'There was a huge amount of blood.'

'Well that figures, because I couldn't find her. I checked relatives, friends, nothing. It's probably safe to assume she's either at the bottom of the bay or in the ground. Anyway, I've done what I said I would do. I'm not going to spend any more time on this case when I don't see any chance of getting paid.'

I swallowed my disappointment. 'Thanks for your help.'

'I'll be sending you a bill. What you do with it, that's your business.'

'I'll pay you,' I said. 'I don't know how or when but I will.'

'That's your choice. It's not like I'm going to come after you.'

He sounded fed up, but not with me. I wondered if the case had gotten under his skin the way it had gotten under mine. 'You spend any time looking for Lucas?'

'That's police business. Out of my league. Risk versus reward. The sooner you learn to balance that equation, the better off you'll be. Enough people have gotten themselves cut up already.'

After we hung up I drank a beer and went to bed. I tossed and turned for a few minutes, then fell into a sudden deep sleep. I was in a bicycle race. It seemed to twist on and on downhill. I had no teammates and the pack was at my wheel. I would slip ahead of them on the curves but on the straightaways they would catch me, nudging my back wheel. Then, without transition, my bike was gone and I was running, chased by a dog, a big husky with a head like a bull's, one eye milky and the other blue, silent except for its breathing. I felt its warm breath and smelled the stink of the Pontiac's trunk.

I woke up sweating, twisted in the sheets, a scream frozen at the back of my throat. Teddy still wasn't home, I saw as I crossed to the bathroom. I pissed, then went out to the kitchen and popped a beer, drank it standing in the cold light of the open fridge, my heart still racing. My mind, though, was beginning to range back over something the dream had triggered. The dog, I realized. Wherever Lucas was he would have that dog, with the cast on its leg that needed to come off.

I would have to call every veterinarian's office in the

Bay Area, maybe in the state, and then what would I do if I found him – call Campbell?

I couldn't sue a missing man. He had to be served with papers, and that meant he had to be found. Except it wasn't my job to find him, I told myself. I wasn't the one charged with enforcing the law. I was a criminal defense attorney; at least that's what I was as long as I worked for Jeanie.

I was at the office by six thirty, and had my desk packed by seven. I took the DUI files and put them on Jeanie's desk, dead center where she'd see them as soon as she came in. Then I went back to my office and sat running the math in my head: the balance of my savings and my few paltry investments plus the limits on my credit cards against what it would cost to set up a practice. Even if I planned on working out of our living room, it wasn't enough. It was nowhere near what it would take to do it right.

Jeanie came in around eight fifteen, called, 'Good morning, Sunshine.' I heard her briefcase thud to the floor, then a pause, then the chime of her PC starting up. Still I waited. I had the scene blocked out in my head, where she would stand, how I'd sit waiting for her to come in, what I'd say, then how I would rise and walk out past her. But she didn't come. Finally I rose and went in to her. 'I'm quitting,' I said. 'I know you don't want this case, but I have to take it.'

She was at her computer, facing half-away from me, the sun in the window on her other side, making it impossible to gauge her expression. She clicked her mouse to close a window and turned. 'Okay.'

Her face was blank, like a stranger's.

When I didn't move she turned back to the screen. 'What do you want me to say? Don't quit? You do what you want. Take that crazy case. There's no way I'm going to fund it.'

I had a plunging feeling, and I realized that I'd expected her to talk me out of it. Quitting was what I wanted, but it was the end of something more than this job, the last strained umbilical breaking. She wasn't going to help me, wasn't going to make it easy; in her passivity I read resentment. She had every right.

The only thing I could do was leave.

I was at the kitchen table with my laptop and the telephone when Teddy came back later that morning. I'd changed out of work clothes into jeans and a T-shirt and flip-flops. If he was surprised to see me there he

312

didn't show it. 'Where've you been?' I asked. 'At Tamara's?'

'Yeah.' His voice was hoarse.

'How'd you get home?'

'Bus.'

I was impressed. It was a long ride with a transfer. 'Get some sleep,' I said. 'You look like you've been up all night.'

'Nah. Think I'll just go into the office.'

'Got some work burning a hole in your desk?'

I saw a ripple of anger cross his face, something wild and uncontainable, reminding me of the way Teddy had been before the accident; though rawer now, the spark was still there.

'You'll have to go without me,' I told him more gently. 'I quit this morning. I'm taking Jeremy's case with me. I'll be representing Tamara and Mrs Walker.'

'Won't that cost a lot?'

'I don't know. Depends.'

He looked at me for a moment, then said, 'I'm working on something, too.'

'A case, you mean? You don't have a license to practice law anymore.'

'You do,' he said with a look of challenge and reproach. 'And besides, I can get it back. The same way

I got back on the visitor list out at San Quentin.' There was an accusatory edge in his voice, and I realized with a sudden chill of inevitable insight that he was talking about our father. Wrongfully imprisoned all these years. My premonition that my brother would want to revisit the case that had nearly killed him might explain why I hadn't wanted to hear Car's suggestion that he could practice law again.

By the fifth or sixth call I had my approach down. Veterinarians' offices tend to have helpful receptionists, guileless, with no expectation of subterfuge. 'It's about Trigger,' I would say. 'The big husky mix. He came in to get the cast off his leg.'

They would ask for the owner's name; the first few times that threw me off. I played dumb. 'He's huge, head the size of a bull's. Blind in one eye. You can't miss him.'

I made call after call, talking myself hoarse, each conversation a variation on a tiny theme, my little mechanism of deceit. I called from morning to night for two and a half days. In the evenings I drank beer and watched TV with Teddy, trying to drown the sickening feeling that I'd scratched my lottery ticket.

Technology gave me the illusion that I was doing

314

something, but the validity of that illusion depended on a guess that was no more valid now than it would have been thirty years ago, before a chump like me could find all the veterinarians' offices in the world from his kitchen table. Thirty years ago, to enjoy the illusion of accomplishment, I would have had to get off my ass and do something. Call it progress, but I wasn't convinced.

On the third day I scored. 'Trigger. Yes, the big husky mix. He's doing just fine. He's got quite a fan club,' said the woman who answered the phone. 'Are you still planning to pick him up tomorrow?'

'Are you the one who was there when I dropped him off?' I asked.

'No, that was Lisa, but she wrote everything down. We do ask that you give advance notice of any changes. Our kennel is very full right now. We don't have many spaces for a dog that size. Will you be needing to leave him an extra day?'

'No, tomorrow,' I told her, then confirmed the address. They were in Kings Beach, on the north side of Lake Tahoe not far from the Nevada border.

The table was strewn with the detritus of my search, lists of numbers and cities checked off or question marked, scrawled over in pencil. I brought over the garbage can, cleared it all off, and next dialed another number, one I knew.

'I found him,' I told Car when he picked up.

'Say what? Found who?'

'Lucas. At least I found the dog. Or I think it's the dog. At a vet's office in Tahoe.'

He figured I was out of my mind. I had to explain it twice to him and still he didn't believe me. 'That's why we have to check it out in person,' I said.

'We?'

'I wanted to give you the chance to tag along.'

'If this pans out, it's the luckiest guess you ever made. And I don't mean good luck. You go up there you're going to get your guts spilled out.'

'He's not going to know I'm there.'

Car breathed into the phone. 'Why'd you call me? Why didn't you just go? You already got Jeanie pissed as hell at me. She thinks I've been helping you poach her clients. Now she gets to blame me for whatever happens if I let you go up there alone. If I come along, same thing.'

'You can't win, I guess.'

'I sure as hell can't.'

'So you might as well be where the action is.'

He was silent for a moment. Then he said, 'You're

sure there's a case here. And by that I mean a case that pays my bills.'

'There's a case,' I told him. How I was going to prove it without witnesses was another question.

'Tahoe,' he said skeptically.

'I'm going to get a rental car,' I said. 'Why don't you tell me where you want me to pick you up.'

Chapter Twenty-Seven

I'd called ahead and reserved us a room at a motel just down the street from the vet's office, a block from North Lake Boulevard on a narrow, pine-shaded street. We checked in a little after midnight. The temperature was just above freezing and the wind spit pellets of rain, but in the morning when we awoke there was a fresh cap of snow on the mountains across the lake and the sun was out. We could see the vet's office from our window.

We had a better view from the picnic table outside the motel office. We sat playing cribbage for a dime a point, taking turns watching the place as we drank the coffee and ate the donuts Car had picked up. The vet's office couldn't have had much space for a kennel. The sound of barking came from the small fenced run in back.

'So you left Jeanie,' Car said as we studied our cards.

'She didn't want this case. It was either leave or stay and represent drunk drivers for the next year.'

He looked up at me over his cards. 'I was wondering when you'd get around to it.'

'I was hoping for a few more years' experience before I made the leap.'

'You don't know what the fuck you're doing, but that doesn't mean you won't make it. I'll say this much: I don't want to see you fail. That's the least I owe Teddy. I'll help however I can.'

'Thanks,' I said.

'I don't work for free, but I've been in this business a while. You got a question, I probably know the answer.'

'I don't even know what the questions are.'

We played a few more hands. Then a big pickup turned at the next block and came toward us, moving slow. It was black, with dual tires in back. I froze, the cards suddenly slick in my hands. Lucas probably didn't know what I looked like, I reminded myself. He wouldn't think twice about a pair of tourists sitting outside a motel, and besides, his wasn't the only black pickup in the world.

The truck slowed, about to turn in to one of the clinic's parking spaces. Then the driver hit the brakes. The engine gunned and the truck raced toward us, cutting across the lane. Car and I jumped up, me hobbled by the picnic table. At the last instant, the truck veered back to the correct side of the road. 'Shit,' I said, catching a glimpse through the driver's window of a face registering fear and astonishment. 'She's alive.'

It was Lavinia.

Car was already halfway to the rental car, a few feet away. I ran after him and jumped in on the driver's side.

I reached the lake road in time to catch a glimpse of her fleeing eastward. I followed, but kept my distance on the busy undivided highway that climbed up the mountain from Kings Beach. She put distance between us, going faster than I dared through the resort town. But as we neared the state line she slowed.

Car made a sound of frustration. He sat pressed back in the seat. I could tell that he wanted to be driving. 'What now?' he said, his voice tight.

'Keep following her.'

'And then what?'

'What else? We can't lose her.'

'The alternative is we let her pick the place where

we confront her, somewhere nice and secluded. She's probably on the phone to Lucas.'

'You think they're up here together.'

'That's the only explanation I can see. She's not dead, but according to you she knows everything he's been doing. That means they're in it together.'

'So what do you think we should do, if you don't want to keep following her?'

'Call the police. She already tried to kill you once.'

'You think it was her driving the pickup that night?'

'Doesn't that make sense? It's her driving it now.'

'What are they going to arrest her for, low gas mileage?'

'Call your buddy Campbell. I bet he'd be interested to know where she is, who she might be with.' He was right.

I took out my phone, started to dial, then dropped it in the center console. 'She knows we're here and she's not trying to get away. I think she wants to talk. If we call Campbell now, we'll lose that chance.'

'You'd make a hell of an investigator, with reasoning like that,' he said.

We crossed the state line. Nature gave way to casinos and fifties-era motels. She kept just below the speed limit, and faster drivers passed us both.

'Maybe she doesn't realize we're behind her,' Car said.

'She knows.'

'At some point we've got to peel off, kid.'

'Whose blood was that in the trunk of her car? If she killed Nikki, that explains the blood on the front seat, but not the blood in the trunk. Someone died back there. It was sprayed across the underside of the lid.'

He glanced over at me, maybe realizing that I'd been holding out on him, that I knew more than I told him. 'She's on the phone with Lucas, man. She's telling him where to go. She's setting us up.'

'I don't think so. I think she wants out and I think she'll talk.'

'Keep thinking that. Blind faith seems to work for most people.'

In Incline Village she turned off, and I gripped the wheel tighter, but she just circled to the lake road and headed back the way we'd come.

I could only speculate what must be going through her mind. I imagined her loyalty torn between Lucas and the need to escape, between fear and bravery. I imagined all sorts of things, but in the end Car was right: I didn't know her. The confidence I pretended was wishful thinking. She retraced our path to Agate

Bay and Trigger, waiting for her. I parked a few slots down from the spot she chose.

'Look, I only want to get my dog,' she said as we got out. 'Won't you just let me do that and let me leave here, please?'

'Who's stopping you?' I said, keeping my face blank, my heart racing.

Car stood leaning against the rental, his arms folded. She studied him warily, then looked back at me. 'What do you want?'

'There's a lot of people looking for you. Probably a few others who are hoping you don't get found. Campbell thinks you're dead, and so did I until ten minutes ago. It's evidently not your blood in the trunk of that car, but it's somebody's. You're going to have to explain that.'

She glanced at Car again. 'Not to you.'

'Maybe not. I want to help you if I can. We've got some time. I haven't called Campbell yet. I will before this is over – I promised him that – but first I want to give you the chance to explain some things. We've got a room across the street. Why don't you and I sit down there and talk.'

Her eyes narrowed, her body going rigid. 'I'll give you five minutes.'

I tossed Car the keys. We crossed the street, Car following a moment later in the rental. I opened the door and held it for her to follow me in. We hadn't made the beds; my jeans from the previous evening lay wadded on the floor. The smell of Car's cigarette smoke hung in the air.

'Please,' she said, catching the door. 'I can't. Not in here.'

Car was at the picnic table. When he saw us come back out he rose wordlessly and moved away to lean against the wall near the manager's office. I wondered if he was really armed or just trying to make it seem that way. If he'd brought a gun, I hadn't caught sight of it.

There was no one else around. We sat at the table, the cards still scattered where we'd dropped them. Some had blown to the ground in the light mountain breeze, dry and insubstantial, cool on my cheeks and scalp, smelling of pines and dust.

In the sunlight I noticed the ashy cast to her skin. She had a scrape on her forehead, the swelling of a bruise. She wore a denim jacket and jeans, boots with a low heel. Traveling clothes. Clothes for running away in?

A maid came out from behind the building with her

cart and went into one of the rooms on the other end.

'You're unlucky,' I said. 'If you hadn't stopped for the dog, everyone'd think you were dead. You'd be home free.'

'Why are you tormenting me? It doesn't have anything to do with you. I got you involved, and that was a mistake. I'm sorry about that, but you're out of it now. I don't know how to convince you just to forget you saw me here.'

'I may be out of it, but my clients aren't. Debra Walker and Tamara deserve justice for Jeremy's death.'

'I don't know what you're talking about.'

'Of course you do. That's why you're running.'

'I'm not running. I'm leaving. There's a difference.'

'Fine, let's call it leaving because you know you'll get killed if you stay. Only why bring the dog? It's just going to make it easier for him to find you.'

'Easy for who to find me?'

'Who else? Lucas. Your boyfriend. He killed Nikki Matson, and he tried to kill me when I homed in on you. You're next. That's why you have to leave. In your situation, I'd do the same.'

I watched her face for a reaction but there was none. If anything, she seemed to become calmer. It was a disconcerting calm, and I wondered if Car was right, if she could have been the one in the pickup the night Nikki was killed.

'What did you think you would accomplish by finding me?'

'You ought to be able to answer that one yourself. We've got the same problem. We're both dead unless we can get Lucas off our backs. You know he's serious. He killed Jeremy, after all.'

I flipped over one of the cards on the table. The three of clubs. I swept it to the ground with the others.

I went on. 'She deserves to know what happened, don't you think? Her daughter-in-law is disabled. Jeremy was their only support. They ought to get some compensation, don't you think? Some money to help them live.'

'Compensation. That's a joke.'

'The department ought to pay for what Lucas did. Lucas ought to pay. But first Mrs Walker needs someone to tell the truth.'

'Tell me, what does a criminal defense lawyer care about the truth?'

'Like I said, I represent Tamara and Mrs Walker. It'd be a civil case.'

She tried to regain her composure. 'So you've heard

some rumors, you see a chance to make a score, and you want me to help put on the squeeze.'

'You know where to find Lucas, don't you? Or maybe you're still with him. Maybe he's waiting for you now. You make any calls during our little tour of the state line?'

'What makes you so sure he did these terrible things?'

'In Jeremy's belongings at the house, he had a statement written out. Telling how he saw Damon's men raiding a house, and there Lucas was. Just sitting there in his car, like he was standing guard or something.'

'You're making it sound like this big scandal,' she said, something finally seeming to crack open between us. 'It wasn't like that. It was policy. It wasn't written down but that's what it was. If we don't have probable cause, or if some judge won't give us a warrant, we'd get out of the way. Stand back and let Damon and his men clean up. We'd be on the perimeter to make sure no citizens got hurt. It wasn't my idea, and I wasn't the one in charge.'

'That's not my point. What matters to me is that Jeremy saw something that day that got him killed. Unfortunately, he then talked to the wrong person about it.'

I studied her face very closely and was rewarded by a glimpse of something dark, a look of dread and shame.

'So I guess Jeremy must have known you were a cop?'

'It was what broke us up.' Her voice was hard, still angry after all these years. 'He didn't think women should be police officers. Or not his woman.'

'Were you there when he was killed?' I asked.

'No. I found out about it from – from my husband.'

'Jeremy came to you, didn't he? From what he wrote, he would have wanted an explanation for why the police were just standing by, letting black men kill each other. He must have thought he could trust you.'

She didn't say anything. Her expression said it for her.

'I'll tell you what I think. I think it's your fault Jeremy's dead. I think that's what you're running from. I think he came to you and told you he was thinking about filing a citizen complaint, and you went to Lucas and told him what Jeremy said, and next thing your old boyfriend is gunned down on his walk to work.'

'I—' She shook her head, eyes shut. Her body shook faintly.

'You've got to own up to it. Campbell hasn't stayed on the case this long because he wants to see you locked up. You may be responsible, but you aren't the one who pulled the trigger.'

Her eyes were shining; her shoulders slumped. 'Who's going to be my lawyer?' she challenged me. 'You?'

'No way. I've got another dog in the fight. For now the priority is getting Lucas off the street. You know where he is, don't you? You know how to find him?'

She looked away. 'I know where he is.'

'Campbell will listen to us. He'll have to. He wants Lucas for Jeremy's murder.'

'Campbell's very angry with me,' she said. 'You have to realize—'

'He'll be glad to know you're alive. Believe me. And he wants nothing more than to bring Lucas down. I'm not saying you can solve all your problems, but you can solve this one.'

'He doesn't know how it was. I started taking the money. Then Lucas decided he was going to take me.' She stopped, shutting her eyes again. 'He made me believe I didn't have a choice, that he could end my career.' A shudder ran through her. 'He was ... violent. When I decided to become a police officer I told myself that at least I would never have to be a victim . . . but with him that's exactly what I was.'

'Where is he now? Is he expecting you?'

'He's dead.' She straightened her shoulders and looked me in the eyes.

Now her gaze was steady, without remorse. 'He's up in the hills near the Briones Reservoir.'

The air went out of me like I'd been punched. I should have felt relieved. Instead, I was dismayed beyond all expectation. 'When did this happen?'

'A few days ago,' she said. 'That's his blood in my car. It's his truck I've been driving.'

'So who are you running from?'

'I don't know.'

'You don't know who you're hiding from?'

'I'm not going to prison.'

'I don't want you locked up.'

'You're not the one who decides.'

'You killed him?'

'If anyone else asks, I'll say I haven't seen him for months. So why don't you go home now, Leo. You're safe. It's done. No one's coming after you. Go home and keep your illusions.'

She swung her leg out from the bench and started to rise. I sat as if stunned. I was here because I couldn't be safe until Lucas was out of action. Now she was telling me that he was.

I caught her wrist as she started to walk away. 'That's not good enough. A man was murdered because of you. What am I going to tell his family?'

She jerked her wrist free but didn't walk away.

Car had moved over to stand beside the rental.

I turned sideways on the bench to face her. 'You leave here now and you won't even get out of town. I think Lucas is still alive, and you're protecting him. And I think that's what Campbell's going to believe.'

'Let him believe what he wants. I'll take my chances.' She pulled free.

'There's another answer,' I said. 'If you hadn't killed him, Campbell would have. He basically told me that's what he was going to do if he ever found him. If Lucas really is dead, Campbell will protect you. I'm sure of it.'

She stopped. 'What are you saying?'

'I'm offering you a deal, if you'll let me try to set it up. I want Lucas. If he's dead, I want to see his body, and Campbell will, too. You bring us there, and you give me a sworn statement telling what happened to Jeremy, enough to make a civil case. And in exchange, your husband makes sure Lucas's killing stays unsolved.'

She stood for a moment poised to walk away. 'Call him,' she finally said. 'I'm not promising anything, but you can call him.'

'Your wife's alive,' I said when I got Campbell on the phone. 'I found her.'

'Thank god. Where?' It was the most emotion I'd ever heard in his voice.

'In Tahoe. She says Lucas is dead.'

'Do you believe her?'

'When I see the body I will. She's promised to take us to it, but in return she needs a promise from you. Most homicides in Oakland go unsolved. She doesn't see why this one should be any different.'

There was a pause. Then he said, 'She's a cop. This idea come from her or you?'

'What does it matter? She'll go along. It's the only chance she's got. There's nothing to connect her to that car. It wasn't registered in her name. I'm the only one who ever saw her driving it.'

'And you're going to keep quiet about this?'

'I just want to know he's dead. And after that I want your wife to testify about the stuff she knows he did.

How he ended up that way is police business. I'm sure he deserved it and I'm glad that's where he is.'

I was taking myself off the hook and putting him on it. He must have known that, but then again he'd been on the hook all along – ever since he'd first made the decision not to remove himself from the invest-igation. I told him we'd call him later to set up the meeting.

Across the street, tethered in the bed of the pickup, the dog whined. It had been crying off and on all afternoon. We'd moved into the hotel room, but I'd come out to the parking lot to make the call, keeping my distance from Car, who sat in the rental, a book propped on the steering wheel. Ignoring Trigger, I went back into the room. Lavinia lay on her side, facing away from me. 'He went for it,' I said. 'Now it's your turn.'

She lay still for another moment. Then she unfurled her long body and sat against the headboard.

She talked for maybe two hours. As she spoke she gazed longingly into the distance somewhere behind me, beyond the wall of the room, like a creature caught in a trap. Sitting on the floor at the foot of the bed, I made notes on a legal pad. I had a tape recorder running.

* * *

I, Lavinia Perry, am over eighteen years of age and competent to testify in a court of law. The following is true and correct and based on my own personal knowledge. I declare under penalty of perjury that . . .

In separate, numbered paragraphs I wrote the essential facts of what she told me, the symbiosis between Lucas and Damon, the raids and the payoffs, the dead written off as casualties of the drug wars.

I was personally present and witnessed at least three separate attacks carried out by Damon Watson and his associates as a result of tips from Oakland Police officers, including Christopher Lucas. One such action took place on May 29, 2001, near Fifty-Ninth Street and Bancroft Avenue. On this occasion, Sgt Lucas received information that suggested a considerable quantity of drugs was being stored temporarily in a house in East Oakland. The information was of sufficient quality to develop probable cause for a search warrant; however, when I asked Sgt Lucas if he would obtain a warrant, he told me he would just call Damon.

It was standard practice for officers who were involved with Damon to station themselves at a perimeter around the action to deter bystanders and in case backup was needed. I accompanied Sgt Lucas as he took up a position in his squad car a few blocks from the house. A man named Jeremy Walker was present in the vicinity and witnessed the attack on the house and the exchange of gunfire. Fleeing the scene, he came across Sgt Lucas and me. Jeremy and I had gone to high school together, and he recognized me. Sgt Lucas ordered him to vacate the area and Jeremy complied; however, a few days later he contacted me and told me that he intended to file a citizen's complaint about what he'd seen. He had guessed rightly that members of the police had condoned the illegal raid, or even coordinated with Damon's men.

I told Sgt Lucas what Jeremy had said to me about wanting to file a complaint. Sgt Lucas said he would take care of it. A few days later I learned that Jeremy had been shot dead as he walked to work. I confronted Sgt Lucas and asked him if he'd killed Jeremy. Lucas laughed, and said that Jeremy had gotten what was coming to him and so would I, if I ever betrayed him.

I asked Lucas again if he'd killed Jeremy, and he said yes.

I'd sent Car to find a notary. Lavinia made corrections while the woman waited. Then she signed her name to the statement I'd composed as she spoke.

'I can feel you watching me,' she said when the notary I'd called had gone. She was lying on her side on the bed again, facing away from me.

'I was just wondering how you got into this.'

She rolled over onto her back. I forced myself to meet her eyes. 'I was a good cop,' she said, holding my gaze. 'At least I would have been.'

'Yeah? What was stopping you?'

'If it weren't for the money we might have gotten through it. Once you have it, once you take it, it has to go somewhere. And what about the drugs? Later it turned out that they were being turned around to favored dealers, put back on the street. The money got spread wide enough for the people who mattered to accept that it was what we claimed it was, a unique answer to Oakland's unique problems.'

'Some people think that novelty is overrated.'

'The secret to a thing like this is you keep giving people reasons not to ask questions they don't want the answers to. Then suddenly it's too late for them not to know what's really happening, and they're on the inside looking out, wondering how the door got shut behind them, with no choice but to keep their mouths shut. That's what it feels like, Leo, like you've just been walking along this long hallway, telling yourself with every step that you're going to turn around and start back, and then the door slams.'

'Is that what happened?' I asked.

'I've always wanted a car like that. But I couldn't drive it. I couldn't stand to look at it. Even before—' Her voice broke off.

After a moment I said, 'What happened, exactly?'

'How did I kill him? I thought you didn't want to know.'

'The tape recorder's turned off. It's just me asking.'

She looked at me, then shrugged. 'I made up some excuse, pretended I needed to get something from the trunk, then called him. I had him sit on the bumper and I started giving him a blow job. This was in Marin, the Headlands. Anyone could have driven by. That was what fooled him. Otherwise he would have been suspicious. He thought it was some kinky thing. Before he came I took out that little gun he gave me and shot him in the face, rolled him in and slammed the trunk.

'It was what he always did to me, you see,' she said. 'He liked to take out his gun and hold it to my head when he was fucking me, pull the trigger, and hear the click right there at the end. So when he saw what I was doing he must have thought I was playing around. Then when I got where I was going to dump him, it turned out he wasn't dead, and the gun jammed when I tried to shoot him again. I had to take that knife of his and stab him over and over and over.'

Her eyes filled. I looked away. Time to go.

Chapter Twenty-Eight

Car was dozing in the passenger seat of the rental. It was early evening, the sun down, the chill setting in. I knocked on the glass. 'I'll ride with Lavinia,' I told him. 'We're heading back.' He just glared at me through the window.

The passenger footwell of the truck was filled with several evenings' food wrappers. Dirty clothes lay mounded in the narrow back seat; clean clothes on hangers hung by the rear passenger window. In the bed of the pickup Trigger now slumbered.

Instead of heading to the lake road, she crossed over to the motel and stopped beside the rental, driver's side to driver's side. She rolled her window down and drew a gun from beneath the seat. I lunged but she blocked me with her elbow. Car was in movement before she had the gun out, throwing himself across the seat of the rental. She fired, moved her arm, fired again. As sound came back into the world I heard the hiss of air escaping from the shot-out tires.

I lay against the side door. A shell casing rolled on the dashboard. My heart was racing. She slid the gun back into the holster and took her foot off the brake, the pickup rolling slowly down the darkened street. I glanced in the mirror but saw nothing.

'I don't want him along, you don't want him along, and he doesn't want to go where we're going. We don't need a chaperone and he doesn't want to be one.'

It was a long, silent ride. It simply isn't possible to make chitchat after gunfire, on your way to dig up a body.

I could just take her word for it that Lucas was dead, I told myself as we came down the long unwinding from the mountains into the gold country. I had her sworn statement. We stopped for fast food and gas. I stayed in the truck while she went into the restroom. As soon as she was out of sight the dog began to pace and whine, its nails clattering on the metal surface, the suspension faintly rocking.

'Call him now and tell him where to meet us,' she instructed when she emerged. She gave directions. My conversation with Campbell was terse. I repeated her directions, saying that's where she wanted him to meet us. He didn't ask to talk to her, though he must have known she was right there. If he were going to betray her, I thought, it wouldn't happen until he saw Lucas dead.

Again I told myself that I wouldn't go through with it. Car could be right, I told myself. It could have been Lavinia all along. She could have been the one who killed Nikki. Tonight she might intend to kill me, but I didn't think so, didn't want to believe it. I had little more than faith to justify any such belief.

It was after midnight by the time we reached the place, a fire-trail gate on Bear Creek Road in the hills between Lafayette, Orinda, and Walnut Creek.

At first I thought Campbell wasn't there. Then I saw his car parked behind a stand of brush. I knew the country, of course, had been here on my bike plenty of times. All around was water district land, dry hills, and cattle. Few cars would be coming along this road so late at night.

Campbell walked up to the truck. Lavinia rolled down the driver's side window. The cloying scent of dry sage grass was thick on the air, miles of it all around us. In the hours since I'd first called him he seemed to have mastered his joy at learning that his wife wasn't dead. 'I see you've met Leo.'

'I've given him what he wants,' she said with subtle mockery. I was seeing a new side to each of them. 'You're not really going to make me go through with this?' Campbell stood rigid in an apparent effort not to look at me, not to hear her implication. She went on, 'Just tell me what you really need and I'll give it to you. I'm here now, aren't I, baby? I came back just like you wanted.'

From the bed of the truck the dog growled. 'You ought to have shot that animal when you killed Chris,' Campbell said, as if coming to some decision. He smacked the roof of the truck. 'Lead the way.'

The chain on the gate was not really fastened; it only looked like it was. Campbell slipped the loop off the post and opened the gate. We drove through, headlights off, only the light of a half-moon to guide us, Campbell following close behind in the police sedan as Lavinia negotiated the rough road.

'Are we going to have to do much digging?' I asked.

'Not unless somebody came and buried him. Not if he's where I left him. There are coyotes, vultures, wild dogs. Maybe even the cattle. I wouldn't get your hopes up. There may not be much.'

'I don't know how you can be so cool about it.'

'Because there's nothing to worry about now,' she said.

I didn't know what she meant, but I'd come too far at this point to ask.

We followed the fire road over the crest of a treeless hill. The landscape was all shadow without substance under the half-moon. I could see the trees ahead of us only in silhouette against the lights of Richmond below. The dog barked, then again, a strangled note that lapsed into anxious whining. When the road came into the trees she stopped. The dog's whining grew more insistent, punctuated by barks, the yips of a smaller dog, and then I smelled it, too, the corpse stink tainting the breeze.

She killed the engine and we got out. 'Trigger, shut up,' she said.

Campbell's flashlight beam raced past our feet. 'It knows.'

He seemed in good spirits.

'You smug prig,' she said.

'So we'll just follow our noses.'

'This ground is hard as rock. What was I supposed to do, blast with dynamite?'

'There's people up here all the time. And you with that dog everyone knows was his.'

'They wouldn't have found me or the dog.'

Campbell's beam lit the way, picking out tree trunks and boulders. The animal began to bark more fiercely, the smell growing more definite as we moved under the trees. It was more than just a smell. It was the landscape into which we climbed. The dog's barking rose to new heights of frenzied abandon behind us, distracting me from working out in thought the alarm that mounted in me with each step up that hillside.

Campbell stopped. 'You didn't carry that body up here by yourself.'

Ahead of us, Lavinia turned. Campbell was behind me and shone the light on her face. She blinked and flinched away.

'Who helped you?' he demanded.

'Why do you have to make me say it?'

'Who?' All the smugness was gone from his voice, replaced by fear.

'Who do you think? Your best buddy, Damon. Loyal to the end.'

I heard the breath wheeze out of him. 'So Damon killed Lucas.'

Her voice was sharp. 'Is that what you want me to tell them?'

When he didn't answer, she turned, kept climbing.

I followed her, the beam wagging along. I didn't dare look back at Campbell. We came to a mass of rock and Lavinia climbed atop it. 'Here,' she said, poised above us, looking down the other side.

We climbed up after her. The ground rose steeply to a sort of cliff where the shadows from Campbell's flashlight beam danced. At the base of the cliff, slabs had fractured and pulled away, creating a series of cave-like hollows. In one of these cracks, beneath the spreading leaves of a bay laurel, the body was wedged, not visible from below, accessible only by clambering over broken rock.

In the night, until the light hit it, it looked like part of the rock, a gray slab. Campbell shone his light on the face, a twisted, swollen leer of tissue and gristle. The eyes were gone, the wound in the cheek also eaten out by something, the lips drawn back over yellow teeth. I couldn't even tell what race the man might have been. If Campbell was dissatisfied with what he saw, he didn't show it.

'So you decided to trade up,' Campbell said, holding the beam on the ghastly face.

They seemed able to stand the stink, but I couldn't. For all the space around us, I might have been sealed up in a box, in a coffin. I held my breath as long as I could. It was like drowning. At last I plunged down the slope, stumbling from tree trunk to tree trunk, retching as I ran but not stopping until I was clear of it. I came out of the trees fifty yards from the vehicles and paused to gag it out of me, my hands braced on my knees. Finally I straightened, wiped my mouth. Then I noticed the silence. The dog had stopped barking.

I didn't see the dog anymore in the back of the truck. My first thought was that it'd gotten free, and I glanced around worriedly but saw nothing. I took a few steps toward the truck, expecting Trigger at any moment to leap straining at the end of its chain. But the silence only seemed to deepen.

A few paces from the truck I caught the hot, coppery stink of fresh blood. Peering over the tailgate, I saw the animal on its side in a glinting dark pool. Its throat cut.

I turned and ran a few steps back down the fire road the way we'd come, then froze as I heard a cough above. On the hillside Campbell's flashlight shone waveringly on the undersides of the trees. Again from closer by I heard something, the clatter of small stones and a metallic clink, then a muttered curse. I stepped into the shelter of the trees. You idiot, I told myself. Run while you have the chance. Shout, warn them, do something. I took one step up the slope, then another, holding my body rigid. Was it possible he hadn't heard me?

Campbell and Lavinia were arguing as they made their way down toward us, their voices weary, as if replaying some played-out argument, too low for me to catch what they were saying.

I took another step up the slope. The half-distinct shapes in the darkness resolved and I glimpsed the killer's silhouette not more than fifteen feet away, on the other edge of a small clearing in the trees that covered the hillside. The man crouched against an oak, holding a rifle pointed uphill. It was Damon Watson.

He was armed and I wasn't; he'd kill me if I revealed myself, and even if I'd been armed, I doubted I was capable of killing him before he killed me. I had no idea what I was doing, but I crept closer, and closer still, moving into the clearing now and through the tall grass on the balls of my feet, hands out to catch myself. It didn't seem real to me, somehow. I was a ghost; my body had melted into the darkness.

It could have been Damon's voice on the phone, I realized, Damon who posed as Jamil and fed me information about his meetings with Campbell. At every turn I'd been set up, and so had Campbell.

He and Lavinia were closer now, coming down the

hill on a line that would bring them into the clearing. Still they were arguing. 'This is just like you,' came Campbell's voice. And Lavinia said, 'You always make it seem like—' Her voice dropped and I didn't catch the rest. As they neared the clearing, the flashlight went out. Damon swore again, searching with the gun in the blackness.

He lowered the rifle and moved away from the tree into the grass, something glinting in his hand: a blade. He was no more than five feet from me now, but still he didn't see me. We were both in the open. I took a step, skidded on a patch of gravel, flinched, and caught myself, but it was too late to run. Damon whirled at the noise. 'Campbell!' I shouted.

I heard the knife hit stone. Damon must have dropped it. He still had the rifle, but he was aiming downhill and I was hardly more than a body length away, a few feet below his contour on the slope. He missed, but the sound of the shot at close range was deafening. I staggered, then scrambled, moving on instinct, knowing that I had to reach him before he could aim again. I heard footsteps and Campbell yelled, 'Hold it!' I grabbed the gun in both hands as Damon tried to get it up again, one of my hands on the barrel and the other down near the stock.

There was a shot from above, but it missed. Before I could set my feet, Damon gave a shout and flung me away. I tumbled spinning onto my hip and kept rolling all the way down to a clump of bushes at the clearing's bottom edge. Too far, I realized with a rush of sadness, struggling for a panicked moment to get my feet under me. He wouldn't miss with the second shot, I knew.

The sound was muffled, and as I rolled over in panic I saw Damon standing in the middle of the clearing with the gun pointed away from me, toward Campbell, who was feeling for something in the grass, Lavinia on the ground beside him. I thought I heard the impact of the bullet, a percussive *thunk* that made my fingers tingle in the sympathy of flesh for flesh. Campbell swung around as if on a pivot and came rolling down, flattening a broad swath of dew-wet grass, sliding to a stop beneath Damon just a few feet from me.

'I got this motherfucker!' Damon yelled, evidently to Lavinia. Then he lowered the gun and hurried to Campbell's side. He struck a flame from a lighter and held it over the dying man. Panting wheezes came from the back of Campbell's throat as the blood spilled out into the dry grass. Damon clucked his tongue and straightened, chambering a round, taking his time. He didn't even bother to look in my direction until he turned and raised the rifle, drawing a careful bead on me.

I saw Lavinia straighten and aim her weapon behind him. He didn't seem to sense the danger. He was savoring the moment. Probably he thought she was still on his side. She fired three times, the sound of the shots blurred together by their returning echoes. Damon stumbled forward, caught himself by planting the gun barrel in the earth, then sat down heavily beside it.

Lavinia, lowering her service revolver, shouted for me to call the police.

I didn't tell them about the car in the impound lot. I didn't suggest they check if there was a pay phone at the gas station where we'd stopped on the way back from Tahoe, or if any calls had been placed from there to the cell phone in Damon's pocket. Her version was that Damon had asked to meet Campbell there, that he'd promised to lead them to Lucas's body.

It wasn't much of a story, and I had to swallow a bitter taste each time I heard it, but it was the official line. By then the department was depending on her to testify before a grand jury that the corruption connected to these deaths had been snuffed out, the mercenary cop faction now purged. Lucas's death was supposed to be the end of the scandal. Lavinia's confession was pure penitence.

Later I took her deposition in the civil case I filed on behalf of Debra Walker and Tamara. After Lavinia's testimony, I was able to negotiate a two-million-dollar settlement with the city. A third was payable to me as attorney's fees, a third to Debra Walker, and a third to Tamara. Blood money, people say, hush money. Who cares what they call it.

Still, they're right.

Teddy is dripping wet, his umbrella tucked under his arm. He remembered to bring it but must have forgotten to use it between the bus stop and my office.

We go upstairs, I pour him a coffee, and he produces an offering from the pouch pocket of his hooded sweatshirt, a sheaf of paper curled with damp. He thumps it down on the desk.

'Produce the body.'

'What?'

'Produce the body. Habeas corpus.'

At first I think he's telling me something macabre; I think of Lucas's body up on the hill. Then I see the caption of the document on the desk. It's a brief to the Superior Court of San Francisco.

'You drafted this?'

The pride on his face is my answer. 'I had a start on it from before . . .'

He and Tamara have a little house in South Berkeley, within walking distance to the grocery and the bus line. They married a few months ago, the swelling of her belly telling the world that Teddy wasn't just in it for her money.

Later, when I read the brief, I will see that it is a competent piece of legal reasoning, painstakingly assembled from scraps of ideas. Somehow, out of his fragmentary thought processes, he has managed to connect the pieces into a coherent whole. He will never again address a jury, but against all odds, my brother is still a lawyer, and the first task he has set himself in his phoenix-like career is to overturn my father's conviction and obtain his release from prison.

He has an affidavit for me to sign, attesting to his fitness to practice law. I put my signature down.

MAXWELL AND ASSOCIATES, the new sign outside my office says, although I have no associates, not even a secretary.

MAXWELL AND MAXWELL, it will need to say.

Acknowledgments

Thanks to Gail Hochman for sticking with me, reading and rereading until we got it right, and to Otto Penzler for taking the big chance. Michele Slung's fine editorial eye helped me avoid many mistakes I would otherwise have made the second time around, and I'm proud to be part of the team led by Jason Pinter and the editorial staff at Grove/Atlantic. Nothing would be possible without the love and support of my wife and first reader, Sarah Moody, and our families and parents.

Bear is Broken

Lachlan Smith

Leo Maxwell grew up in the shadow of his older brother, Teddy, a successful yet reviled criminal defence attorney, who racked up enemies as fast as he racked up acquittals.

The two are at lunch when Teddy is shot, the gunman escaping through a crowd. As Teddy lies in a coma, Leo realises that the search for his brother's shooter falls upon him, as Teddy's enemies are not just among his criminal clients but embedded within the police department as well . . .

Leo must navigate the seedy underbelly of San Francisco, but the deeper he digs into his brother's life, the more questions arise: about Teddy and his estranged ex-wife, about the ethics of Teddy's career, and about the murder that tore their family apart decades ago. And somewhere, the person who shot Leo's brother is still on the loose, and there are many who would happily kill Leo in order to keep it that way.

Praise for *Bear is Broken*:

'A riveting debut' Linda Farstein

'Grabs the reader by the throat and doesn't let go' *Publishers Weekly*

'An exciting read' *New York Journal of Books*

978 1 4722 0118 8

headline

The Ophelia Cut

John Lescroart

Defence attorney Dismas Hardy takes on his most personal case yet.

When Moses McGuire's daughter is raped by her ex-boyfriend, Rick Jessup, he vows to get his revenge. So when Rick is found dead the next day, Moses is arrested for murder.

Dismas Hardy has no hesitation in defending his old friend but as the evidence against him starts piling up Hardy can't help wondering, what if he's actually guilty? And to make matters even more complicated, the case threatens to bring to light an old secret that could destroy Hardy's career.

With the trial going against him, Hardy must draw on all his legal ingenuity until he sees a new way forward that might just save them all. But at what price?

The Ophelia Cut pits lifelong friends against one another, where truth does not always lead to justice and where long buried secrets still have the power to redeem or destroy.

Praise for John Lescroart:

'The best legal thriller I have read in years' Brad Thor

'Today's best legal thriller series' Lee Child

978 0 7553 9322 0

headline

The 500

Matthew Quirk

Mike Ford was following his father into a life of crime, when he chose to go straight. Now he's landed the ultimate job with the Davies Group, a powerful political consulting firm run by the charismatic Henry Davies. But he's about to discover that power comes with a price, and being on the side of the lawmakers doesn't mean your work is legal.

Caught up in a deadly chase, Mike needs to lie, cheat and steal to survive and possibly, even kill . . .

The 500 is a fast-paced thriller that takes the reader on a journey through the corridors of power to the crack dens of Washington and the corrupt underbelly of politics.

'What an absolutely phenomenal, kickass thriller' Joseph Finder

'A riveting page-turner in the tradition of John Grisham' Jeff Abbott

'High-octane political drama with an up-to-the-minute edge' *Daily Mail*

'A superior debut' *Guardian*

978 0 7553 8742 7

headline

Fire and Brimstone

Colin Bateman

When billionaire's daughter Alison Wolff disappears following a massacre at a party, nobody knows if she has been kidnapped or killed. Dan Starkey is hired to find the missing student but instead is drawn into a violent struggle between rival gangs.

A drugs war is tearing the city apart and in response, a new church movement has sprung up. But when a controversial new abortion clinic is firebombed, Dan is asked to prove their involvement.

In a Belfast rapidly descending back into chaos, Dan is left with an impossible choice – betray his client or risk losing his family . . .

Bateman. The word on the street:

'He just seems to get better and better. Funnier as well as gripping' Ian Rankin

'Bateman has a truly unique voice . . . He is a dark and brilliant champion of words' James Nesbitt

'Sometimes brutal, often blackly humorous and always terrific' *Observer*

978 1 4722 0121 8

headline